Praise for *Pegasus*

Pegasus is an edge of the seat, can't-put-the-book-down kind of story that puts the reader in the action. Vince wrote this as if he was recounting real events, hitting the highs and lows in the battle to take Iraq.

— Sergeant Chris Gonser, U.S. Army, OIF Veteran

Simply put, Vince Guerra's *Pegasus* is the apogee of his story telling. Building on the story lines of *Beyond the Golden Hour* and *The Stars in Their Places*, Vince amps up the human capital of his characters and his consummate storytelling to produce a riveting, outstanding story of troops overcoming their limits to go above and beyond to defend their country, its interests, and their fellow troops.

— Lieutenant Colonel Wm. Brendan Welsh, United States Army Special Forces (Ret.)

Vince's newest book is a thrilling story of contemporary military aviators and operators. The characters are especially compelling and realistic. The families are treated equally with respect, and together they make an engrossing story of our contemporary warriors and their world. I can't wait for his next book.

— Anonymous, Captain, United States Air Force

Vince Guerra is a great new voice in military techno-thrillers. Action packed storyline; believable, humanized characters; plenty of high tech military equipment. As a former A-10 driver, I appreciate his authenticity and accuracy. As a lifetime reader of the genre, I give it five stars – highly recommended.

– Anonymous, former A-10 pilot, United States Air Force

This book points to the need of God in our lives. In the midst of a story of people in war for different reasons, it shows how God is near us ready to help, and uses all people who are willing.

– David Eubank, Founder, Free Burma Rangers

Vince Guerra is an author hitting his stride and *Pegasus* is his best book yet. As an old Vulcan/Stinger soldier, I especially appreciated the tactical details.

– Colonel Clifford Brown, U.S. Army (Ret.)

Also by
Vince Guerra

Beyond The Golden Hour

The Stars and Their Places

PEGASUS

VINCE GUERRA

✝

Cover by Copperlight Wood
Cover image by Levi Clancy
Cover background image by Specna Arms
Illustrations by Vincent Guerra V

Printed in the United States of America

Published by Copperlight Wood
PO Box 870697
Wasilla, AK 99687
www.copperlightwood.com

ISBN 978-1-7345978-3-7 (paperback)
ISBN 978-1-7345978-9-9 (hardcover)
ISBN 978-1-7345978-6-8 (ebook)

For those who have walked through
the fire.

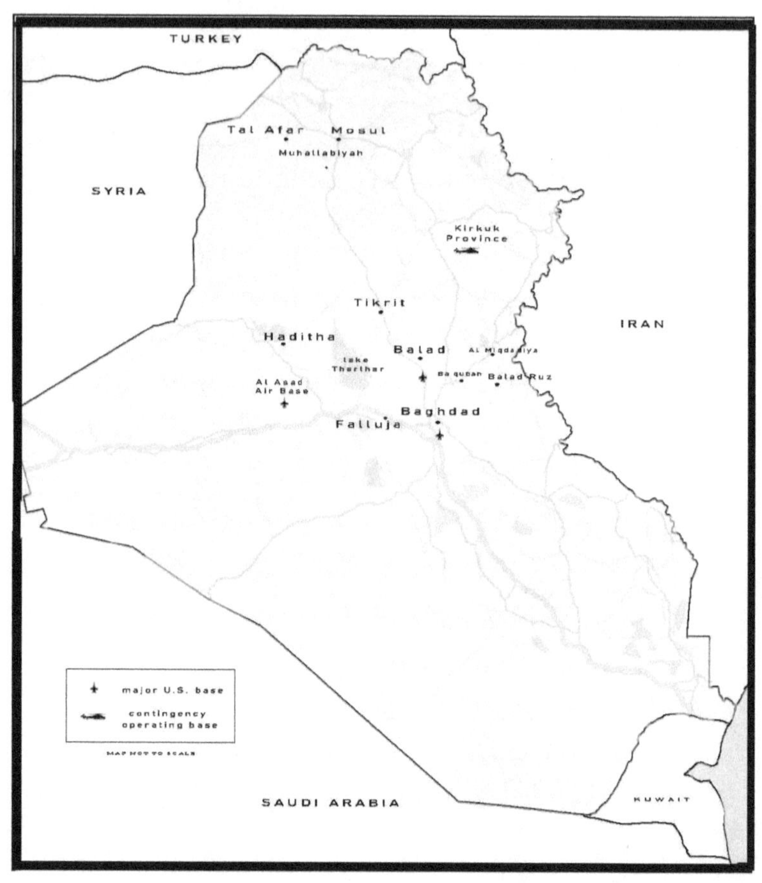

TURKEY
SYRIA
IRAN
SAUDI ARABIA
KUWAIT
Tal Afar
Mosul
Muhallabiyah
Kirkuk
Province
Tikrit
Haditha
Balad
Al Miqdadiya
lake
Tharthar
Ba quba
Balad Ruz
Al Asad
Air Base
Baghdad
Falluja
major U.S. base
contingency
operating base
MAP NOT TO SCALE

CONTENTS

STORY NOTE

This is the third part of a four book series. Book one, *Beyond the Golden Hour,* covers events in Afghanistan in 2003 and focuses on special operations forces, including pararescue jumper Aiden McCoy and US Navy SEAL Porter Dawkins.

Book two, *The Stars and Their Places,* follows Aiden's path after those events, and furthers the story into Iraq in 2007 and 2008.

The book you are about to read is set parallel to the events in *The Stars and Their Places*, and focuses on what Porter was doing over the same period of time in 2007 and 2008.

PROLOGUE

Los Angeles, 1980

"Oh, come on. Move over, ninny," Marcus Cooper said, more to himself than the driver in front of him. Their brake lights flashed again. Marcus groaned, slowed, and looked for an outlet in the stop-and-go traffic.

"What's a ninny?" his daughter asked from the passenger seat.

"A slow as molasses, hippie VW owner, who doesn't know how to drive."

"Ninny, ninny, ninny," she sang, fishing in her Happy Meal box for another French fry.

"Here we go," Marcus said, maneuvering his Chevy Nova into the right lane, accelerating through the gap between a van and a delivery truck. Once clear, he moved back into the far left lane and regained his cruising speed around 80mph. He glanced at his daughter and noticed her head out the window, looking into the sky.

"Ginger, sit back."

"Daddy, look! An airplane!" she said, pointing her finger out the window, too.

"Girl, sit down before you fall out," he said, grabbing the back of her pants and pulling her into the seat.

She sat, but still leaned her head out the window, chestnut hair flying, never taking her eyes off the sky. Marcus leaned forward and looked up through the windshield. "That's not an airplane, sweetie. It's a helicopter."

"What's a helencopter?" She asked, looking at him from behind her star-shaped pink sunglasses.

He grinned. "Like an airplane, but it can fly in lots of directions, not just straight." He held up his right hand and mimicked the motions as he described them. "It can go up or down, move sideways, or pivot in midair. You know the hummingbirds that eat from the feeder outside the kitchen window?"

"Uh huh."

"Helicopters do the same thing. They hover."

"Helencopters eat sugar juice?" she said, with the wide eyes of an incredulous four-year-old.

"No," he laughed. "They just fly the same way."

"Huh," she said, quiet for a minute. "Where do they fly to?"

"Lots of places, it depends on the helicopter. That one up there's probably lookin' at the cars on the highway and watching for traffic," — he braked and slowed the Nova to a crawl again — "so it can tell us how long we'll be stuck here," he grumbled. "Some helicopters can lift heavy things and carry them around. There are helicopters that pick up people who have really bad owies and take them to the hospital. And then there military ones, like Hueys and Cobras that soldiers use to fight bad guys."

"The helencopter is named Huey?"

"No, Huey is a type of helicopter. Remember your uncle Sammy? He used to ride in Hueys."

Genevieve Cooper watched the helicopter until it disappeared from view. She turned her attention back to the food in her lap.

"I'm unnah fly a helencopter," she said, eating fries and bobbing her head to the music on the radio.

"Can I fly in it with you?"

"Okay," she said, bouncing in the vinyl seat.

"What kind of helicopter are you going to fly?" Marcus asked.

She reached into the box again. "A pink one."

Marcus grinned and hit the accelerator.

1

Silver Spoon

Al Asad Airbase, Iraq 2007

Porter ate the last bite of scrambled eggs off his plate, pushed it away, and leaned back to finish his coffee. Most of his team was elsewhere, but plenty of people were in the chow hall even at this hour; most of their operations were conducted in the middle of the night.

Porter looked at his watch. *02:25.*

He drained the cup, took his dishes to a plastic bin near the trash cans, and went back to his sleeping quarters.

He took his time getting dressed. He knew anxious energy would soon envelop him — it always did — but not yet, not this early. A dozen years and hundreds of missions ago, the simple act of tying his boots got him amped up. But these days everything blended together; the operational tempo never let up and Porter rarely got anxious. Giving a mission briefing sometimes caused him stress, but even then it was only because he feared someone might drop the ball and someone else might die as a result. He was long past worrying about what the higher-ups thought, mainly because they respected him enough to give him full authority in planning — or at least, as much as possible within his rank.

Tonight's mission was planned by someone else, but he'd scrutinized every detail, approved it, and was confident his men had it right as usual.

Porter considered the four color-coded cases under his bunk, taking a last-minute appraisal of what he'd need tonight. Each case was filled with unique gear necessary for various mission profiles, but the gear he used every day was on a three-tier plywood shelf to his right. He stood in front of it and stretched his back before starting his routine.

He put on layers of clothing and filled specific pockets with little things he might need: bandages, batteries, precision tools for picking locks, plastic chem lights that glowed in the dark when you cracked their tubes, even small stuffed animals and pencils that could come in handy on a mission. Kids were almost always present.

He tightened his belts and harnesses, picked up his tactical vest. He inspected the back of it, with its custom-designed configuration of coiled radio antennae, and hoped it would work as well as it usually did. When he put the vest on he felt all sixty pounds with the added weight of the ballistic plates. He did a quick visual inspection on each of his magazines, starting with his Sig Sauer P226. He holstered the pistol, then checked each of the mags for his suppressed Heckler and Koch 416 assault rifle and inserted them into the vest. He opened a box of cartridges and filled two additional mags he hoped he wouldn't need. If everything went perfectly, he wouldn't have to fire a shot, but that was rarely the case. Every additional pocket was filled with extra ammo. He attached the rifle to its harness.

He put on his fingerless gloves that were reinforced at the knuckles and the back of the hand — perfect if he had to punch something, but allowing the dexterity necessary for working with delicate gear.

His last act was to remove his old Red Sox cap. It was a part of him, and he wished he could wear it on these kinds of missions. He placed the hat in its temporary home on the shelf and picked up his helmet, paused, then set it down again.

Next to the hat on the shelf was a letter he'd read several times since receiving it a week ago. Porter pulled it out of the envelope and unfolded it. He didn't read it all, just scanned the handwritten lines until he got to the part he was looking for, halfway down the page.

I went on a date tonight. The guy was a complete tool. I would have had a better time scraping the grime from the bottom of the refrigerator.

Porter smiled, folded up Jen's letter, and put it in its envelope. He placed it back on the shelf in front of her other letters and picked up his helmet. The SEAL lieutenant closed his eyes, took a deep breath, and walked out.

———

Porter stood in the hangar next to the rest of his team, waiting for their ride. Nobody spoke. But for all of the weapons and high-tech gear, they could have been six strangers, casually waiting for a subway train to take them to work.

They didn't have to wait long.

An MH-6M Little Bird landed on the tarmac just outside the hangar. The small helicopter's rotor never slowed and the six men moved as one, out from the bright lights of the hangar toward the dark helicopter. Porter's team hopped onto the benches above the skids on each side. The pilot looked at Porter, who gave a thumbs-up. In the blink of an eye, the Little Bird whisked them off to another night's work.

———

Haditha, Iraq

"Must be hot tonight. A lot of people are sleeping on the rooftops," Craig Allen said over the internal communication channel of his Apache.

"This could get interesting," Ginger said from the seat behind him. "Pegasus One Three, see any movement?" she said on another channel.

"Negative, Eight. I see zero targets. Sleepy time on the top decks, it seems. Probably hot as hell inside the buildings."

"Copy that," Ginger said.

The pair of Apaches hovered over the east bank of the Euphrates. Across the river in front of them lay the city of Haditha. Craig looked at the infrared images of families on his monitor, searching for movement, but mainly looking for weapons as he trained in on each rooftop beginning with the ones nearest the western bank of the river, then to the ones behind it, and so on toward the target building, ten streets inland.

His counterpart in Pegasus One Three was doing the same check of the quiet streets and alleyways of the neighborhood. The only movement came from an occasional vehicle on the main road and at the gas station a few blocks from the target. The Apache front-seaters took in every detail.

Craig finished his initial search of the rooftops and focused in on the target building. He looked at each window facing him, the courtyard, the surrounding terrain, and a vacant lot twenty meters to the west.

"Looks clear," he said to his pilot.

"Alright, let's get it on," she agreed.

Ginger toggled a different radio frequency. "Star Niner, this is Pegasus Eight. Eyes on target, looks clear."

"Copy, Pegasus," replied the pilot of another helicopter.

Ginger increased elevation and flew slowly across the river, along with her wingman. The Apaches watched a Little Bird move into frame on their cockpit screens. It came in fast from the dark sky, and Craig could see three men sitting on both benches of the relatively tiny egg-shaped helicopter. Ginger maneuvered her Apache closer, and Craig could make out the men's legs dangling above the skids as the Little Bird swooped into the vacant lot, and landed just long enough for the six men to jump down before lifting off and disappearing out of the frame.

The figures left in its wake immediately moved in two columns toward the target building.

"Touchdown," said Craig.

———

Porter took a knee and scanned his side of the landing zone from behind the four lenses of his night vision goggles as the helicopter took off behind him. He stood and led his men across the courtyard toward the two-story residence.

They reached the concrete wall surrounding the building, then separated – three operators moving along the base of the wall to the left, Porter and the other two going right.

Porter's column reached a steel door set within the concrete wall. He halted, whispering into his radio, "Titan One in position."

He gently pulled on the door handle. It was locked. He waved one of his men forward and pointed at it. Porter moved out of the way as Mario tried pushing the door. Though locked, the rusty handle produced some give. Mario pulled out the sledgehammer, a tool he was privileged to carry as the newest guy on the team, and positioned himself to smash the lock and looked at Porter, waiting for the order to swing.

"Titan One ready for outer breech," Porter whispered into his mic.

———

Farther along the wall, the rest of the team stood at another entry point, an iron gate secured with a sturdy handle and a deadbolt.

"This is Titan Two, standby," Denny said.

He lifted up his night vision goggles and looked at the gate with his naked eyes, rubbing them as they adjusted. He felt the knob, looked at the gate and its hinges, and frowned. He reached into his leg pocket and pulled out a breeching charge, peeled off the film to expose the adhesive, and stuck the explosive to the door next to the deadbolt. He set the primer and detonator, then took several slow steps to the right. Denny put his back against the wall and pulled his night vision lenses back over his eyes.

"Fire in the hole," he whispered to the two men next to him. They took several steps sideways and paused against the wall.

"Titan Two ready to breach on your order, Titan One," Denny said.

—————

"Execute," Porter said without hesitation.

Mario swung the sledgehammer into the flimsy doorknob. It crashed through with a clang and the door swung hard on its hinges, wide open. Porter moved through it and scanned left as Jonathan followed him scanning right. Mario put the sledgehammer back into his pack and followed behind, pointing his rifle at the second deck of the building, then at the roof as he walked.

Denny triggered the breeching charge on the gate at the same moment Mario swung the hammer. The explosion blew the heavy door across the courtyard and it smashed into the building, falling with a clang that Denny feared would wake the entire neighborhood. The three SEALs entered the inner courtyard opposite Porter's squad, searching for targets from the other direction.

They could see the other team and the laser beams emanating from their rifle scopes in their night vision. Both teams took up positions at different doors to breach the next tier of the building's defenses. The noise had eliminated the element of surprise and they moved fast.

Porter checked a door — also locked, and much sturdier that the first. Taggart set a breeching charge identical to Denny's and the scene replayed as it had at the gate.

Taggart and Jonathan raced to set new charges on separate exterior doors. They didn't wait to coordinate their breeches; speed was all that mattered now.

"Firing in three, two, one," Taggart said, and blew his door off the hinges, followed almost immediately by Jonathan's charge.

All six men disappeared into the building.

———

Craig watched both teams enter the building, then scanned back to the roof. Several figures had stirred when the first gate detonated. Now, two of them sat up as the building was breeched. Craig watched them look around; he could see they were unarmed and remained sitting.

"Movement on the roof," he said over the radio.

He increased magnification and studied the man through the Apache's lens. He could clearly see his outline, headdressing, and a blanket covering the lower portion of his body. Craig could even make out his beard, but he saw no weapons.

Craig looked at the other figure, a woman vigorously shaking the shoulder of the man sleeping next to her. He rolled onto his knees and Craig saw her shuffle over to the wall and gesture toward the ground.

Craig rubbed his finger on the trigger of his 30mm cannon. A single burst would easily disintegrate that quadrant of the roof and everyone on it, including three small bundles laying at the man's feet, most likely children.

He zoomed out and quickly scanned the seventeen individuals he had already counted on the roof, mostly still sleeping, but as the seconds passed more of them seemed to shift, possibly waking up.

"Better hurry, guys," he said, thinking out loud.

He tried to see their faces.

Which one is he?

———

The SEALs followed Porter through the door and down the hallway, peeking into rooms as they went. Every room was empty. The second team moved through another corridor along the first floor, looking through the kitchen and into other rooms on that side of the house, but finding nothing.

Porter slowed and all six men mimicked his pace, their boots hardly making a sound as they swept through the ground floor.

Light shone from a room ahead, revealing a staircase across from it, and a man emerged, turning off the light. Porter crept up behind him, his rifle's laser beam centered on the man's back, quickly followed by four other beams. Porter was three feet behind him when the man turned around, unarmed.

The man's face had the terrified expression of one suddenly confronted by a four-eyed monster in the middle of the night. Porter let his suppressed H&K dangle from its harness as he stepped forward and punched him in the jaw. The unarmed man fell like a sack of potatoes.

Denny and his men rejoined Porter at the foot of the staircase. He whispered in his radio, "Lower deck clear."

Porter nodded at Mario to deal with the unconscious man on the ground, then made a tomahawk chop gesture toward the staircase.

As the five SEALs climbed the stairs, Mario flex-cuffed the man's hands behind his back, then pushed him out of the way, rejoining his team, periodically turning his rifle toward the ground behind them as they climbed.

———

Ginger's eyes looked in two different directions, an unnatural and freaky talent unique to Apache pilots, one that took her hours of training and countless headaches to master. Her left eye was free and worked normally as she inspected the ground out the cockpit window on that side. Her right eye, however, moved independently, covered as it was by a large monocle attached to the helmet-mounted display (HMD), which fed her a dozen different instrument readings as she looked at the rooftop. She could flip a switch and superimpose weapons targeting data or change the image character to reveal infrared or heat signatures with her "Predator helmet," as she called it. It also had crosshairs which slaved the retina of her right eye to the 30mm chain gun under the helicopter's nose. Whatever she looked at with her right eye was always on target. Right now it was looking at a man standing on the roof.

The gun sighted on his back, then to his wife and the bundle of children she was huddling over.

Out the window, Ginger saw the bridge over the Euphrates illuminated by street lights. She also saw several Army vehicles come to a stop on the east side, just before crossing the bridge.

"Pegasus, this is Viper Three Seven," she heard over the radio. "In position, over."

"Copy, Viper. I have visual. Standby."

Ginger changed frequencies. "Titan, you have movement on the rooftop. Several unarmed individuals, including children."

"Man, this sucks," she said to Craig.

"Come on, lady," Craig whispered to the Iraqi woman on his monitor. "Everybody back to bed now."

Denny led his team from room to room along the second floor.

Still nobody. They must all be on the roof.

They passed through rooms, pointing their laser beams at beds, dressers, and little else. They usually saw weapons of some variety, but none tonight.

Wrong house? he wondered.

They finished the second floor sweep and Denny whispered, "Middle deck clear," into his radio as he moved toward Porter's team, already at the top of the last set of stairs.

Porter's laser beam was fixed on the door to the roof, just to the left of center at chest height, should the door suddenly open.

Jonathan knelt next to him, put his left hand on the doorknob, and waited to open it inward.

Denny watched from the rear. *Here we go again.*

Porter placed a hand on Jonathan's shoulder, signaling him to turn the knob. Jonathan opened the door wide enough for them to rush onto the roof.

Porter immediately sighted his laser beam on the unarmed man looking over the wall. His wife and children were sitting up at his feet. Porter spoke from behind him in a quiet, firm voice.

"On the ground. Now."

The man turned, terrified and dumbstruck. His wife let out a yelp, but was silenced by the hulking shape of Taggart pointing his rifle in her face. She turned her attention to her children and huddled over them. Tag swept his sights over the mass of humans, looking for a weapon.

Porter put his hand on the man's shoulder and forced him to his knees facing the wall, then motioned for Tag to cover both the father and his family, and stepped to the left to survey the rest of the roof. Denny and Mario were pointing their weapons at a group of men sleeping near the opposite wall, a line of three AK-47's next to them. Porter took a slow step over a high bundle of blankets, the sleeping Iraqis oblivious to the laser beams passing over them. Porter walked around them looking for the right one.

"Fadhi," Porter said a little louder as he looked around.

All of the sleeping men were covered by the SEALs, who could kill the entire roof before any of the Iraqis lifted a head. Porter raised his voice to a shout.

"Fadhi! Wake up!"

———

"Movement. Looks like everybody's awake now," Craig said, watching figures scramble out of their bundles only to be kicked and shouted back to the ground.

"Viper, this is Pegasus. Roll out," Ginger said to the convoy parked beside the bridge.

"Copy that, Pegasus," the commander replied.

———

"Fadhi, I said get the hell up! I swear I'll leave you here," Porter said to the crowd, still not sure which one was Fadhi.

A young man crouched with his hands in the air and rose a few inches, unsure whether standing would get him shot. He was too scared to speak.

Porter saw and made a beeline toward him and pulled him to a standing position. He lifted the night vision goggles to look at Fadhi face to face, then turned on his helmet-mounted flashlight and shined it in Fadhi's eyes, causing him to wince.

Fadhi looked away to avoid the glare. "You're American," he said surprised, in English.

"Affirmative. Now shut up," Porter said, before he keyed the open frequency to broadcast across the radio net.

"This is Titan One. Silverspoon. Repeat, Silverspoon," he said, then took Fadhi by the scruff of the collar and shoved him toward the door.

"We're leaving, kid. Pronto."

———

Al Asad Airbase

Rear Admiral Buchanan gave a thumbs-up to his senior officer, who took the information to the conference room.

Upon entering, a well-dressed Iraqi couple sprang to their feet. The man put his arm around his trembling wife as they waited for the American to speak.

"We got him," he said.

The couple let out a cry and hugged each other as tears filled their eyes.

Fadhi's father asked, "Is he here?"

"No. He's alive, but it's not over yet."

———

Porter walked Fadhi to the door and paused so Jonathan could flex-cuff his wrists.

"You are American. Why are you handcuffing me?" Fadhi said in perfect but accented English. "They kidnapped me."

"Don't care who your daddy is, bro," Porter said. "Till I get you home, keep your head down and shut up."

The SEALs had flex-cuffed everyone but the children. Porter moved Fadhi down the stairs faster than the terrified young man thought was possible. All Porter cared about was catching a ride, and they were right on time.

———

After the Americans disappeared through the door, Ginger turned to watch the small convoy of vehicles crossing the bridge over the Euphrates.

"See that truck, Craiger?" she asked.

"Got him," Craig entered a distant fuel truck into the Apache's computer. His fire control system was now locked onto nine separate targets — essentially everything that moved along the mostly deserted streets — just in case.

"No bad guys. Maybe we can get home before dawn for a change, eh?" Ginger asked.

"I'll bet you $50 on that."

Ginger scoffed. "No way."

"Eddie'd tear you a new one if you came back loaded."

"We can shoot some water buffaloes on the way back?"

"Clear it with Atwood and I'm game."

Ginger switched to a formal British accent. "I thought we agreed that none shall speak that name when I'm holding a weapon."

She cued up the Apache's weapons menu, and Craig saw her scrolling back and forth from Hellfire missiles to Hydra rockets, as if trying to decide between them.

"My apologies, Madam."

"Here we go," she said, more serious as the convoy approached the target building. *It's only a matter of time before the real shooting starts.*

———

The first Bradley M3 fighting vehicle bounced as it came off the bridge at 50 mph. Its driver slowed just enough to verify the planned route and make a slight pivot, then crossed the intersection and regained speed. Two Humvees followed, with men aiming their top-mounted .50 caliber machine guns at the rooftops along the route. Each gunner watched a different side of the road but saw nothing other than concrete.

Another Bradley, two additional Humvees, and a truck followed, making six Viper vehicles in all. They moved as one, fast enough to cover the distance before anyone could get a drop on them. They knew they had Apache cover, but also knew better than to rely on their continued availability.

The lead Bradley saw the green plastic chem lights on the ground and slowed as it passed by what was left of the iron gate. It stopped with its rear hatch facing the hole in the wall, the big diesel engine idling.

"Titan, this is Viper Three Seven. Ready for handoff," the Army officer said.

Mario and Jonathan crouched with their rifles aimed toward the street and saw the Bradley come to a stop.

"Titan One, Viper has arrived," Jonathan said.

Porter stood just inside the main entrance. "Alright, Fadhi, keep your head down. That way," Porter said as he pushed him forward. The Bradley's back hatch opened as he moved toward it.

Almost done.

Porter was focused on one single purpose: To get Fadhi on that Bradley. After that he'd worry about getting his men out, but at this stage everything else was subordinate. Until Fadhi was surrounded by the armor plating of the Bradley with a quad of Rangers around him, Porter would not let him go. If the convoy was ambushed, if the Apache's got called away or shot down, or if all of his team was killed around him, Porter would get Fadhi home or die trying. If he had to shield Fadhi with his own body to slow down enemy bullets, if he had to carry the man all the way to Baghdad, Porter would see his mission through. He knew almost nothing about the son of the Shiite leader, and he didn't care about him at all. Fadhi was a mission, his mission, and tomorrow there would be another.

The SEALs parted to make way for them. Porter shielded Fadhi with his body till they reached the hatch, and tossed him in like a 150-pound sack of potatoes. Two

Rangers caught him and sat him down while an Army medic began looking him over.

Porter didn't say goodbye, didn't speak to the Rangers, didn't give Fadhi a second thought. He turned away from the Bradley and joined the other five SEALs who were pointing their weapons outward.

"Titan, this is Star Niner, inbound," Porter heard the Little Bird pilot say.

Mission complete. Let's get the hell out of here.

"Copy, Star Niner. On our way," he said.

"Fall back to the LZ," he said to his team. The SEALs moved in the shadows, backing away from the building, scanning their weapons in all directions.

———

As the Bradley and the first two Humvees pulled away, the Rangers dismounted the remaining four vehicles to deal with Fadhi's captors. They stormed the roof, sorted them out, and moved the military-aged men by gunpoint and boot heel to the bed of a five-ton box truck. The soldiers tossed the Sunni thugs into it like cordwood, then climbed up behind them for the drive back to base.

———

The Little Bird swooped in and landed on a different patch of ground than it had ten minutes earlier. The SEALs hopped in as soon as it touched down and were in the air almost before they were even strapped in.

It picked up speed but maintained a low altitude, flying straight and fast along the dirt road toward the desert until clearing the row of buildings, then pulled up hard. A second later it was alone over open desert. It increased altitude and turned left in a wide half-circle, high above the Euphrates.

Porter surveyed the city he'd grown to hate. He didn't hate many things, but a city full of deadly men intent on killing was one of them. They kidnapped, killed, bombed, and tortured as many people as necessary to solidify their distorted version of harmony. Porter looked away.

He knew the city was full of good people, some of them were even working with his teams. Like Fadhi and his family, they were trying desperately to combat the insurgents, to establish a new government.

How many more of these kinds of missions?

He was tired, tired of war, tired of training incompetent Iraqis, tired of seeing the ones with promise get cut down by sectarian violence. The situation was maddening.

You don't have to do it much longer, you know. Screw 'em.

As his feet dangled high above the landscape, he wasn't contemplating quitting. *SEALs never quit, but we don't do this stuff forever.*

He thought about the truck sitting in his garage that he rarely ever got to drive. He thought about going to a Sox game with his dad again. *How long has it been since I've been back home? Four years? Three?*

Porter thought about retired team guys he loved but almost never saw anymore, and about the civilian business opportunities some of them offered.

He thought of Jen.

An Admiral had once told him he would know when it was time to hang it up. "Till then, just focus on your boys, and get through the next mission."

Porter looked to his left where Tag and Jonathan were riding along next to him. He looked to the horizon, the sky just beginning to change to the color of dawn — time for bed, unless there was another mission to roll into.

The only easy day was yesterday.

———

The Apaches watched the Little Bird swoop in and pick up the SEALs in a swift, beautiful motion that made Ginger smile. She turned the helicopter, and the Apaches followed the convoy until it was almost to the base gate.

"Pegasus One Three, I think we're done here," Ginger said to her wingman.

"Copy that," the other pilot said.

Ginger took up a new heading to fly back to their base. After ten minutes, Craig asked her, "How's your butt doing?"

"Shut up, Craig." She rolled her eyes.

"Mine feels amazing," he said. "So soft, so cushy. I could almost take a nap." He raised his arms and yawned.

Ginger squirmed in her seat and focused on flying the marvel of modern weaponry, with its sophisticated systems worth thirty-five million dollars, all surrounding the cheapest seat cushions the Army could buy.

Fifteen minutes later they were almost to the base when they received a text message:

PEGASUS EIGHT CONFIRM FUEL AND WEAPONS STATUS

Craig replied with the numbers that confirmed the Apaches were fully loaded on weapons but almost dry on fuel.

PREPARE FOR HOT PIT

"So much for breakfast," Ginger said.

"I'll take that $50 bucks."

"I never took it."

The Apaches landed next to each other with their engines running for a hot pit refuel. Two men in chemical firefighting suits stood by holding fire extinguishers while other men pulled hoses toward the aircraft, lifting a fuel nozzle attachment to shoulder height and fastening it in place. Ginger watched through the side window to ensure there were no accidents or spillage.

"I'm gonna take that nap now," Craig said, faking another yawn.

Their new coordinates came in as the aircraft topped off its fuel tank. The ground crew removed the hose and gestured to Ginger that she was good to go, and she radioed to her wingman. They lifted off together.

Ginger radioed, "Pegasus Eight, proceeding to objective. What do we got?"

"Copy, Pegasus. TIC." *Troops in contact.*

She angled the nose and throttled her way up to full power. "Better wake up from that beauty nap, Craiger."

2

Rhino

Tikrit, Iraq

The orders were simple: Find the enemy and engage him.

It was the same mission American rifle companies had conducted for generations, in every environment on earth. They'd hunted their elusive enemies across farmlands, through cities, into dense forests, and within gorgeous chalets and palaces. They slogged through bloody surf onto treeless volcanic islands, chasing their enemies through miles of tunnels that bombs couldn't penetrate. Riflemen rode helicopters over miles of rice paddies to hump through lush tropical foliage and exotic cities, searching. Always searching.

Riflemen fought dysentery and yellow fever, leeches and camel spiders, the boredom of fruitless patrols and the terror of sudden ambushes. They searched in rugged snow-peaked mountains, in deserts, and in dilapidated cities that all looked the same, like this one in the middle of Iraq that could just as easily have been the one they were at yesterday, or the week before that.

The Army rifle company was aggressive, because aggression drives the enemy to make mistakes, which ends wars, and ending wars meant the riflemen could go home. But to win they first needed to find the enemy, and so they searched.

Has this place ever looked good? Or has it always been this way? Corporal Lewis surveyed the town as he rode in the open top vehicle. *Surely it was new once, years ago maybe. But this place looks like a scene from a zombie movie.*

It was always the same. They drove through the desert, sweating under gear, riding in smelly, cramped Infantry Carrier Vehicles until they came to a new town where he'd see more broken walls, trash in the streets, burned or abandoned cars, and people.

Wait. Why aren't there any people?

His heart raced a few beats faster and an age-old ally told him something was not right. The ally was fear, and the fear said *ambush.*

The ICV bounced along and he started looking closer at the buildings as he passed them. He noticed an unusual feature — small holes in the walls, holes that were all the same size and fairly evenly spaced. Not in one house but in all of them. He passed a window with sandbags stacked behind broken glass.

And still no people anywhere, and no children. There are always children.

In a special pocket he had small stuffed animals and candy for the children they routinely encountered. But no people could only mean one thing.

They're waiting for a signal, drawing us in. Find the enemy and engage him. They're here, alright.

The thought was like a trigger. Suddenly a blast, and three vehicles ahead a massive cloud of black and yellow dust lifted the Fire Support Vehicle off the ground. The soundwave hit him and shook everyone as they watched the vehicle spin in midair.

What kind of explosive lifts a sixteen-ton carrier with nine guys that high off the ground?

Bullets ricocheted off the armor of his ICV and he aimed his M240B machine gun to meet them. Every man in the platoon had the same thought as their radios chattered up and the world exploded around them: *Engage.*

Gunfire rained down from rooftops and up from dugout trenches in the alleys.

They were smart, they got us. Damn.

The enemy had taken full advantage of the terrain and devised a way to hit them and then reposition without being seen, establishing perfect fields of fire for maximum damage.

They probably fed our commanders some bogus tip to get us to come here.

Lewis unleashed his weapon on the building closest to him. Several muzzle flashes came from holes in the wall, but the firepower advantage of the Americans made them scatter. Yet they repositioned and continued to attack, and he realized this road was probably littered with IED's.

The Stryker Infantry Combat Vehicle was fully armored, easily absorbing and deflecting the small caliber rifle bullets. The column's vehicles maneuvered to attack the enemy fire positions they could identify, but were slowed in one direction by the burning vehicle, and Lewis saw burning men falling out the back as medics from another vehicle assisted them. A medic went down as he was dragging a man away from the wreckage.

Twelve soldiers dismounted from the backs of two Strykers, running to assault both sides of the road.

"Dismount to protect the casualties," his own vehicle commander said.

"Wilco," Lewis replied, meaning *will comply.*

He contacted his rifle team leader in the rear compartment of the Stryker. "Deploy to defend the casualties." He watched all six of his infantrymen run to the burning vehicle, spreading out and concealing themselves as they intermittently returned fire into the buildings.

Shooting started again from the right and he felt the force of the Stryker's top-mounted MK 19 grenade launcher firing next to him, its gunner sighting the building through a camera from inside the Stryker, hurling 40mm shells that flew through the shoddy concrete walls like rocks through paper.

Heads popped up from behind lines of sand bags up ahead and the two forward Stryker's machine guns fired into the rooftops, which looked fortified all down the street. He realized his company had no choice but to dismount and fight the town.

Find the enemy and kill the enemy.

"Bring up the MEV," his vehicle commander said over the radio.

His vehicle made way for the company's Medical Evacuation Vehicle trying to get to the burning Stryker, and suddenly he heard a familiar sharp whistling from above.

It got louder as the first mortar round came in humming. It landed to the right of the Stryker, sending a plume of sand and steel flying, bowling over two infantrymen who were lucky to be far enough away. More mortar rounds flew in.

They've got us dialed in, probably planned this weeks ago. He looked at all of the garbage in the street. They'd have to drive over piles of it to maneuver, and that was only after they got the casualties mounted. *And how many more pressure sensors are waiting to be triggered when we scramble?*

Another mortar landed close enough to shower him and shake his Stryker, followed almost immediately by two more. He smelled smoke after the second explosion and heard screaming in his earphones. *The rifle team leader?*

As Lewis looked over his shoulder he was thrown forward, blinded, ears ringing. He felt the heat from the engulfed vehicle and smelled burning diesel.

He struggled to regain himself and prayed he wasn't missing any body parts, putting his hand to his head, feeling his neck, and looking at his arms and legs.

Am I alive? We took a hit. I'm alive.

He looked behind him. Black smoke poured out of his vehicle.

"We're on fire," he said on the radio. *Get out before the ammo starts cooking off.*

"Get clear. Get clear. Move!" he said to the driver and the vehicle commander. He grabbed his rifle and jumped out the top hatch. Bullets rained around him as he struggled to clear it, leaping to the ground. At the rear of the vehicle he found his rifle team leader's lifeless body just inside the hatch. Lewis dropped his rifle and jumped in, searching in vain for the fire extinguisher as flames licked the vehicle's interior. He threw the fallen sergeant out the back as he jumped free, then grabbed him again and fireman-carried him to the nearest cover he could find, a small car parked near the building on the left.

He got down on a knee, put his back to the wall and looked at the building across the street. Americans were moving in and out of it but enemies were still on the roof. Another mortar exploded, obscuring his view. Two medics assisting the burn victims looked over at him, unsure where to go.

"Here! Over here!" he called.

The medics acknowledged and ran toward him, carrying a badly burned soldier on a litter. Several soldiers from his squad started toward him but he waved for them to stay put.

"There," he said to the medics, pointing to the nearest open door. "Move him there. Follow me."

We need more ammo. We need cover.

"Pop smoke!" he shouted to the soldiers nearest him, then turned to the medics. "Gather the casualties here till the MEV comes up."

The medics acknowledged and ran back to the burning Stryker. Another mortar exploded farther down the road to his left, and he saw the forward Strykers' guns pounding away. Another one approached, slowing as it moved around the wreckage of his ICV.

Suddenly another explosion lifted the approaching Stryker off the ground before slamming it back to earth. Lewis watched it in slow motion, tires spinning in midair. Now there were three dead vehicles, with shell-shocked, bloody men pouring out of the most recent one.

Scattered infantry crouched in the street, trying to shoot from any cover they could find, and every minute another mortar round landed. He waved to the injured men but they didn't see him in the confusion and smoke that filled the street. He ran to a soldier fumbling to put a tourniquet on a man's arm. Lewis smacked him on the helmet.

"There," he pointed to where the stretcher lay, "gather there." Then he ran to the next man.

He saw the red and white cross on the MEV as it neared, and farther down the road through the smoke he thought he caught a glimpse of the missile vehicle moving off the street, between the buildings.

Good, I hope it's going out to hunt down that mortar.

He ran back to the newly-damaged Stryker, grabbed its fire extinguisher and doused the flames, wondering if it was still driveable.

He slung his rifle and picked up as many ammo cans as he could carry back to the building, where the medics were struggling to get the worst burn victims inside the MEV. The street reeked of charred flesh and spent ammunition.

"What do you need?" he asked the nearest medic.

"Bandages. Lots of them, and IVs," he replied.

Fully loaded with critically wounded burn victims, the MEV started backing out as a barrage of rifle fire came down on it. The infantry returned fire.

Lewis ran to the disabled Stryker, rummaged around, and grabbed an armful of med kits. Another mortar exploded as he jumped out, knocking him off his feet. He got up with ears ringing and regathered his supplies, dizzy and disoriented.

He stood and looked around, confused about which way to go. Between the buildings ahead, he saw an old pickup with a long tube mounted in the bed. The tube spun, pointed directly at him, and fired.

Lewis dove, rolling away as it impacted the Stryker. It tipped to the side but the armor held, and it righted itself.

He stumbled back to the casualty collection point, dumped the supplies just inside the door, ran back to the street and leveled his rifle.

Where the hell did the technical go?

He ran across the street, back to the alley, and sighted in on the pickup. Several men stood in its bed, loading another round into the tube. Lewis fired as he ran, shooting each man several times as he got closer. Before he could get a clear shot at him, the driver hit the gas and sped off, abandoning the dead bodies of the gun crew as they fell from the bed.

He stared at the dead men in the street and realized he was alone. He backed up to the nearest wall and looked around, hearing gunfire from almost every direction. Suddenly the truck reemerged behind him, now facing the opposite direction with a new crew manning the gun. It slid to a stop in the same spot.

The truck-mounted recoilless rifle pointed straight at him and he sprinted away as it fired. A 105mm projectile hurled past him, into the building. The explosion threw him forward and through the flimsy wall of the opposite building, where he lay stunned under a light layer of debris, ears ringing.

He heard faint rifle fire, yelling. He rolled onto his knees. His back seared and he wondered if he was on fire as he regained his balance. He stumbled toward the hole he'd flown through just in time to see another projectile fly down the street toward the men he'd left. Wincing from pain, he stepped through the hole in the wall, looked to his right, and saw the gun crew reloading.

Lewis was furious and his adrenaline kicked in. He quick-stepped toward the pickup, shooting first at the man who was aiming the M40 gun at the Americans. He went down but the others fired back a spray of AK-47 rounds, several hitting him in the feet and lower legs. He fell to his knees, then onto his side. While laying on the ground he returned fire, hit the Iraqi rifleman and the gun barrel while trying to hit the third man. He was about to shoot the driver when the truck pulled away again.

For a moment it was quiet. His feet were bleeding and he pulled himself along on his elbow, lifting his head to try to find some cover. He had never felt so alone.

He would need to crawl back to the medics, over a hundred meters away. But then he heard the truck again.

Not again.

It came to a stop in roughly the same location, but the new crew didn't notice the injured American as they lined up their gun for another shot. Lewis summoned his strength, got onto his knees, and pulled a grenade out of his pouch. He tossed it in a high arc toward the truck but whiffed it, and the grenade landed in front of the truck, blowing open the hood and pulverizing the front left tire. He ducked as sharp metal peppered his neck. He heard voices again and looked up, saw the man in the back of the truck pointing his AK skyward, shooting on full auto.

Lewis rolled over to pull another grenade and saw a shadow overhead, then heard the thumping of a 30mm cannon. He looked up and saw the moving image of an Apache.

—

"Bingo. He gone," Ginger said as the truck exploded, and she was answered by several pings on the side of her helicopter. "Taking fire." She throttled the bird away from the buildings.

"Pegasus, this is Rhino Six," the company commander said on the ground channel, "we're getting hammered by mortars here."

"Copy that, Rhino. Do you have a grid for me?"

"Negative, Pegasus. Probably three teams at least."

"Copy that, Rhino."

"Find 'em Craig," she said, making a wide circle around the center of the action.

Craig saw rifle flashes all over the battlefield. Smoke rose in every direction from burning Stryker vehicles, rockets, and grenades. He clearly made out the two burning Strykers; a number of the others were fully engaged. Infantry exchanged gunfire with enemies in the alleys, across opposing rooftops, and from behind the cover of various buildings.

"I can't tell who's who down there," he said.

"Rhino, we're having a hard time pinpointing your locations," Ginger said into her mic.

"Copy, Pegasus. We've got dismounted infantry in two buildings and a casualty collection point in a third. I'm gonna have 'em pop smoke on the roofs of those locations."

"Copy that," Ginger said.

"Pegasus, I've also got four intact Strykers and dismounted squads supporting them on the street," the captain said.

A few seconds later Ginger saw a smoke canister emitting a blue plume from the top of a building with several rooftop shooters. Then two additional smoke canisters opened on the roofs near the burning Strykers. Enemy fighters ran to and fro, and more trucks like the one she'd just taken out were all over the area. It was a mess, but at least she had an idea where to start.

"Pegasus One Three, do you see the smoke?" Ginger asked her wingman.

"Copy Eight, I got 'em," Donovan said.

"How about you just kill everything to the north and I'll kill everything to the south?" she said.

"Sounds good, Eight."

"I got the mortar. One of them, anyway," Craig said. "The ditch, 300 meters from Rhino building Alpha."

"Splash 'em, Craiger," she said, plugging additional targets into her computer.

Craig flicked his thumb switch from the gun position to the missile, raised the safety, and pulled the trigger. A Hellfire missile flew from its rail toward several men crouched in a ditch, holding a large diameter tube. The ground erupted in debris and smoke.

Ginger pulled the trigger on the chain gun and cut down three men holding AK-47s as they ran down an adjacent street. More targets scrambled away, terrified of the Apache bearing down on them.

"Pegasus, we're taking RPG fire from the building across from us."

"Copy that, Rhino," Ginger said.

"Craig, you got 'em?"

"Copy." Craig locked on the building. Muzzle flashes came from several openings on three floors.

"Rockets away." He pulled the trigger, sending two of his twenty-four Hydra rockets into the ground floor, followed immediately by two into the second floor and another two onto the roof, then sent one of his four remaining Hellfires past the building into an enemy truck as it sped along a parallel road.

The building rumbled and half the roof caved in. All movement ceased from the standing sections that remained.

"Yeah, that'll do it, Pegasus," the captain said on the radio. "Nice. Still taking mortar rounds."

"Craig?" Ginger asked.

"Yeah?"

"Find that other mortar team…and find that Chachie who took a shot at me earlier."

"Uh, everyone's shooting at us, Ginger."

"Yeah, but I want the little punk who started it."

"I'll see what I can do."

<hr>

Two buildings away, the dust from the collapsed building enveloped Lewis. He rubbed dirt and sweat from his eyes and tried to stand but his feet gave way. The searing pain almost made him pass out. He took a few deep breaths and rolled onto his thigh, propped himself on his elbow, and dragged himself to a pile of concrete rubble.

He could hear gunfire all around him but only saw smoke and debris. He could hear helicopters circling but they were out of his frame of vision.

Fear creeping in, he inspected his feet. Blood pooled around his legs.

I need to get to the medics.

He crawled, leaving a trail of blood behind him. When he got to the wall he sat up with his back against it, pulled out a bandage from his pouch and wrapped it tight around his ankle. Blood soaked though, but the bandage seemed to abate the flow.

Do I need a tourniquet?

The thought was interrupted by a whining sound of an incoming mortar.

———

"How we lookin'?" the lieutenant asked his medic.

"These two are stable, this one's gonna need a medevac ASAP, burns all over. Where is the MEV?"

"Took the first load away. Gonna have to wait. We've got air support now."

"Rhino Six, Rhino Five, Copy?" the XO called his captain over the radio.

"Go Rhino Five," the captain answered from the command Stryker.

"I've got three critically wounded here and one who needs immediate evac."

"Copy, Rhino Five," he said.

Another round of mortars exploded in the street, jarring two of the Strykers but their armor repelled the blasts. The force sent a cloud of dust into the casualty collection point.

The lieutenant patted his medic on the shoulder.

"Keep on 'em, I'm going back to the roof. I'll get you word if we can get a medevac in."

"Affirmative," he said, knowing full well they wouldn't call in a rescue bird while the firefight raged outside. They'd have to wait for another Stryker to carry them out, hopefully before shock killed the man.

The lieutenant ran up the stairs amid gunshots, stopping on the second floor to check on his sniper team. "How we doin'?"

Two of his men lay in front of a window looking through scopes toward the field. "Might have one of the mortar positions. I see smoke."

"See a tube?" he asked.

"Negative, there's a bunch of debris and grass, but I swear I saw a smoke plume from it for a second."

The lieutenant crept up next to his sniper with binoculars. He saw the pile of logs, maybe an abandoned wooden cart, surrounded by tall grass. He got on his radio.

"Rhino Six, Rhino Five. We may have located one of the mortar positions."

"Pegasus One Three, I've got ten combat minutes left. How's your fuel?" Ginger told her wingman.

"Same, ten minutes left," Donovan said.

"Copy that."

"Pegasus, we have a potential location on one of the mortar teams," the company commander said on the radio. He gave the description as relayed to him from his lieutenant, and Ginger maneuvered to inspect it.

"All Rhino call signs, this is Pegasus Eight. Be advised we've got ten minutes remaining on station. Prioritize your targets."

Ginger could almost hear a collective groan from the soldiers on the ground. She knew that she and her wingman were holding back a tide of well-equipped, creative enemy fighters who obviously chose and prepared this battleground long ago. It galled her to have to break off. She still had plenty of weapons but only enough gas to sustain flight for an hour and twenty minutes total, some of which she'd used to get here. She needed an equivalent amount to get to the nearest refueling point.

She looked at the fields surrounding the main buildings and saw insurgents fleeing into the open, running away from the destruction she and Craig kept bringing. She looked at the wood pile Rhino Five had called in, and flipped on the targeting acquisition system. Heat signatures came from two figures hidden within the pile.

"Copy, Pegasus. Priority is the mortars," the captain said.

Craig studied the figures. He couldn't make out a mortar tube or weapons, but the men were moving. "What do you say, Ginger?"

Ginger inspected them. She had the pile in the crosshairs of the monocle, her finger on the trigger of the 30mm cannon. Craig had a Hellfire on deck, but he needed a positive identification. It was almost certainly one of the mortar positions, but if it happened to be just two Iraqi kids hiding from the battle and she gave the order to fire, she and Craig could very likely end up watching this gun camera video at their prison sentencing. This was a different kind of war.

"Hold fire," she said, but continued to stroke the trigger while her other eye scanned for threats out the window. *Come on, just make a move. Go ahead, pick up a mortar round. I dare you.*

Rifle shots pinged against the side of the helicopter. Ginger's eye searched for the shooter as she banked her bird left.

There he is.

She lined the crosshairs on two insurgents spraying rifle fire toward her. They were too far away with weapons too small to do the Apache much damage. A single 30mm round would be enough to obliterate a human being, and her gun averaged more than five rounds per second. She gave the slightest tap to the trigger and eliminated both targets.

Crag never took his eyes off the woodpile. He watched the thermal image of the men at work, handling something that looked like another projectile, and knew he had them. All he needed was to see a launch tube — or even just a rifle slung on a shoulder — and the Rules of Engagement said he could shoot. Everything was recorded, and Craig and the rest of the Pegasus pilots would eventually sit in on a debrief where this video would be shown to cockpit crews as a tactical lesson. Every minute detail would be scrutinized. He had to be sure.

One of the men stood and looked over the top of the woodpile directly into the rear of the helicopter, directly into the camera facing the opposite direction.

That's right, buddy. I'm turned around. I can't see you from behind, right? Craig smiled.

The man dropped down, picked up something, and turned back to his partner. Both men turned away from whatever they were holding and put their hands to their ears.

Gotcha.

A small shape launched from the woodpile, leaving a trail of smoke from its ejection. Craig pulled the trigger and a Hellfire missile dropped from the Apache's wing mount. The solid fuel ignited and the 100-pound weapon first flew straight, then turned in midair as it locked on to the grid behind the helicopter Craig had designated.

From the ground, the men at the woodpile would have been startled to see the missile's seemingly chaotic flightpath, and then terrified when it turned directly into them, if they'd had the chance.

"Target destroyed," Craig said.

"Nice one," Ginger said.

Craig looked at his screens and saw the mortar land and explode next to one of the Strykers. He shook his head in frustration and swore.

"I'm gonna tell your mama you said that," Ginger said.

—

"Rhino Six, this is Pegasus Eight. Gotta hit the gas station, be back ASAP," Ginger said.

"Copy that, Pegasus. Hurry back."

"All Rhino call signs, Apache cover is leaving to refuel," he said over the unit radio frequency, then swore out loud.

"How long?" his lieutenant asked, surveying the fields to the west through the vehicle cameras. Something moved in the distant smoke.

"Who knows?"

The fighting was tapering off. *They're regrouping.*

He'd have a few minutes to reposition before the next wave, and he tried to anticipate their next move.

Two mortars taken out by the Apaches. The others went silent, now they probably know better than to reveal their positions. But the helicopters are gone. How long till they figure that out? Not long, couple minutes.

He thought about his casualties near the location of the ambush.

"Rhino two. Update on your casualty status."

"Rhino Six, three stable, one critical in need of evac," was the reply.

"Copy, Rhino Two, the MEV is in route."

"Captain, I've got multiple trucks converging," the lieutenant said.

Here they come again.

Four insurgents stood up in the open field at once, each with an RPG on their shoulder. They simultaneously fired at the command Stryker.

—

Lewis took a moment to catch his breath after crawling another twenty feet. He sat with his back against the wall and saw four rockets streak up from the field. He heard the explosions and couldn't see where the RPG's impacted, but he clearly saw where they were fired from, and watched as the shooters ducked down to conceal themselves in the tall foliage and reposition.

He raised his rifle and caught a glimpse of an insurgent through his scope, running with a launch tube as he ducked behind a small shed. Lewis heard machine gun fire and saw dirt kicking up in the location the RPG's had launched from, pointlessly shooting at the vacated position.

He paused and looked in the direction he thought the medics were, then back to the field where he knew the enemy was.

Find the enemy, kill the enemy. That's your job.

He tried to stand and put weight on his foot. The pain almost made him vomit and pass out, but the foot held his weight; it wavered, but held. He used his rifle as a support and pulled himself up to standing.

Turn off the pain. Get to work.

He hobbled on with excruciating, methodical steps that took him ever closer to the shed. He leaned against the remains of the truck, didn't bother looking at the men he and the Apache had killed. He kept going, tripped and fell forward, cursed and got back up. He saw a second insurgent run to the shed and duck behind it. He looked over the field and saw trucks driving behind the smoke near a far tree line.

His foot gave way. He caught himself as he slammed hard into the grass; tried to stand but couldn't. He leveled his rifle at the shed and scooted along on his knees toward it, leaving a trail of blood as he went.

—

Four well-aimed RPGs didn't have the firepower to destroy the Stryker, but the damage limited its mobility. The sound of its gears grinding was nauseating as it tried to maneuver. The lieutenant recognized one of his men, scooting toward a small structure. He increased magnification and saw the man was injured but engaging the shed. Rifle fire again rained in on the damaged Stryker as it moved to attack, and the lieutenant lost sight of the lone soldier and the shed.

—

Lewis walked on his knees in the tall grass. All he could hear were his own breaths as his heart beat faster and sweat poured down his face. His head pounded.

Range is good, no angle.

He needed to move to his right so he dropped to his elbows and crawled, just like he'd done as a kid in the backyard when it was all a game. A few more feet and his line of sight was clear. Two men with RPGs were about to turn from behind the shed and fire.

Lewis steadied his rifle and fired three round bursts at each of them. They fell dead and he got back to his knees, pulled a pin on a grenade and tossed it at the small shed. The grenade exploded, splintering the frail wood and catching something else; almost immediately, explosions from inside sent a ball of flames skyward. The repercussion knocked him onto his back and flames washed over him. He rolled over several times and patted himself frantically to extinguish the flames and escape the burning grass.

Where is my company?

He saw no vehicles. The ringing in his ears masked the sound of battle, and the pain from gunshots, shrapnel, and burns would no longer submit to duty. His strength drained like air from a punctured tire as his organs began to shut down, and shock accomplished what the enemy could not: his defeat.

———

Ginger changed her heading caught sight of the burning shed, and noticed a soldier alone in the field.

Farther out she saw a convoy of enemy trucks behind some trees, driving in a line toward the fight. She looked at her fuel status.

No time, damn.

She gritted her teeth, resigned to the situation and said nothing to Craig; they both knew.

"Rhino Six, breaking off to refuel. Be advised, you have…" she paused.

"Six," Craig said.

"Six enemy trucks behind the tree line to the north east. Recommend you hit 'em fast."

"Copy, Pegasus. Thanks."

Either the soldiers could hold them off till the Apaches returned, or more men would die. There was nothing she and Craig could do about it.

Just get the gas.

———

Another mortar hit near the casualty collection point, sending concrete fragments into the windows and breaking what little glass remained. From the roof, Rhino Two looked across the expanse of single-story rooftops to the west, a thousand hiding places for a mortar team to conceal themselves in. And he was dealing with at least two.

"Say goodbye to our air cover," the sergeant manning the radio said.

"They'll be back. Just find those mortars," the lieutenant said.

The three damaged Strykers were mostly charred. In the absence of the Apaches, the mortar teams seemed to be trying to zero in on the command vehicle limping around and the building the lieutenant was standing on. If they couldn't neutralize the mortars before the enemy adjusted, the entire building could collapse.

"Sir, the MEV is loaded and pulling away."

The captain scanned the street below and saw the MEV speed away with its second load of casualties. To the north he saw the Anti-Tank Guided Missile vehicle speeding toward the command vehicle.

The ATGM is gonna deal with the trucks. We need to find the mortars.

He turned back to the east, trying to catch movement, a smoke plume, anything that might betray the mortar position so he could walk the infantry in to attack it. He had two snipers on the second story beneath him, mostly taking shots at individual runners as they repositioned from house to house.

"Rhino Six, I need Rhino Four to come forward 100 meters and engage the building on his right."

He heard another mortar round coming in. *We can't stay here.*

———

Ginger landed and stretched her back in the seat. She allowed herself a few seconds to close her eyes and take slow, deep breaths, refocusing on the next leg of the mission that had started at sunset the night before. As the helicopter swallowed 3000 gallons of fuel in six minutes, Craig checked his systems and inventoried his remaining weapons.

Ginger looked out of her right window and saw Donovan refueling his bird. She texted him, using the Apache's keypad:

RACE YA BACK. WISH I HAD A DECENT STEREO

Donovan replied with a text of his own:

NEGATIVE. LEARNED MY LESSON IN WOFT

Donovan had once teased her during their time together in Warrant Officer Flight Training, a hundred years ago, or so it seemed. She challenged him to a race on her Kawasaki motorcycle, made him look stupid, then took their pilot class to dinner with Donovan's 300 bucks and made him order from the kids menu.

She typed again:

TELL RICO GOOD SHOOTIN

Out the window, she saw Donovan's front seater blow her a kiss.

AWW, she mouthed, and put her hand to her chest.

The refueling crews disconnected the lines and backed off, and the ground crew leader gave the Apache pilots a thumbs-up.

She typed:

LETS GET IT ON

Donovan replied:

AFTER YOU MILADY

———

A nearby explosion brought Lewis back to consciousness. He lifted his head a few inches off the ground to see over the grass, saw the vehicle tires nearby. *They don't know I'm here. Or maybe they think I'm dead.*

The truck's shooters poured torrents of bullets into the building, and fury raged within him. He saw his men return fire, one of them from a grenade launcher. The truck exploded, and the occupants scrambled in different directions, one running straight toward him.

Lewis got up on his knees and shot the man in the face, then went full-auto and mowed down every insurgent he saw until his mag went dry. He scrambled to change his magazine as those he missed turned their weapons on him, their attention now divided between him and the rest of his squad near the building. He fired again with controlled, three-round bursts, dropping three men before noticing the recoilless rifle from the third truck fire into the building next to the Americans.

He grabbed his last grenade and heaved it toward the truck, falling facedown in the grass from the effort of throwing it. He heard shooting all around him and he tried to raise his head but everything was too heavy, the pain too strong. There was nothing left but to wait and die.

Ginger looked out the window and saw the soldier fall forward. Craig immediately fired a line of 30mm, destroying the remaining trucks and every man in them.

"Is that the same guy?" Ginger asked.

"Who knows?" Craig said.

Ginger passed over them and saw the command Stryker fighting it out around another corner. Craig identified the shooters and sent a series of Hydra rockets into three positions silencing them, allowing the command Stryker to limp away.

"Rhino Six, this is Pegasus Eight, what are your priorities? Over," Ginger asked.

"Pegasus, Rhino Two is still taking mortar fire. Kill the mortar asap."

"Copy, Rhino Six. Any input on the mortar's location?"

"Pegasus, Rhino Two says it's in one of those houses to the northeast of his position."

"Pegasus Eight, I think I have him," Donovan said, making a fast, wide turn around the neighborhood west of the street.

"Copy, One Three," she said.

He's all yours, Rico.

"Craiger, how we doing on ammo?"

He looked at his screen: 600 rounds of 30 mm, 22 Hydra rockets, and 3 Hellfires remaining. "We're good."

"Good, use 'em up. I don't want to hear it from Eddie again," Ginger said.

"Right. It's not like they're gonna expire, ya know."

"Dare you to tell him that."

"No thanks."

Craig fired off another round of rockets. "There you go, Eddie. And I think I've got the other mortar."

"Where?"

"Here." Craig highlighted a dumpster on the targeting computer. "A dude just jumped into it."

"Maybe he's just hiding from all the gunfire?"

Ginger saw another man toss a bundle into the dumpster, then run in the house next door and return with another armload before jumping inside, closing the lid over him.

"Ah, that's him alright."

The lid cracked open and a man peeked out. A second later, the lid flapped open just long enough for a mortar round to streak skyward before closing. Craig didn't hesitate; he sent a Hellfire into the dumpster, destroying it and the building next to it in a cloud of debris.

"Bingo," he said.

"Pegasus One Three, one mortar down. Need help finding the other one?"

"Negative, Eight. Target destroyed," Donovan answered.

"Copy that. Rhino Six, this is Pegasus Eight, looks like the mortars are gone. Which grid you want us to plow for you?" Ginger asked.

"Pegasus, clear a path to the east if you can."

"Copy, Rhino Six. Standby."

Ginger few over the field where the corporal lay, and zoomed her camera at the prone figure.

"Craig, is that guy still alive?"

Craig flipped on the thermal imaging. "Affirmative, but probably not for long. Gonna need a medevac, probably."

This LZ is too hot for that, Ginger thought. She could see the other soldiers running to him.

"This is Rhino Six, I've got a critically wounded in need of immediate medevac."

She and Craig took turns hitting various targets on the ground for another two minutes before she heard the reply.

"Rhino Six, acknowledged your request for medevac. Standby."

Nobody's coming anytime soon, though.

The Apache pilots were already eying their fuel gages again.

The medic set a tourniquet just below the knee as shots rang out from the soldiers covering them, and then started patching the other holes.

"He's gonna be gone in the next thirty minutes if we don't get him medevaced now. Tell 'em again."

The sergeant toggled his radio.

"Rhino Six, repeat, I need an immediate evac. Critically wounded. No time left."

Craig fired another round of rockets, and another hellfire. He was almost out of missiles.
Ginger radioed her base that they would have to break contact to refuel, "Ten minutes remaining on station."

"Copy, Pegasus Eight. Pegasus Six and Pegasus One Zero en route to relieve you."

She listened in on the open frequency as the captain attempted to vector in a medevac for the critical injury. She heard *acknowledged* and *stand by* repeatedly from different sources across the communications net.

"Fire from the windows. Rocket away," Craig said.

She saw a man with an RPG duck behind a car. Her eye centered on the side door and the cannon tracked in on the target. She flipped over the fire control, squeezed the trigger, and heard a jerking mechanical sound followed by silence. Ginger and Craig both checked the 30mm ammunition status — 340 rounds remaining.

"Fire control failure," Craig said, switching to rockets. He held the laser on the door of the car, released another Hydra, and watched the car explode.

"I'm gonna kill Eddie," she said.

"Eddie's gonna kill you for breaking his gun."

Ginger looked at the remaining weapons payload — one Hellfire and two rockets.

"Pegasus One Three, my gun's broke. Almost out of rockets. A few more shots and I'll have to break off."

"Copy, Eight," Donovan said, not masking his frustration.

"Rhino Six, this is Pegasus Eight. Gonna have to re-arm. I'll take out whatever I see till we run out."

"Copy, Pegasus." The captain's voice betrayed his irritation after repeated requests for a medevac. "If you can keep the wolves off my men till we can get a medic, I'd appreciate it."

"Affirmative," she said, and banked hard to the right to get a better angle on the four men huddled in the grass, taking and returning intermittent fire from several directions.

Craig lined up the source of one of them, released a rocket, and destroyed a group of insurgents. An American on the ground gave the Apache a thumbs-up.

They could see the medic doing compressions, and heard on the radio, "This is Rhino Six, we're losing him. Either we get a medevac soon or don't bother."

"Copy." It was the same reply they had heard all afternoon. Ginger watched the medic through the window as he slammed his fist into the ground and shook his head in disgust.

Three minutes seemed like an hour as she hovered and kept her laser painted on Craig's last targets of the day. They had played their part, could have done more for the men on the ground but for the broken gun. She watched the targets disappear one by one in clouds of dust with one of her eyes, and watched the tragedy unfold on the ground with her other.

"Last Hellfire," Craig said with detached professionalism as he also watched the soldier dying. "Ginger?"

Ginger stared out the window, and made a decision.

"Pegasus One Three, move to cover my landing. Rhino Six, I'm going to extract your man."

———

Donovan smiled.

He and Ginger had entered flight training together. They had competed, failed and studied, failed again and grew. By graduation they'd learned to love each other's wildly different personalities. He knew tomorrow she would face the battalion commander in the mission debrief and defend her actions without apology like she always did. The responsibility for Craig's life and the 30 million dollar aircraft was on her.

Protecting Ginger as she set the Apache down in a hot landing zone was now on him. Nobody was going to touch her.

"Copy, Eight. I've got you."

———

The medic felt a surge of dust from behind him as he leaned over his patient, struggling to keep the IV bag from flying out of his hand. The Apache landed almost on top of them, its engines screaming — he could almost reach out and touch the port side rocket launcher.

He wondered how they would secure his patient to a helicopter that was designed to carry all variety of weapons, but not a person. Two clocks were ticking; the attack helicopter was a sitting duck, and his patient was dying.

The canopy opened and the front-seat occupant scrambled out and ran to them.

"Can we lift him?" Craig yelled over the engine noise.

"Yeah, where are we going to put him?"

"In the front seat," Craig said.

The medic was surprised but relieved. He followed Craig's lead as he motioned to two soldiers for help. Craig and the medic got on the helicopter and the soldiers passed the wounded man up. Craig guided the injured man's bloody, bandaged feet into position, leaned him back, and found a place to secure the IV bag. Then he turned off his controls so the sedated man wouldn't affect the flight or weapons operations if he woke up.

It then dawned on him that he and Ginger hadn't discussed where he would go.

He leaned over to her. "I'll stay and help them out. Catch a ride back later."

Ginger almost smacked him. She admired his courage but she also knew he wouldn't last five minutes in a firefight. He'd be killed, and his mom would kill her for leaving him there.

"Strap yourself to the fuselage," she said. "And if you fall off and die, I'm gonna kill you," she added, lowering the canopy.

Craig opened the side hatch and retrieved a length of webbing. He strapped it to a large carabiner on his flight suit and then to a handle just in front of the wing outside the cockpit doors. He got situated and looked around, noticed three of the soldiers staring at him. He gave a thumbs-up.

One of the soldiers shook his head, ran up to him, pulled out a length of paracord and two carabiners from his own rucksack, and secured Craig to the helicopter like a frustrated mom strapping her toddler into a carseat. The soldier smacked him on his helmet, gave him a thumbs-up, and jumped down to rejoin his men.

Craig looked through the window at Ginger. With her visor down he could only see her smile as she shook her head and mouthed, *Hold on.*

———

Lewis woke in a haze to the sensation of floating. Through slit eyelids he tried to reconcile his last thoughts with what he was seeing: clouds and terrain in the distance, sunlight shining in his eyes.

Am I dead?

He looked at his legs. They were obscured by several mechanisms, dials, controllers, video screens, and keypads. He looked to his left and saw the ground passing under him, felt a surge of pain, and his head fell against the headrest waiting for it to pass. He turned to the right window and saw a man with a large helmet, with rounded dark glasses resembling bug eyes that made him even more confused.

The bug man looked at him and smiled, then gave a thumbs-up.

I must be dead.

———

Against every instinct, Ginger kept a level, moderate speed as she flew with Craig attached to the outside of her bird. She wanted to go full throttle to get the soldier to the hospital sooner, but feared that flying too fast would flick Craig off the wing like a bug. She was also banking on an invite to the Allen's Thanksgiving table, and feared killing one of Cecilia Allen's children might jeopardize her invitation.

She relayed the tactical situation to the pair of Apaches relieving her and Donovan, then made visual contact with them. They came straight toward her and as they got closer, she heard Tim Miller's voice in her ear.

"This is Pegasus Six, we'll finish up for ya. See you at home."

———

As the pairs of Apaches got closer, Tim Miller was astonished to see a person sitting on top of Ginger's rocket pod. As they passed each other, Tim recognized Craig, screaming as if at a rock concert, swinging his legs, and giving him hang-loose signs with both hands.

Tim turned back to his instrument panel and his fingers went to the keypad. He sent a quick text to Ginger:

THE HELL?

A few seconds later Ginger texted back:

HES IN TIMEOUT

———

After dropping off the soldier and letting Craig back into his seat, they finally landed at their own base, refueled, and taxied the Apache to the rearming point. They would still have to remain in their seats with the controls running to allow the weapons to reload. Their arming team would do a visual inspection of the unused munitions — in this case, a single remaining rocket.

Ginger stretched her aching back and rubbed her neck while yawning. She had been in the seat for eleven hours.

"Uh oh," she said to Craig. Eddie, their ground crew sergeant, stopped just outside the canopy and stared at her with his arms crossed. She raised the canopy and offered a weak smile.

Eddie's booming voice rose above all the other noise.

"Went and broke my gun, eh, ma'am?"

3

Porter

Al Asad Airbase, Iraq

Porter leaned back in the lawn chair and flipped open the book Aiden had sent him. He didn't read much, but his friend sent a few classic paperbacks every month anyway, along with two large bags of M&Ms.

Porter struggled through two pages before checking to see what page he was on. He flipped to the last page, saw the total page count was 349, and sighed. He went back to page 41.

Denny walked into the room, saw him reading, and went to Porter's bookshelf. He perused the titles for a minute.

"What the hell is a *Pimpernel?*" Denny asked.

"I have no idea," Porter said without looking up.

Denny sat on Porter's bunk and helped himself to a handful of M&Ms.

"Want to go for a run?" he said while chewing.

Porter closed the book, grateful for an excuse. "Sure." He grabbed his own handful of M&Ms before hiding the precious candy in a crate under his bunk. He tossed the book on the bed. The thieves could have all the books they wanted.

It was near sunset when they finished their run, but barely midday by their internal clocks. They pushed themselves just enough to stay agile, maintain focus, and to be ready whenever something might come up. Something was always coming up.

Porter and Denny made their way to the chow hall, ate a hearty lunch, and went back to their platoon headquarters. As they entered the room, an Iraqi soldier quickly got off the sofa and stood.

"Sirs," he said, saluting. None of the other SEALs moved or even seemed to notice their officers; several of them were watching a movie on a television in the corner.

"Sit down, Ozzy," Porter said, sinking into the cushions and laying back with his eyes closed.

"Sorry, sir. The informality is rather new to me," he said with accented but discernible English.

"It's Porter." He closed his eyes again.

Ozzy regained his seat and waited a few minutes before speaking again.

"I'm very pleased with the outcome of the last mission. Fadhi is a good man."

Who the hell is Fadhi? Porter had to think for a minute before he remembered the name of the man they'd rescued the night before. He opened one eye.

"Friend of yours?"

"No, sir. I know of the family. They are very good for Iraq. They are very..." Ozzy searched for the word. "Targeted."

"Don't know anything about 'em," Porter said, closing his eyes again. "Glad he's alright."

Ozzy smiled at Porter and opened his mouth to continue, but read his disinterest and thought better of it. All their conversations up to this point had been brief discussions on tactics — specifically, Porter chewing out the Iraqi translator for one mistake or another. But Ozzy learned faster than any of the Iraqis in the pool. He had an operational aptitude that stood out, and all of the Americans who had worked with him, including the top tier SEALs in the room, had adopted a margin of respect for him. And yet Porter remained skeptical, and Ozzy felt it.

"If I may ask, sir? You instruct me to call you Porter, this is a nickname, correct?"

Porter stifled a litany of curse words with a deep breath. "Yes."

"I do like my American nickname, Ossy."

"Ozzy, not Ossy." Shep and Jonathan said at the same time.

"You see?" he said.

Mario joined in. "I thought Ozzy was your name?"

"No, my name is Zayno."

Porter almost got up to excuse himself, regretting his choice of seat, but Mario chimed in again.

"Why do they call you Ozzy?"

"I don't know exactly. When I first volunteered to train with the Americans, we stood for roll call. The commander stumbled with my surname, then said something I later learned was a profanity. He then called me simply Z. Eventually it became Ossy."

"OZZZZZY," Mario stood and leaned into the Iraqi. "With Zees, not Esses."

"You are Mario. Yes? Is Mario your family name?" Ozzy asked.

"Negative."

Three of the SEALs called out, "Maaaahrio" with a strange, high-pitched inflection.

"This is a joke?" Ozzy asked.

"They're jealous of the stash," Mario said.

"Your mustache? Yes, they all have thick beards. Why is that?"

"Frogmen wear beards," Mario explained, "but my last assignment was a mixed unit, SEALs and Rangers mainly. The CO decided to enforce strict military regulations with respect to that stuff, made all the SEALs shave their beards. But we found a loophole, the regulations allow for mustaches. Ain't it sexy?" Mario stood up and held his arms out, fishing for approval, only to be met with a cascade of candy pieces and half-empty water bottles.

"So where do they get Mario from?" Ozzy asked.

"It's from a video game. The character has a thick mustache."

"Ah yes, I think I know this game."

Denny leaned forward and looked at Ozzy. "You've got kids, right?"

"Yes, two. I only see them occasionally now. But they are happy with what we are doing."

"Well, I hope you get to see them soon." Denny said, getting up. He gently kicked Porter's boot. "We should head on over."

Porter rubbed his eyes and refitted his tattered Red Sox cap on his head. "Right."

Ozzy stood too. "I think I will go as well."

From the sofa, the rest of the men heard Ozzy call out from behind as he walked out.

"Mister Mario, tell Luigi I said hello!"

———

Porter and Denny surveyed the rows of tables, settling on one near the exit. Officers from various branches filed in and found seats, and notepads and pencils came out as the room got crowded. Two operators walked in, searched the room, and immediately made eye contact with the SEALs.

Porter nodded to Jenkins, and the Delta officers took seats at their table.

"You gals come here often?" Eric asked his special operations counterparts.

"Practically every night. The bartender is lousy," Denny said.

"You might have a problem. May want to get some help," Jenkins said.

"He's beyond help," Porter said.

As more officers trickled in, Porter leaned over to make eye contact with Jenkins down the table. "You guys getting any replacements soon? Heard you had to send back three this month."

"Maybe four. Two on the same mission, then Peetie goes and breaks his leg, now Jimmy's got some crazy fever thing. Practically died from dysentery on the last op. See how the next day or so shakes out. How 'bout you guys?"

"We're good. Pretty amazing, considering the tempo."

"Right," the Delta officers agreed.

The crowd quieted as the general in command entered and went straight to the front of the room.

"Okay, I know you all have pressing matters to attend to, so we'll keep this as brief as possible. First I want to give you an update on what we know as far as the sectarian violence you've all been encountering. I know it's messy, but we're starting to see some tribal leaders play ball. More on that in a sec. Second, we'll go over a couple of significant enemy innovations we've seen pop up, and we'll finish with a breakdown of the overall campaign so you can start planning your areas of responsibility." The general paused, scanning the attentive, professional audience.

"Alright, let's get to it."

———

Three hours later, Porter and Denny were huddled around a computer screen going over mission details. Soon they would be conducting a presentation of their own for their team.

"I don't remember the Navy recruiter mentioning anything about PowerPoint," Denny said, working the mouse.

"I don't remember the last time I swam anywhere."

"I'll bet Shep does." They laughed, remembering the op where Sheppard fell into a ditch of sewage and spent a week in sickbay as a result. They clicked several slides and became serious again. Decisions made now meant life or death later. Porter started thinking about the last year's worth of ops.

"Think it's getting better?"

"Must be. Less bombs going off."

"Ever think of hangin' it up?" Porter said, taking a sip of coffee.

"Every damn day," Denny said. "Still plenty of war left. You're almost up, though. What are you thinkin'?"

"Who has time to think? It's just onto the next mission, but I know it's out there. Lingering." After another minute he said, "Some admiral will probably just tell me to re-up, and I'll just say, 'Sure whatever,' ya know?"

"No plans for after?"

Porter put his hands behind his head and stared at the wall, thinking about Jen's letters. "Negative."

"Probably best not to."

"I don't mind thinking about it. I just don't want to leave this stuff for someone else to clean up. Might as well stick with it till it's over."

"Not me, bro. Someone else broke it, they can clean it up. The sooner we get outta here, the better."

"Well, you better figure out that insertion point then, or we ain't going anywhere," Porter said, looking at the satellite image on the screen.

"I still think we should use this portage here." Denny pointed to an area of vegetation on the lake's shore. "Be a hell of a lot quieter and faster than fast-roping it in the parking lot, and maybe we can finally break out the dive gear."

"Better confirm it's not the friendly neighborhood toilet, first."

"No problem. I'll have Shep recon it," Denny smiled.

4

Ginger

Contingency Operating Base (COB) Foxtrot
Kirkuk Province, Iraq

Ginger walked out of the mission debriefing with less enthusiasm than usual.

Tim Miller caught up to her. "It was perfect."

Ginger didn't slow down, or even look at him.

"Yeah, I know."

"So why are you upset?"

Ginger scoffed. "I'm not."

Tim laughed. "Okay, let me rephrase that. Why are you acting like a whiny brat?"

Ginger paused and turned to the older pilot, intending to lay into him. The smile on his face and the direct question made her hesitate, causing the slightest hint of a smirk to show on her lips. It was all he needed.

"See? You know I'm right."

"So tell me this then, oh Jedi Master," she asked. "If it was so perfect, why was Atwood dressing me down for it?"

"Because Atwood's a dirtbag, but who cares? Everyone in there would have done the same thing, including him. That's not new."

Ginger kept walking in silence.

"What? Do you need a lollipop? Poor little Ginger got her feelings hurt," he continued.

"Keep your lollipop," she smiled at the dig. "Geriatric old man."

"That's better," he said putting his arm around her in a fatherly way and roughing up her hair. "Good job, kiddo."

"Thanks."

———

"Alright, run through it again," Eddie said to J.T., whose laptop was plugged into the Apache. The Pegasus Eight arming team had spent the better part of the morning running diagnostics on their bird, assessing damage and fixing issues as needed. Fixing the 30mm chain gun was the only thing left. J.T. uploaded programming code into the fire control system on the chain gun. After a few keystrokes, the gun started humming.

"I told you there's nothing wrong with it," Tony said, spinning a socket wrench.

"So it's a software glitch, not mechanical?" Eddie asked.

"Yeah, computer must've got confused, or components overloaded," J.T. answered.

"I'm still gonna blame Ginger for breaking it," Eddie said.

"Seems good now," Craig said, climbing out of the seat he'd spent the afternoon scrubbing with baby wipes and towels – a delicate task with all of the electronics, even if it wasn't another man's blood.

"Yeah, but I wouldn't trust it," J.T. said. "I'll replace the motherboard and run it a few more times, then you can test it for reals."

"Gonna have to get you a new 'roid pillow too," Tony teased, holding up the deflated, donut-shaped seat cushion.

"Have Mama Allen send some Preparation H with it," Eddie added, laughing.

"And cookies, bruh," J.T. added, typing on the laptop.

"Oh yeah. Mama Allen's cookies are dope," Tony said.

"I'll ask her," Craig said, examining his seat cushion. He opened the valve and blew it back up, only to watch it deflate again from several holes he'd tried to patch with duct tape.

"Any chance of ordering us some new seats?" Craig asked Eddie in between breaths into the valve.

Eddie gave him an are-you-kidding-me look, and picked up a string of ten 30mm shells out of an ammo crate. "Do you have any idea how much one of these costs?"

Craig shrugged and went back to working on his seat cushion as he watched Ginger and Tim approaching from across the tarmac.

"Hey!" Ginger hollered. "You fix my gun yet?"

Eddie whipped around, held up his massive index finger. "Don't even."

She walked right up to him, stood with her hand on her hips, and smiled, inviting a comeback.

He bit his tongue. "I'm gonna forget I heard that," he said, turning back to the helicopter.

Ginger looked at Craig blowing into his pillow. "Come on Craiger, have some self respect."

Craig closed the plastic valve, admiring his work. "Jealous," he said. He set the pillow on a crate and sat down, leaning back with his hands behind his head and putting his feet up, then pulled his sunglasses over his eyes.

"Chief Cooper, you tell Allen's mama you hung him out to dry yesterday?" J.T. asked.

"Nah, but she'd say he deserved it."

"Let's do it again with a GoPro," Craig said from his makeshift recliner, soaking up the shade provided by the Apache's tail.

Ginger looked over J.T.'s shoulder at the screen, and he felt her next question.

"Couple hours, good as new, ma'am," he reassured her.

"Good deal. Get me back in the air. It's too hot down here." She was already sweating through her t-shirt.

"Whatever. Get the princess outta here," J.T. teased.

She smiled and walked away. As she passed Eddie, he gave her a dap.

"Go on. I got this."

—

Two hours later, Ginger passed Tim in the hall on her way to take a shower, giving him a familiar nod. Tim waited, then turned around and walked back toward her room — just enough to see her door from a distance.

Maybe I was wrong?

He breathed a sigh of relief and was about to walk away when he saw her door open.

Oh, come on, Ginger. You know better.

Tim pretended to turn his attention to the papers in his hand and looked the opposite direction. But in his peripheral vision he saw an Army lieutenant he barely knew slip out of Ginger's room. Tim was sure the man hadn't noticed him, and it took every ounce of restraint to stifle his desire to walk up, grab him by the throat, and throw him through the plywood wall.

—

Ginger started in on her sandwich. Tim walked up with his own tray of food and sat across from her.

"Long day yesterday, everyday lately. How ya doing with that?" he said, taking a bite of his lunch.

"Bring it on. I'm good," she said. "How're *your* old bones doing up there, old man?"

"Like hell, actually. But what else is new?"

They ate in silence for a minute. Tim had no idea how to broach the subject, or whether he even should. *Will she think I'm spying on her? Is it none of my business?* He decided to try another tact.

"Talk to your Pops lately?"

"Last week, yeah. He's got a new girlfriend," she said while chewing. "Seems happy with her. How's Renee?"

"Dealing with our last teenager, and wishing she were over here instead of me," Tim said, laughing. "She sent me an email, said she wanted to borrow my bird to follow her around town."

"How old is your daughter?"

"Seventeen."

"Guy trouble?"

"Better not be," Tim said, taking another bite.

"Says the dad, thousands of miles away." Ginger laughed. "At that age I was driving my dad craaazy. I had a long leash and believe me, I used every inch of it. But you've got good kids. She'll be fine."

"Yeah." He saw an opening. "How did your Dad warn you about messing around with guys?"

"He didn't. I did."

"That's not very reassuring."

"He was just trying to survive on his own. I put him through the ringer. We made it, though."

Tim wanted to tell her outright to get her act together. He wanted to give her the direction she lacked, but he wondered if it was his place. *I wish Renee were here to talk to her with me.*

"He did alright," Tim said. Ginger smiled and took another bite, and he decided to leave it alone. He already felt awkward. Maybe it would play itself out, and if not, he'd run it by his wife first.

Keep her mission-focused. That's the point. That's your job.

"Stay sharp, kiddo. Got an important mission coming up."

"Relax, pops. Go grab a nap or something," she grinned.

5

Hammer Fall: Lake Tharthar

Lake Tharthar, Saladin Governorate, Iraq
Thursday 02:00:00

Two Chinooks flew high in the perfect blackness of a moonless night. They were all alone as they made a gradual turn above the desert, just north of a massive lake. They flew an additional four miles before making another pitch to the right, then squared up with the lake and increased speed.

Once over the water, the Night Stalker pilots plunged toward the deck and all twenty Navy SEALs aboard grabbed their mesh seats to steady themselves. They leveled out as suddenly as they dropped, skimming ten feet above the water until they reached the center of the lake.

Porter looked at his watch and stood, followed by the rest of his nine-man team. They walked to the back of the helicopter wearing LAR-V gear — a Light Amphibious Rebreather system, similar to scuba but with the benefit of no bubbles — on their chests. Denny and the nine other SEALs did the same in the other Chinook, and waited for the flight engineer to open the back ramp.

The Chinooks pulled to a hover and the pilots gave the signal. The interior lights turned green as the ramps lowered.

Both helicopters tilted up slightly as the flight engineers pushed a large plastic, rubber crate roughly the size and shape of a refrigerator onto each ramp. The pilots compensated for the weight loss by increasing power as the deflated Combat Rubber Raiding Crafts fell into the dark water, followed by the SEALs. In seconds all of the cargo and men were unloaded, and Operation Hammer Fall, the most massive combined offensive since the surge, was underway all over Iraq.

Porter put his fins on underwater, then swam to the dark mass in front of him and linked up with two of his men. Together they undid the restraints on the deflated vessel, attached a tank to fill the rubber ballast tubes, and held on as it inflated and rose to the surface.

Nobody on shore could see or hear the rafts surfacing, nor the smaller shapes climbing into the pair of F470 Zodiacs. The twenty men removed their LAR-V gear, assembled weapons, and distributed ammunition from their various containers. On the back of each vessel, a SEAL attached a 55-horsepower engine to a pump-jet propulsor, set himself on the stern, and waited for the signal to fire up the impeller beneath the simple but sturdy landing craft.

Porter took off his diving hood and replaced it with a black knit cap, put on his night vision and adjusted it. He scanned his men who were doing the same, then gestured to the man on the stern who nodded and signaled to his counterpart in the other Zodiac. Roughly four minutes from the time they left the helicopters, twenty Navy SEALs motored across a dark lake toward an unsuspecting shore.

Balad Air Base
Thursday 02:08:00

Rear Admiral Buchanan watched the monitor as he listened in on the radio channel. The crafts neared the coastline of Lake Tharthar, and on the drone-fed image he saw the men slide over the sides of the Zodiacs and pull them onto the shore with beautiful precision.

"Titan touchdown. Proceeding to target," he heard Denny's familiar whisper.

"Copy that, Titan," the officer on the other end of the radio acknowledged.

Piece of cake, Porter, make it quick.

Buchanan turned his attention to another monitor, one of several feeds from missions currently underway. He paused, then looked back at Titan's feed and lingered on it. Porter's wasn't the most important mission of the night, but it held the potential for a big intelligence payoff, and it was also more sensitive.

He recalled the simple mission goals. *Get in and see what's there. If it's paydirt, hold it till supported. If not, get out as quietly as you got in.*

There was nobody he trusted more than Porter. He turned his attention back to the other missions, but couldn't stop thinking about Titan.

Denny scurried up the bank, the ground becoming firmer with each step and the other SEALs right behind him. Porter's team followed until they reached a sand dune, and both teams paused. Both leaders surveyed the distance between them and the target, an industrial building complex two kilometers away. To the right of it were several one-story outbuildings, as well as large water tanks and miles of piping connecting them. There were also lights, lots of them, shining all over the complex.

But lights also meant shadows, and Porter selected a line to the nearest outbuilding that was well-concealed in them. He gestured to the group. They stood, and moved as one.

Soft, rapid footsteps soon brought them outside the first building. They looked inside two parked trucks as they passed, and had yet to see a single security guard or worker anywhere among the power plant. Everything was quiet. Porter moved to the next building and stood near an attached ladder that went to the roof. He waited for the rest of his men to catch up and flipped up his NVG's. His men followed suit.

"You're up, Shep," Porter whispered.

The sniper took out a pair of bolt cutters and snipped the padlock off the covering that blocked access to the ladder. The metallic pop sounded like it would wake the dead but no one in the compound seemed to hear. Sheppard took off the lock and handed it to Jonathan, then he and Ozzy went up the ladder. Once past the first few rungs, Jonathan closed the cover over the base of the ladder again and put what was left of the lock back in place, giving it an appearance of having been undisturbed.

On the roof, Sheppard lay down and adjusted his sniper rifle. He visually acknowledged the other sniper team on a nearby connex before surveying the parking area, the pipes, the other buildings, and the target building. He keyed his mic.

"Titan Five in position," he whispered. "All clear. Proceed to target."

"Copy that," Denny said, and began a hurried trot toward the target while Sheppard watched from above.

Next to Sheppard, Ozzy lay with a spotting scope and watched the outbuildings for any sign of movement. He had a bullhorn for crowd control if necessary; so far it seemed like extra weight.

Sheppard saw two SEALs take up a firing position to cover the entrance of the building, and the remaining sixteen SEALs moved to the target building entrance.

Denny tried the steel doorknob. Locked. It was centered in a large metal box that had four numbered push buttons underneath it.

Might as well try. Maybe it was coded by an idiot. He pushed 1-2-3-4, but the handle didn't turn. *Oh well. The hard way, I guess.*

He motioned for Jonathan, who came forward and pulled out a large pry bar, then had another idea as he looked at the keypad. He pulled a large magnet out of his pack, held it alongside the keypad until he heard clicking, then motioned for Denny to try the knob again.

The handle turned. Denny smiled at Jonathan.

"$500 security handle can't beat a $4 magnet," Jonathan said.

"Nice." Denny made a mental note to change the locks on the unit's gear lockers at home.

Everyone repositioned their NVGs. Jonathan looked to Porter, who nodded. Fourteen SEALs entered the building, leaving two men to guard the entrance.

———

On the roof, Ozzy heard a faint but sustained tone. At first he thought his ear might have been ringing, but after rubbing it with his finger it remained, not loud, but constant.

"Shep, do you hear a ringing?"

Sheppard was watching through his scope, and listened.

"Affirmative, it's an alarm."

"Titan One, this is Five, be advised we hear an alarm," Sheppard said.

"Get ready for some company, Ozzy."

———

The SEALs in the building cleared the ground floor, moved up the stairs to the second floor hallway, cleared a large conference room, and heard the humming. A few more feet down the hall, they entered the control room and saw four panicked men looking at a computer monitor.

"Turn off the alarm," Porter said, pointing to the ceiling. The operative next to him echoed the instruction in Arabic, then yelled several more things Porter didn't understand, but the facility crew responded by putting their hands up — all except one man, who frantically started typing on his keyboard.

The operative pointed his rifle at the man's forehead and shouted again. The alarm stopped.

"On the ground. Cuff 'em," Porter said.

"Wait," the operator said in English, then asked a question in Arabic.

One of the Iraqis raised his hand. The operative gestured him to a different terminal while commanding the rest to get facedown on the ground, where they were flex-cuffed. The American let his rifle dangle, whipped out his pistol and held it next to the man's ear while giving him more instructions in Arabic.

Porter knew his translator was an ex-SEAL, but he had little experience with CIA operatives and how they conducted business. Up to this point he had wondered if the man could physically manage the dive, the approach, and the assault; now he knew, and all of his concerns evaporated. The operative was clearly a frogman — a frogman pushing fifty, but a frogman. Porter said nothing.

"How long do we have?" the CIA operative asked Porter in English, referring to the alarm.

"Not long. Get what you can," Porter said.

"This is Titan One," Porter said on the radio. "Target secured. Collecting intel. Titan Five, how we look?"

"Titan One, this is Five, alarm is off," Sheppard whispered. "Getting some lights in the outbuildings. No targets yet."

Porter and the CIA operative shared a look. "Your show for now, boss," he told the older man.

"Take the hard drives from those," the CIA operative pointed to a bank of computers, "and any papers you can find."

He watched over the Iraqi's shoulder as he brought up security camera footage of the power plant, looking for evidence of illegal oil sales and transportation. The plant had dozens of cameras, and after clicking several archived video feeds he became frustrated.

"This is taking too long," he said to Porter.

"What do you think?" Porter asked.

"It could take weeks to go through it all."

"Say the word and I'll call in the QRF. Uncle Sam can own this place as long as you want, right?"

The CIA operative pondered the weight of the decision, whether it was worth it to commit a platoon of Rangers to occupy and exploit a politically sensitive target with little hard evidence of wrongdoing. On the other hand, they were already there with full access, and would probably never get the green light again.

"Call 'em in," he said.

Porter had to trust the man's instincts, knowing that despite the CIA man making the call, it was ultimately his decision, and whatever fallout occurred would come down on him and him alone.

Over the command frequency, Porter gave the mission call signal that triggered a Quick Reaction Force. Two Chinooks full of airborne soldiers would fly to the target, secure all access points, and take over the compound from the SEALs. Additional CIA intelligence operatives would fly in after it was deemed safe enough to do so. How long all of that would take on a night when sensitive operations were being conducted all across Iraq was anyone's guess.

———

"This is Titan Five. Getting hot out here," Shep said.

"Shep, lights coming on Four Alpha," Ozzy said.

"Copy that, I see 'em," Shep said, honing in on the grid Ozzy called out. Three armed men emerged from a construction trailer.

"Titan Five. Engaging targets," Shep said, then shot one of the men before the others knew what was happening. The two remaining men stared at the body, and Shep took out the second man. The third ducked back inside the building. More people were coming out of two other buildings, but he couldn't tell if they were armed or not.

"This is Five, I've got multiple individuals on the move," he said on the radio. Then he turned to Ozzy. "Check the deck below us. Better get that bull horn handy, too."

"Roger that, Shep."

Outside the building, the SEALs guarding the structure watched lights coming on all over the compound.

"Titan One, this is Titan One Five. We've got a lot of movement out here."

"Copy," Porter said.

He went to the window overlooking the compound and saw several buildings with lights on. Some of the people stumbling out of them seemed to be workers, but it was too dark to tell if any of them were armed.

"Great," Porter muttered.

Denny stood next to Porter. "Nothing?"

"Negative," Porter said.

"Why am I not surprised?" Denny said with a sarcastic laugh.

Porter realized none of the intel was correct. There were no terrorist leaders on site, probably very little useful intelligence from their scared prisoners, no obvious insurgent force, and he had two dead Iraqis that Shep just took out. Porter knew they were legitimate targets or else Shep wouldn't have fired, but that wouldn't stop the foreign media from calling them all murderers. Unless they could contain the site and document the evidence, it would be another messy operation with his SEALs thrown under the bus. But the QRF wasn't even en route yet, and the time was getting late. He made another command decision.

"Five minutes, move it ladies," he ordered. He then pointed to the scared workers. "Take them down to the lower deck."

Where are those helicopters?

Balad Air Base
Thursday 02:20:00

"What do you mean, rerouted?" Buchanan asked the subordinate.

"That's all I was told, sir. Troops in contact. The QRF was rerouted."

Buchanan was one step away from being furious, but knew it was pointless. He could have called his bosses, but with everything else going on he knew it wouldn't make any difference. He had nineteen SEALs and one CIA operative at the compound; they should be able to hold it for as long as they needed to. They'd done it before. He kicked himself for trusting other units for support.

I guess the Army doesn't want this site very bad after all?

Now he had to consider his options: either reinforce Porter, or order them out of there.

"Let me talk to them," Buchanan said.

Porter and Denny shook their heads. Buchanan himself had just told them not to expect the QRF.

"Exploit the target for intelligence for only as long as you deem appropriate, then extract," Buchanan had said.

Porter made up his mind and turned to the CIA operative. "Sorry boss, time's up. We're moving out."

The site was a bust, and chances were they wouldn't be reinforced anytime soon unless they got air support, and the Air Force wasn't going to start shooting up a civilian power plant, terrorist black site or not. There were dozens of facets of war Porter could stomach, but squandering his men's time and resources on shady intelligence was not one of them.

"This is Titan One. Prepare to move out."

—

"Titan One, I've got seven armed Muj grouped around that line of trucks," Shep said. "Count eleven others, unarmed and walking toward the parking lot in between our positions."

"Basically a nightmare," he said to Ozzy.

"More coming out," Ozzy said, then pointed to the far left, "Lights up in the desert, north."

"Damn," Shep said, wheeling his sniper rifle in that direction.

"Titan One Two, you have a visual on those lights?"

—

Through his scope, Titan One Two saw four beams of light bouncing along in the dark.

"Copy that. Titan One, we've got four —"

"Six," his spotter corrected.

"Correction, we've got six vehicles moving fast toward your position from the north."

———

"Copy that," Porter said, turning to the window facing that direction. He looked at Denny, who shook his head.

"Titan Five and Titan One Two, hold your current positions to cover our withdraw."

"Wilco," Shep said.

"Wilco," the other sniper repeated.

"And these guys?" Mario asked, standing guard over the workers.

"Leave 'em," Porter said, and walked out. His only remaining care was to get his men home alive.

———

A third shot rang out, followed shortly by a fourth. Through his binoculars, Ozzy watched the bodies fall. The remaining men took cover behind the trucks, no doubt wondering where the shots had come from. He watched a man peek out from behind a tire, crouching, getting ready to lunge for his fallen comrade's weapon.

Go ahead, buddy.

The man made a dash for the AK-47, and as soon as he picked it up Shep put a round through his ribs for kill number five.

Ozzy had no compassion for the foolish men, rather, he had hatred for the men who recruited them, lied to them, fed them vitriol, and got them to leave their families to embrace the death cult overwhelming the country he loved. He'd tried to reason with so many of his countrymen, but with little success. It was dangerous enough to merely speak positively about the Americans and the West, but Ozzy had had the audacity to join them. He was one of the few men in his family who didn't fear the jihadists, his wife Dwura was another. His father and mother cautiously respected his decision to join up when the Americans began recruiting for local policemen. It was good money. Planting IED's paid better, but this was honorable. Both vocations were equally hazardous.

But Ozzy's parents were dead now, along with the few friends who had dared to side with coalition forces. Ozzy was discovering every day, along with the Americans who trained him, that he had a natural gifting for this kind of work. He had quickly been assigned as an interpreter for American Special Forces, and within a year the operators who trained him went from considering him unwanted baggage to an asset that leadership wanted for themselves. He was respected more and more by increasingly elite units, earning every bit of it in the face of skeptical opposition. That opposition evaporated every time Ozzy revealed some kernel of intelligence that only a local would know, or suggested a particular tactic that saved American lives.

Every step up the ladder found him staring in the faces of men who either scoffed at him, discounted him, or openly scorned him, and Porter was no different. But every unit also learned they could rely on him, though trust was perhaps a bridge too far.

Ozzy tapped Shep on the shoulder. He held up four fingers, then pointed toward the ground below them.

Shep nodded, quietly gathered his MK 12 sniper rifle, and packed his gear. Ozzy did the same, then whispered on the radio.

"This is Titan Six, our position is compromised. Preparing to displace."

"Copy that, Six," was the reply.

Shep and Ozzy crawled to the edge of the roof. Ozzy held a rod over the edge with a small mirror attached to the end of it. Below them, four men stood next to the ladder they had used to access the roof.

Ozzy removed a grenade and looked at Shep, who nodded. Ozzy pulled the pin and dropped it over the edge as they quickly rolled back from it. The grenade landed directly among the men below and exploded. He looked over the edge at the ghastly remains.

"Let's go, Shep," he said, betraying no emotion.

———

The noise of the grenade set off a panic among the non-combatants, and they scattered in an uncoordinated slew of directions. As Buchanan watched the feed from the drone, he had a hard time distinguishing his own men.

What a mess.

The video feed showed six vehicles in the upper left quadrant, closing in on the main building. Waiting for them were two groups of SEALs in defensive positions. Buchanan watched the trucks slow down, and as soon as they were in range, the SEALs fired a pair of M72 shoulder-fired rockets, destroying the lead vehicles with bright white splashes on the video monitor.

"It's on," Buchanan announced to the room.

———

Porter watched waves of flames roll out of the vehicles, the light catching everyone's eye. The SEAL machine gunners opened up, laying down fire on the next vehicles, which swerved to avoid crashing into the burning trucks. Porter checked the opposite direction and saw a dozen people running in as many directions. He also saw three men running toward his position with rifles at their hips.

Porter kneeled, leveled his rifle, and dropped two of them before another SEAL mowed down the third.

"Let's move, now!"

The SEALs gathered their gear and began a steady retreat toward the beach, firing as they withdrew, taking full advantage of the confused enemy and hitting them from a number of directions.

The remaining sniper team dropped two figures as they covered the withdrawal toward their position.

"Time to move," the sniper told his spotter when they were almost to him.

He swung one last look toward the other sniper position and watched Shep and Ozzy crest the side of their roof. Shep got to the ground first and turned to cover Ozzy as he climbed down.

Through his scope, the sniper saw Shep fly backward and slam into the wall at Ozzy's feet. He saw bullets hit the wall and chip the concrete as Ozzy jumped from the ladder and covered Shep's body with his own.

———

The second Ozzy threw his body on top of Shep, he knew the SEAL was dead. With fury, he raised his rifle, spotted the shooters, and put them down with three aimed bursts in rapid succession.

He scanned for other threats, but aside from the distant cries of confused civilians, all was quiet.

Ozzy looked at Shep's vacant eyes and felt for a pulse, then keyed his radio. "Man down, Titan Five...," he paused, afraid to say the words out loud. "He's dead."

Ozzy put his bloody glove back on his rifle and searched for threats. He saw people running aimlessly, illuminated by the burning trucks in the distance. He let his rifle hang in its harness, picked up Shep's body, and shouldered his 250 pounds in a fireman's carry. Ozzy was larger than Shep, but he still struggled to balance the weight on his left shoulder while keeping a hand on his rifle.

Two insurgents turned a corner, running in the direction of the lake. They didn't see Ozzy, who cut them down from behind even as he himself was running in the same direction.

An insurgent truck carrying at least half a dozen men pulled out in front of him, cutting him off, then came to a stop directly in between the SEALs and Ozzy's position, its occupants believing they'd managed to flank the retreating SEALs.

Ozzy locked eyes with the startled driver, the only one looking in that direction. He knew the hatred in those eyes, had seen it in people he used to love, and knew there was no reasoning with it. The man pointed to Ozzy and screamed, but the insurgents in the truck were too consumed with their own bloodlust to heed his warning. With Shep's weight Ozzy could only shoot from the hip, but he walked his shots into the driver, then back toward the bed until the magazine went dry.

Unless he put Shep down he couldn't change the magazine, so he unholstered his pistol and fired several shots. The remaining men in the truck ducked to avoid the pistol rounds and returned fire at Ozzy, who continued shooting while he backed up and found cover behind the corner of the building. He was exactly where he'd started as an onslaught of bullets chased after him.

———

Porter heard the radio call and shelved his emotions for later. He started to run to Ozzy and Shep when the truck separated them and started shooting. The SEALs took cover and returned fire but not before one of them was hit, and Mario grabbed the injured SEAL by the vest and pulled him behind the shipping container. The SEALs made short work of the truck, but another drove in from the same direction, also shooting.

"Spread out, take cover," Porter said to the men around him. They took up defensive positions and in seconds shredded the truck with interlocking fields of fire from behind three sand dunes.

Porter saw the building in the distance, but not Ozzy or Shep. He keyed his mic.

"Titan Six, where the hell are you?"

———

Ozzy had never stopped moving. The line of bullets followed on his heels and with every step around the corner he saw more insurgents. He ran all the way around the building with Shep on his shoulder, taking out several men with his pistol in the process. In the confusion he lost his bearings and paused to regain his position relative to the rest of his unit when he heard Porter on the radio.

"I copy, Titan One. Coming to you," Ozzy said through labored breaths.

He moved into a shadow, the muscles in his neck and shoulder burning under the weight of Shep's body.

No. I won't lay him down. Not until he's safe.

He holstered his pistol, repositioned Shep onto the other shoulder, and changed the magazine on his rifle. He lowered his NVGs and looked toward the sand dunes, saw the SEALs in the distance.

"I've got you, Shep," he said as he began to move.

"This is Titan Six, moving toward you. Check your three o'clock."

Porter called the Chinook pilots. "This is Titan One. Prepare for hot extraction. Five Mikes." Then he turned to Denny. "See him?"

"Affirmative." They watched Ozzy run past a cluster of terrified Iraqi civilians, and could tell he was yelling something that caused them to fall to the ground before him. Ozzy increased his speed but was visibly straining under the weight of the man he carried. He paused every few feet to shoot at enemy riflemen, stepped over dead bodies, and limped from his own gunshot wounds.

Porter jumped up and sprinted toward him, followed by Jonathan and Taggart. When Porter was close enough, he told Ozzy, "Here, I'll take him."

"Negative, I've got him," Ozzy said, jogging past.

The assault team fell back to their boats. Ozzy slid into the zodiac, cradling Shep's body against his chest and holding his rifle at the ready.

The SEALs pushed off, fired up the engines, and spun around as shouts from the beach searched for them in the darkness.

The boats flew over the water toward the center of the lake, leaving an unknown number of enemies behind them.

The dark shapes of the Chinooks passed overhead and came to a hover 1000 meters ahead of the speeding Zodiacs. They lowered their ramps and dropped below the surface of the lake, just enough to put a few inches of water between the bottom of the boats and the helicopter's interior; too much and the weight would sink them.

The SEALs adjusted their approach, throttled their engines to full power, and drove straight up the Chinooks' ramps.

As they entered the helicopter, the flight engineers grabbed hold of the rubber craft, secured it with carabiners, and called to the pilots.

"Got 'em. Let's go."

In a swift movement, the Night Stalker pilots angled up and increased power with the ramps open to let the water pour out the back.

As their altitude increased, the ramps closed and Porter felt them make a hard cut to the left. When they stabilized into a moderately level flight the SEALs disembarked from the rafts.

Porter saw one of the SEAL corpsman examining Shep while Ozzy held him. The Corpsman looked at Porter and shook his head. Porter put a hand on Ozzy's shoulder.

Ozzy wiped his knit cap away from his head and ran his hand through his short hair. He looked at Porter as tears filled his eyes. He tried to hold back the surge, didn't want to show weakness in front of the men he so admired. Shame flooded over him and a sledgehammer of guilt pounded him at the realization he'd let one of them die. He'd never cried in front of another soldier, ever, not even when he'd seen friends killed by suicide bombers. But Ozzy couldn't hold it in any longer. In front of Porter, the most feared American of them all, he wept desperate tears of regret.

"I'm sorry," he managed.

Porter leaned forward, put his forehead against Ozzy's, wrapped his arms around both Ozzy and Shep, and wept along with him.

6

Hammer Fall: Sonic

Contingency Operating Base (COB) Foxtrot
02:00:00

Twenty-five men and one woman stood on the dark tarmac with bowed heads. Captain Robinson surveyed his squadron's aviators, wondering if they would all make it back, then closed his eyes and spoke, but not to them.

"Almighty God, who art the author of liberty and the champion of the oppressed, hear our prayer. We acknowledge our dependence on you in preservation of human freedom. Go with us as we seek to defend the defenseless and free the enslaved. May we ever remember that our nation, whose motto is, 'In God we trust,' expects that we shall acquit ourselves with honor, that we may never bring shame upon our faith, our families, or our squadron. Grant us wisdom from thy mind, courage from thy heart, strength from thy arm, and protection by thy hand. It is for you that we do battle, and to you belongs the victor's crown. For yours is the kingdom, and the power, and the glory, forever, amen."

"Amen," the pilots echoed in the dark.

As the huddle broke, an unusual sound filled the air. The opening bass line from "Another One Bites the Dust" got louder in the dark, and all eyes turned to its logical source.

Captain Robinson grinned at Ginger, shook his head, and walked away.

"Let's get it on." Donovan slapped Ginger on the shoulder.

With the music in the background, the pilots gave their send-offs like a sports team firing each other up in the locker room and turned toward their individual Apaches — all except Ginger, who did a skipping dance toward hers.

"Let's go Craiger, make me proud," she coaxed him to follow her.

Craig followed, but mercifully didn't dance with her.

———

"I should have had another plate of chow," Craig said, going over his instrument checklist.

"The last thing you need is another bowl of beans," Ginger said with disgust.

"You can open the window."

"You could eat a freaking salad once in a while and stop stinking up my aircraft. I don't know how Cecilia managed with six of you boys at home. Must have drove your sisters mad, too."

"You don't win friends with salad," he said.

Eddie and the rest of their arming team did their final walk around the Apache, and Eddie waved his index finger at Ginger, like an angry dad warning his kid to be more careful with his tools.

Ginger smiled and blew him a kiss. Eddie crossed his massive arms and frowned, then with zero expression he pretended to catch the kiss and slowly put it in his shoulder pocket.

Ginger grinned. *Don't worry, big guy. I won't break anything this time.* He gave her a thumbs-up to indicate she was flight ready.

"Showtime, Craiger."

"Word up, Money," Craig said.

"You're such a dork."

———

Southwest of Al Miqdadiyah, Iraq
02:00:00

Two Blackhawk helicopters approached the desolate highway that connected the insurgent strong points of Baqubah and Al Miqdadiyah.

"Star Seven, two Mikes," Jenkins heard the pilot say. He held up two fingers in the darkened cabin, and his men readied themselves to make for the door.

One of the helicopters pulled into a hover above a large building on the south side of the highway; the other landed on the sand on the north side, directly across from the building. Two exterior lights on the front of the building were all that illuminated this stretch of the highway, and the door gunners on both helicopters searched in vain for movement.

The coast was clear.

"Over the target," the pilot said to his crew chief.

The crew relayed that to the Delta rope master, who said, "Ropes out."

The bar mechanism of the FRIES fast-rope extended out both sides of the helicopter, and two 40mm diameter ropes were released from it, draping down to the roof fifty feet below.

On the other side of the highway, the operators in the other Blackhawk stepped out onto the ground. They immediately took a knee and scanned the highway and the surrounding desert for targets. The Blackhawk peeled away and the operators waited for the dust to settle.

"Move out," Eric said to his team and led them across the highway toward the parking lot.

Inside the other Blackhawk, Jenkins and his men gripped the ropes with their gloves, their boots encircling the ropes, and exited two at a time. As each man's boots hit the roof, the pilots compensated for the weight shift. Any sudden tilt of the helicopter could cause a man to lose his grip and possibly fall to his death, or knock others off the rope beneath him. The pilot held the machine for a perfect insertion.

Soon the helicopter disappeared above them, and the Delta operators were ready for the next step in their portion of the night's activities.

South of Bald Ruz, Iraq
02:30:00

Tim Miller led the flight of six Apaches as they flew over mostly dark terrain. The horizon suddenly lit up with the first burst of distant bombs. To the northeast, ground attack aircraft bombarded targets and soon a fireworks display of sorts spread out ahead of them.

Tim saw the lights of a city ahead, too many lights for this time of night.

"Look sharp," he told the pilot following him. Suddenly he heard something hit the underside of his helicopter, then another.

"Taking sporadic small arms fire," one of the Apache pilots said.

"Copy that," Tim said as he made jinking turns to avoid the ground fire.

"Pegasus Eight, same here," Ginger said.

"Pegasus One Three, ditto," said Donovan.

Tim was annoyed. He wasn't worried about ground fire from small arms — the Apache could take plenty of those — but where there were rifles, there were undoubtedly rockets as well.

"Keep an eye out for rockets. They've got plenty of 'em."

"Copy that," he heard from a few of the pilots.

Tim waited, sure he would soon hear Ginger's voice.

"We've got more," she said. "But I guess we won't on the way home."

Tim smirked.

He was grateful for Ginger's calm confidence even though a part of him wanted her to be a little more serious. All the same, he knew she could manage levity with precision, but he wondered if she knew when to be quiet.

———

As Ginger passed over a small group of buildings, she caught a glimpse of something out of her right eye.

"Craig, did all of those buildings just go dark as we passed over them?"

"Looks like it."

"Pegasus Niner, you see those lights go out?" she asked one of the two Apaches behind her.

"Affirmative. Confirm all the lights below went out when Eight and One Three passed over."

"Pegasus Six, take her up?" Ginger asked Tim.

———

As the flight leader and the most experienced pilot in the squadron, Tim Miller understood the tactic that was playing out on the ground. Several years earlier he had led a flight of Apaches as they approached a well-lit town, and suddenly the lights went off city-wide — a signal for everyone on the ground to find a weapon and start shooting into the sky. The onslaught of small arms fire had wreaked havoc on the flight of Apaches, and the pilots were fortunate to have run the gauntlet intact.

Good girl.

Tim knew that Ginger was thinking about that now, and her instinct to pull up to a higher altitude was exactly what he would have told them, if he'd decided it faster than she had.

"Affirmative," he said. "High-high six zero, and proceed to target."

"Wilco," the Apache pilots confirmed. Tim and his wingman rose to an altitude of 6000 feet, the next pair behind them leveled out at 5500, and the last at 5000, a tactic to stay far out of range of small arms fire, and just out of range of RPGs. Only large anti-aircraft guns or surface-to-air missiles could hit them now, and if the insurgency had any in this isolated town, at least they'd have a little extra room to maneuver.

The lights from another city came into view, and Tim smiled when he saw them all go dark.

Not this time.

———

Jenkin's men cleared the roof and worked their way down to the second floor. Eric's men assaulted the ground floor entrance, cleared that level, and in a matter of minutes the building was secured. The place was empty.

Jenkins pulled up his NVGs to look at Eric. "Piece of cake."

He looked at the combat air controller and gave the CCT a thumbs-up. "Call your boys."

The CCT made his way to the roof, unpacked an array of radios and batteries, and began setting up a mini air traffic control tower.

"Set up quick, won't be long now," Jenkins said.

"Wilco, boss," Eric replied, and led his team back to the highway.

Jenkins returned to the roof and the CCT gave him a handset attached to a transmitter.

"Zelda, this is Arrow," Jenkins said. "Do you read me, over?"

Thirty-thousand feet overhead, an E-3 Sentry AWACS answered. "Copy Arrow, this is Zelda, read you loud and clear."

"Copy, Zelda. Sonic is open for business. Repeat, Sonic is open for business."

"Copy that, Sonic." Jenkins handed the receiver back to the CCT.

Jenkins briefly listened to the Air Force special operator speak with the E-3 command and control aircraft, establishing what air assets were overhead or nearby, making notes of call signs and their corresponding aircraft so that when the time came, Sonic — the newly established forward operating base Jenkins had just created — would have a full arsenal to play with.

Now we wait. But the thought dissipated as soon as it appeared because he knew that was never true; his men would prepare for a fight. Every minute was an opportunity to dig in, throw up barricades, establish checkpoints and lines of fire, sandbag and reinforce the command tower he was standing on, and a hundred other details that could mean the difference between life and death for his men.

He put up his binoculars and looked down the highway toward Baqubah, and saw flashes from explosions as the Army's offensive got underway. He felt concussions from other directions and knew it was only a matter of time before vehicles began fleeing toward him to avoid the American onslaught.

Insurgents would soon try to pass by him to either flee the Americans from one direction, or engage them from another. When they did, Jenkins and his Delta team would be waiting to either scoop them up and detain them, or unleash the full arsenal of the United States Air Force to destroy them.

Forward Operating Base Sonic's orders for the foreseeable future were now quite simple: Kill or capture every bad guy in sight.

———

Ginger pulled into a sharp climb. The Rolls Royce engines, pulling 38,000 rpm, sent Craig hard against the back of his seat and reminded him why he chose to skip a second bowl of beans.

"The Ginger coaster rides again," he said breathing heavy.

"You didn't want this to be boring, did you?" Ginger said, bouncing the helicopter.

"Oh, no. I'm good." Craig took a deep breath to stave off nausea.

Ginger smiled. Flying the Apache was her second love, edged out slightly by motorcycle racing only because of the technical demands it necessitated, and the fact that, unlike motorcycle racing, she never got to fly it full out. She likened it to owning a luxury race car but never getting to drive it past third gear. She longed to feel speed again; the years spent racing with her dad across stretches of the Mojave desert — first as a passenger hanging on for dear life, then beside him on a machine of her own — were the best years of her life. They rode every chance they got, right up until she left for basic training. Soon after, she found herself racing alone across the highways of Arkansas, Florida, or Georgia, winning a month's paycheck at a time from bombastic soldiers or civilians eager to race the cocky girl from California.

With the possible exception of Tim Miller, Ginger Cooper rode, and flew, better and faster than anyone she'd ever met in the Army or anywhere else. Every member of Pegasus, from Craig all the way up to Major Atwood, and the Apache pilots presently flying behind her, knew her helicopter didn't do anything she didn't want it to.

"You alright Eight?" she heard the Apache behind her ask.

"Affirmative, just a choppy spot," she said.

"I hate you," Craig said.

"I know," she said, quoting Princess Leia.

Checkpoint Sonic
Thursday 03:30:00

Jenkins scrutinized the first vehicles trickling down the highway, small cars with wide separation. They slowed as they got closer to his barricaded checkpoint, manned by six of his men and a German shepherd. They had high-powered weapons and no sense of humor.

"What I wouldn't give for a tank," Jenkins said, looking through binoculars.

"Right. I guess they're all busy down the road," the nearby sniper replied.

"Even a freaking school bus would be nice."

"I could try and hotwire one of those 18-wheelers?"

"I already asked. No dice."

Instead, the Delta team made do with office furniture, a couple of dumpsters, and as much scrap metal as they could find. It was enough to slow traffic and create a bottleneck, which is all they really wanted.

The first car obeyed Topher's command to halt. He waited while the three cars behind it also came to a stop before approaching the driver. The man rolled down his window.

"Where you off to tonight?" Topher asked in English.

The frightened driver said something in Arabic that Topher didn't understand. The Delta operator had thousands of hours fighting, interrogating, and killing jihadists in Iraq, Afghanistan, and Africa, and he knew the difference between an insurgent and a scared civilian. Still, the cars behind him needed to see the show.

Topher motioned for him to exit the vehicle and put his hands on the hood. His partner looked in the vehicle with his flashlight on the end of his rifle, while another walked the leashed dog around it. A fourth operative opened the trunk.

"This guy's a nobody," the sniper said to Jenkins, who was watching the reactions of the other cars' occupants.

In two minutes the driver was dismissed and sent down the road. The operators went on to the next car, wondering how long it would take before they encountered one with the look.

Jenkins saw a large fuel truck coming toward the roadblock from the southwest.

"Arrow Three, Arrow Four, hold 'em up. There's a fuel truck approaching."

Topher stepped into the shadows and looked down the highway. "Copy Arrow One, I see it."

"Let's see what homeboy does," Jenkins said to the men around him.

The Delta operators got the next driver out of the car and made a point of thoroughly searching the vehicle.

"That's right, buddy. We've got all night, not in any rush," Jenkins thought out loud.

Two additional operators came out of the shadows and directed the car behind it to move into the opposite lane, effectively closing the highway from both directions with vehicle barricades. They also took their time, making a show of inspecting their vehicle.

Jenkins didn't bother watching the inspections; he trained in on the fuel truck. It stopped for a moment before turning into the opposite lane. Then it accelerated toward the checkpoint. Jenkins didn't hesitate.

"Take down the driver," he ordered.

The sniper fired into the cab and hit the driver, but the truck continued toward the barricade. It swerved and almost tipped over but righted itself, then sideswiped one of the waiting vehicles and kept going. Eric's men fired as it passed, adding more rounds into the dead or mortally wounded driver, whose foot must have been lodged against the gas because the fuel truck was still accelerating.

Jenkins could only guess the truck's contents. Regardless, it had blown past his checkpoint and was now simply a target that was getting away in spite of the barrage of weapons chasing after it.

"You're up," he said to the CCT next to him. "Whatd'ya got?"

The CCT smiled.

———

"Rapier One Three, this is Sonic. I need you to take out that fuel truck," the pilot heard.

The CCT went through the CAS 9-Line Brief checklist, feeding the pilot heading, distance, the location of friendlies, and other details that would help keep the A-10's weapons on target. Jenkins listened in on the unique pilot/controller dialect, understanding some of it, but trusting it would keep his men as safe as possible.

"Copy, Sonic. Engaging," Colonel Josiah McCoy lined up his A-10 to strafe the truck. He pulled the trigger and the familiar *bruuuup* of its cannon filled the atmosphere while a line of 30mm rounds kicked up sand as they impacted the ground, the road, the truck, and back into the darkness on the other side of the highway.

With its front end torn to shreds, the fuel truck veered into a ditch and tipped over. Its fuel tank skidded on its side and flipped end over end before coming to a stop, fully blocking the eastbound lane.

Josiah made a wide turn and lined up for another run with his finger on the trigger, watching the display screen for any movement. He held his fire.

"Sonic, this is Rapier One Three. Truck looks pretty well disabled, if you ask me," Josiah said.

"Acknowledged, Rapier. Agreed," the CCT said.

Josiah surveyed the highway in both directions as he turned a slow circle over the American checkpoint. He saw a line of vehicles coming from both directions and knew the odds were high that many of them contained threats. He checked his fuel status, and frowned under his oxygen mask.

"Sorry, Sonic. Gonna have to break off to refuel. Anything I can do for you before I leave?"

Jenkins shook his head. "That sucks."

The CCT answered over the radio. "Negative, Rapier. Thanks for the run. Don't be a stranger."

———

Josiah replied, "Sorry Sonic, been a busy night. Running low on ammo as well, but I'll check in with you after I top off. Good luck, buddy."

It was Josiah's fifth action of the night in less than two hours, and he was already pushing the envelope with regard to fuel but he couldn't risk any more. Abby would never forgive him if he had to eject again, and would probably have assigned him to sleep on the sofa permanently if it was because he'd simply run out of gas.

He had just enough fuel left to rendezvous with an aerial refueling tanker. The boys on the ground would have to find some other help for now.

———

"Got another one?" Jenkins asked the CCT.

"Negative, I've got something better."

Jenkins looked at him and frowned. *What's better than an A-10?*

Checkpoint Sonic
04:15:00

"Copy, Sonic. We are a flight of six Apaches, fully loaded. What do you need?" Tim Miller asked.

"Glad to hear it, Pegasus. I've got TIC and multiple targets."

"Just point 'em out and we'll brush 'em off for ya," Tim said to the ground. Then on the Apache frequency, "Pegasus Eight, Pegasus One Three, break off and take care of Sonic. See you back at home."

"Copy that Six," Ginger and Donovan answered.

Ginger texted Donovan:

RACE YOU TO THE DECK

She angled down into a hard vertical dive and took in the scene.

"Now, what have we here?" Craig said.

The highway was littered with small vehicles, some of which were burning, and to the north of them was a disabled fuel truck. Craig inspected each vehicle. Several had armed figures in them, others had men actively shooting from them.

Craig followed their lines of fire and saw they were shooting in two directions: some toward the east side of the highway into what was left of the barricade, others to the west side, up toward the roof of the only building in the area — Sonic's command position.

"Wow," Craig said, "Those vehicles are loaded with civilians." Ginger had noticed, too.

"Sonic, this is Pegasus Eight. Looks like you've had a busy night. How can we help?" she asked.

The CCT handed the receiver to Jenkins. "Pegasus, we're getting hammered from shooters hiding behind human shields."

"I confirm that, Sonic."

"If you can tell us who's who down there so I can direct my guys, I'd appreciate it. Take out whatever you can."

"Gonna have to thread the needle tonight, Craiger," Ginger said, checking her fuel display.

She did some fast math, subtracting the 400 pounds of gas she'd need for minimum landing allowance once they were back at base, then factored in the fuel consumption they'd burn getting there, and came up with her total: 660 pounds of combat gas before they'd have to break away.

"Copy Sonic, I can give you forty, that's four-zero mikes, on station."

"Acknowledged, Pegasus," Jenkins said. "Appreciate it."

"I got this," Craig said.

———

Chad, the Delta sniper on the east side of the highway, lined up a man's chest in his crosshairs only to see him duck behind the front end of the car again. He muttered an expletive.

It was the most chaotic field of fire he'd ever experienced. What started out as a checkpoint was now a battlefield, and a line of cars fifteen deep was stopped behind it. In the other direction, the fuel truck lay across the road and several vehicles behind it were waiting to slip through, for whatever purpose Chad couldn't fathom, unless they were reinforcements coming to join in the fight.

In between was a no man's land of broken and burning vehicles that had tried to run the checkpoint only to be mowed down by Sonic's lines of fire. The jihadists trapped in the middle realized they were fish in a barrel, and desperately made use of the civilians around them. Some ducked into the back seats of cars and fired from rear windows behind terrified strangers. Others laid underneath the cars and forced the civilians at gunpoint — women and children included — to stand in the road between them and the operators.

Chad had taken out one of the insurgents who tried that tactic. Another had just managed to turn at the last second and almost caused him to fire at a kid. He was beyond frustrated; he was pissed.

The smoke from the fires and the dark shadows they cast made the night vision ineffective. His finger moved to its rest position above the trigger, and he saw something slide across the road from under a small car to land underneath a larger vehicle. A second later, the man stood with his hands raised near the car.

"Homeboy surrendering?" Topher asked.

"Not a chance. That was probably his gun," Chad said.

The man walked slowly toward the larger vehicle, then dropped out of view behind it.

"Should have popped him. Damn rules of engagement," Chad said.

"That's one way to reposition," Topher scoffed.

———

"Arrow Six, how's that van coming?" Jenkins asked Chad.

"Loaded with shooters. No shot."

Jenkins called up the Apaches. "Pegasus, that white van has an unknown number of targets inside, but they're using their buddies as human shields. Any ideas?"

———

Craig flipped on the thermal imaging, showing several heat signatures inside the van. Outside the van, several unarmed adults stood on both sides of it with their hands up.

Civilians would run away. These aren't civilians.

Ginger moved the helicopter around to line up directly behind the van. "What do you think, Craiger? Can you put a few rounds straight into the back door?"

"Sure, but it might tear up the guys on the outside, too."

Ginger considered the options. The cannon fired at a rate of 625 rounds per minute, so even a slight tap of the trigger would send a barrage of 30mm rounds into the van. The rounds had a lethal radius of about five feet against unprotected targets, but what would happen to the men standing outside the van was anyone's guess, though she was pretty sure they'd all be injured.

"I've got the gun," she told Craig.

There was a moment of pause as Ginger listened to the engine's hum and they watched the van. A conical shape popped out of the driver's side door, pointed at Sonic's main position.

Ginger pulled the trigger.

———

Chad saw a burst of light and a line of small explosions go into the van from behind, tearing through the roof, the windshield, and the engine. The sides of the van disappeared in a dust cloud along with all of the men standing next to it.

———

Ginger and Craig waited for the cloud of dust to dissipate. The van was in pieces, and the individuals who had been standing outside it were on the ground.

"They alive?" she asked. Then she saw them crawling away from the wreckage.

"Yeah, they're good," Craig said, knowing full well they were likely to die from injuries unless attended to. But the unarmed insurgents were alive for now as the gun camera footage confirmed, and that was enough.

"Good job, Eight," Donovan said on the radio.

And yet, Ginger wondered. *Maybe they were innocent civilians. Will they bleed out? Did I just commit murder?*

She filed it away and focused on the next target. There would be plenty of time to think about that later.

———

"Thanks, Pegasus," Jenkins said, and moved his attention to a long flatbed truck and nearly a dozen men sitting inside it, now approaching the wreckage of the disabled fuel truck. It stopped, and all of the men in the back jumped out. They were clearly empty handed, but three of them reached into the back of the truck and spread blankets over…something.

"Pegasus, you see that flatbed on the northside?" the CCT asked.

"Copy, Sonic. Looks like they're concealing weapons in the back," Donovan answered.

"Can you confirm that, Pegasus?"

"Negative. I can't see weapons yet."

"Copy that."

"See any, Eight?" Donovan asked.

"Negative, One Three, I don't see any either," Craig said.

The men stood next to their truck, as if casually talking over their next move. Donovan's gunner scrutinized each of them for anything that would trigger a green light — a weapon, bomb materials. The fighters were too smart, knew too well what the Americans could and couldn't shoot at. Donovan surveyed other targets, but Rico focused on the men who, he knew, would eventually slip up.

Jim, the Army medic, wasn't going to admit it to anybody, but he was in almost constant pain from the gunshot he'd taken through the arm a few weeks prior. It hadn't fully healed and was still tightly wrapped in a brace, but he played it off as good to go. He had a mission to focus on.

He crouched and ran to the nearest car, following Lance and Eric.

They could see its driver hunkered down on the front floorboard. He looked up as Eric opened the door, but hesitated when Eric beckoned him out.

Eric had no time for waiting, and pointed his gun at him. "Out, now!"

Whether he spoke English or not, the man understood and crawled out onto the street before scurrying away into the dark, joining a line of refugees who streamed away from the battle.

Donovan's gunner still watched the flatbed, waiting to spot any weapon that would provide the justification to pull his trigger and destroy the target. The truck started to inch forward, the men walking alongside, and suddenly one of them opened the tailgate. He grabbed something out of the back and the truck immediately accelerated toward the checkpoint.

"He's making a break for it, Rico," Donovan told his front seater.

"Take out that truck, Pegasus," they heard the CCT say.

"Hellfire away," Rico said on the radio.

A hellfire missile slid off Donovan's rail, closed the distance in a heartbeat, and annihilated the speeding truck just as it passed the toppled fuel tanker.

The rocket ignited the oil-filled tanker. The blast lit up the desert as well as the flatbed, and the percussion knocked refugees and operators off their feet as the flames spread wide, covering the highway.

"This is Arrow One. Everyone check in," Jenkins said.

One by one the Delta operators responded; they had survived the blast.

"Back off and let it burn itself out," he ordered. Jenkins looked south at the scattered vehicles, some were on fire. He looked north at the flames licking into the sky. The highway would be closed indefinitely.

Ginger looked at her fuel display. "Sonic, I don't see any more targets and we're running low on fuel. Gonna have to leave you for tonight. Left you a night light, though."

"Roger that Pegasus." They could hear Jenkins smiling. "Have a nice day."

"Sonic, it has been our pleasure," Ginger said in a British accent.

The Apaches took slow turns over the highway, searching for any stragglers with weapons, but didn't see anyone.

Jenkins flipped a bucket upside down and sat on it. He set his rifle aside, unzipped one of his many vest pockets, and unwrapped an energy bar. He noticed the CCT steal a look, and he reached back into his vest, retrieved a second energy bar, and handed it to the airman.

"Thanks, boss."

Jenkins chewed and looked at the flames. "Need some marshmallows, huh?"

The CCT smiled. "I know, right?" and went back to speaking to the AWACS.

The sky lightened as dawn approached, and Jenkins wondered how hot it would be on this rooftop in the daylight. He might have to hold this position for hours, all day, or even longer, depending on what went down in other parts of the country. He considered the possibility of getting an hour or so of sleep when he saw headlights to the east.

So much for that.

"Sir?" the CCT said.

Jenkins took the receiver. "This is Arrow One, go ahead."

"Sonic, this is Rapier One Three," Josiah McCoy said. "How's it going down there? Looks like you've made a bit of a mess."

Jenkins stood and saw the dark outline of an A-10 Warthog as it passed between him and the last stars of the night.

"Affirmative, Rapier," Jenkins said. "Busy night. What can you tell me about those vehicles approaching from the east?"

"Stand by, Sonic," Josiah answered. A few seconds of radio silence passed. The men on the ground heard the jet engines but couldn't make out the plane.

"Full of bad guys," Josiah said.

From a distance the operators saw the A-10's cannon flash, then saw two explosions on the highway.

"Targets destroyed," Josiah said.

"Copy that, Rapier," the CCT said almost laughing.

Man, I love Hogs, Jenkins thought. He sat back on the bucket, put his feet up on the CCT's rucksack, and pulled his beanie over his eyes.

Maybe I'll sneak a snooze after all. Thank God for Combat Air Controllers.

Central Iraq
05:15:00

The sun wasn't up yet but the features on the ground were clear as Ginger and Donovan flew back to the base. They heard radio chatter from Pegasus birds engaged in action and knew their time on the ground would be just long enough to refuel before setting out for another mission.

Ginger saw a blanket of small buildings up ahead. As she passed over the first building a flash shot skyward, tracers from a rifle on the ground. Then she saw more, several more.

"Pegasus Eight, I'm taking small arms fire," Donovan said.

"Copy that, One Three, same here," Ginger said, taking evasive action, pulling back on the controls to increase her elevation. The Kevlar-reinforced cockpits repelled just about everything smaller than an anti-aircraft gun, and even the fuel tanks had a special design that resealed themselves from bullet holes. But missiles were another matter.

Suddenly the ground threat warning systems in both Apaches sounded; flares fired automatically. She jerked to the right, saw a smoke trail and tried to mentally source its origin.

She heard Donovan on the radio. "I'm hit," he said, breathing heavily. "Pegasus Eight, something hit the tail section…losing altitude…wait…leveling out…"

"Take the tactical lead. I'm trailing on you," Ginger said.

Ginger listened as she watched her wingman's erratic flying. The helicopter bounced and tipped sideways as Donovan struggled to keep the machine in the air. His altitude plummeted, and Ginger saw tracers walking into the helicopter from three directions.

"Craig."

"I see 'em." He fired three rockets, first to the sources of the tracers on the right, then to the one on the left. The guns stopped, only to be followed by more warning alarms that indicated another SAM was in the air. They banked as the automatic flares fell free of the helicopter, masking the heat signature of her engines.

"Where the hell is that SAM, Craig?" Ginger's Apache was flying on its side, turning around again as she maneuvered to get level while simultaneously searching for a visual on Donovan.

"They're hammering him, Ginger," Craig said, watching their wingman absorb more small arms fire.

"I see him," Ginger said while increasing speed. She got ahead of Donovan, high above the town. She angled her helicopter to get the entire town in her field of vision and pulled into a hover with its nose lowered.

Craig entered targets as fast as he found them and fired a rocket, then another, destroying enemies as Donovan passed over the buildings they shot from while limping over the town.

"Talk to me, One Three," Ginger said.

"Trying…trying to fly, Eight…"

Ginger could hear the tension, the physical strain in his voice as he fought the controls.

If he's still in the air he can stay in the air, if he can focus. Focus, Donny.

The machine was doing its job; it was designed to take this kind of beating. But it required uncommon mental clarity from its pilot.

Talk to him, Ginger.

"You're looking good, One Three," she said. The ground fire had ceased; either the enemies were dead or they didn't want to expose themselves to anymore fire from the Apaches. "Almost clear, just keep her level for a few more clicks, I got you."

Donovan's helicopter was past the town, but barely in the air. "Pegasus Eight, I've got control. Can't climb though, without everything going haywire."

"Copy that, One Three." Ginger spoke like a patient teacher. "You've got plenty of fuel. Let's take this slow and easy and we'll keep her over the sand. I'm right behind you. If you need to put her down, go ahead, I'll cover you."

"Thanks Eight, I think we can make it back if I keep her level."

"Just a walk in the park," Ginger said.

———

The sun broke on the horizon as the pair of Apaches lowered their birds onto the tarmac. Ginger let out a sigh of relief when her wheels touched the ground, and she and her wingman taxied to their arming areas. She pulled to a stop with her engine running, paused to look out her window, and saw Donovan had paused before continuing to his arming station.

They locked eyes. Neither pilot spoke. There were no quippy texts, none of the good-natured harassment that postulated their earlier days, first as Warrant Officer Candidates, then as combat aviators. Donovan merely nodded the silent gratitude of one warrior to another. She did the same.

Out her other window, she saw Eddie watching her with his usual posture of dissatisfaction, arms crossed, a frown on his face. It was the same way he always greeted her and she prepared for his scorn at her coming back with unused ordinance.

She rolled her eyes, raised her palms and through the glass mouthed the word, "What?"

Eddie almost cracked a smile, and pounded his fist in a manner of respect. Ginger could clearly read his lips saying, "My girl."

7

Calloused

Baghdad, Iraq
Friday 11:00:00

Porter watched the C-17 load its precious cargo. He alone was dressed like a civilian: khaki cargo pants, and a navy blue collared t-shirt. He pulled his ball cap tight on his head and saw bearded men in uniform walking down the ramp, most wiping away tears and no longer trying to conceal it.

Porter turned to Denny and they shook hands. "See you in a few days, brother. Keep 'em busy."

"Will do, boss."

Porter slung his rucksack, which for the first time in ages held no weapons, merely clothing and a book he probably wouldn't read. He walked to the ramp, took a deep breath, and boarded the flight home.

As he ascended the rear of the cargo jet, Porter saw rows of metal coffins lined in the hull. He purposely avoided finding out which one held Shep's body out of fear he would stare at it the entire flight back to Virginia. He wanted to sleep, needed sleep in order to face Shep's family, to be the rock they'd need to endure the next 48 hours of pain.

Porter took a final survey of the line of SEALs standing near Denny, all of them unwilling to do anything until Shep was on his way home. Porter noticed one man holding a salute, oddly out of place among the rest of the men, and realized it was Ozzy.

—

Sentara Norfolk General Hospital, Virginia

A woman in maroon surgical scrubs paused in the hallway and stretched her back. She put a cupped palm behind her neck and rolled her head wishing she had time to visit a chiropractor.

"Jen, you've got a call," she heard from the nurse's station.

Jen Peterson took a deep breath and walked the squeaky halls to the desk. She took the receiver from the other nurse.

"This is Jen."

"Hey." Jen instantly recognized the voice but didn't respond, waited for more. But he still didn't say anything and the silence became awkward. She sighed.

"Hey. I take it you're back?"

"Got in this morning." Another awkward pause.

"Well, welcome back." Jen was irritated, and tired, and hungry, or else she might have taken less offense at Porter's shortness. This was not how she expected to reunite with her best friend, home from war, but then she remembered his email and realized what Porter had likely experienced since the moment he landed this morning. She felt ashamed, and selfish.

"How are you doing?"

"Hungry," he said. "Got time for some lunch?"

Jen looked at her watch.

She could sneak away for a quick bite somewhere, not much farther than the busy hospital cafeteria, or a fast food joint. But she also knew it was unlikely she'd get to see Porter twice before he was back on a plane to Iraq. And she preferred to greet him in something other than sweaty scrubs and a messy braid.

"Maybe, but it'd have to be short. Do you think you'd have time for dinner instead? I'll buy."

There was a long pause on the other end of the line.

"Tonight? I can call you around…sevenish?"

"Perfect," Jen said, smiling.

"Alright, call you later," Porter said, and hung up.

Jen looked at the receiver and slowly hung up the phone.

"Date?" one of the nurses asked, raising her eyebrow.

"Porter," she said still looking at the phone.

"Oh," her friend said, more serious now. "So, date?"

Jen had no idea what to expect from Porter. She never really did.

"No," she said, and went back to work.

———

Porter put down his phone and checked the emails on his laptop, realized most of them could wait, and shut it. He laid down on the sofa in the apartment he rarely saw. He'd never owned a home, had lived on base housing or in nearby apartments since graduating from the Naval Academy, and that seemed like a lifetime ago.

He had no family save his aging parents up north in Maine, and his men.

And Jen. But Jen was more than family, she was *…What? A responsibility?*

But that was insulting, and also untrue. Porter couldn't seem to explain it, even to himself. He loved her, but was never quite sure how. She was the wife of his best friend, and then his widow. In the four years since Gator's death, they became more than friends but not lovers, as others seemed to think.

Porter was a lieutenant, and more than that, a DEVGRU SEAL, a leader of the most elite special forces development groups on earth. He was almost always either training or operating, and in places Jen had no business knowing about. At any moment he could be whisked away on a very secret — or very public — counter-terrorism mission anywhere in the world, for however long. How could he subject her to a lifestyle of waiting around for him to get back?

It was why he didn't date, and it was one of the reasons he had a hard time knowing what to think about Jen. The other reason was Gator.

Gator wasn't the first friend Porter had lost in war, but he was the first man he'd loved, aside from his father. He was a brother. And watching him fade away in his hospital bed as battlefield injuries slowly killed him from the inside out, and watching Jen by his side, sending him off gracefully and courageously, but then weeping in Porter's arms with gut-wrenching sobs for weeks afterward, was the single hardest thing he had ever experienced in a career characterized by hard experiences.

It nearly broke Porter; it did break Jen.

But Jen recovered with time, and largely because Porter was there to take every desperate phone call, to listen to every tear-filled outburst, to patch the holes in the sheetrock after Jen heaved a frying pan at the poorly constructed walls of her Navy housing.

But then Porter was deployed again to Afghanistan, and later to Iraq. Leaving Jen was the second hardest thing he had ever done, all the more so because she hadn't come to say goodbye. Porter knew why, and didn't blame her.

Over the past four years he watched men die in greater numbers than he'd ever imagined as a young officer coming out of the academy that had known two decades of relative peace. But he trained to be a warrior, and warriors, like Gator and Shep, die.

Porter had almost died as well, wounded alongside Gator on that day. The awards for valor and the promotions that followed seemed to come by the dozen. But so did the funerals.

Jen had attended a few of those funerals when Gator was still with her, but not one since they handed her a folded American flag. The pain of association was too much.

Porter recognized it, and though he hated their silent mutual agreement to keep each other at arm's length, both of them only had one person in the world who understood, and that was each other. And so they were inseparable, though ironically almost never together, and both feared it would always be the case.

Porter shelved the emotions and put Jen in a virtual crate alongside the other facets of his life, things he didn't have the luxury to enjoy, like his parents, his guitar, and his rarely used apartment.

He set the alarm on his watch, pulled his ball cap down till it almost covered his closed eyes, and put Jen back in the box for a few hours. Soon he'd awaken, open the Naval officer box, don his dress blues and prepare to hammer yet another SEAL trident into another coffin of an operator he hardly knew. Then he would be the strong presence Sheppard's family needed. He didn't have the luxury of feeling sorry for himself.

Jen sat in the booth, twiddling her fork in the over-priced bowl of pasta, hoping it didn't spatter, and wishing she had worn an old flannel instead of an expensive white blouse.

Porter sat across from her in a black t-shirt and his dirty ball cap, savoring a pint of beer. He smiled. Jen hadn't seen him smile in a long time. It made her do likewise and she no longer felt overdressed.

"I thought you'd like it," she said, referring to what a colleague had suggested as the best beer in town.

"Sure do," Porter said, taking another draft. "This place new?"

"I don't know. First time I've been here."

"Thought maybe one of those tools you mentioned might have brought you here," he said, referring to her last letter.

"No, that guy was more interested in…" She paused.

"What?" Porter asked, looking her in the eye.

"Himself," she answered.

Porter sat back against the cushion and took another swig while he looked away. They sat for several minutes in silence, slowly eating, both wondering what to say, but not really wanting to say anything.

Jen knew Porter wouldn't break the silence, so she summoned her inner extrovert, honed by years of nursing, and asked a question she really didn't want to discuss.

"How did it go today?"

"Sucked," he said, hoping that would suffice.

"Of course it sucked," she said, annoyed at the flippant response. "How did it go?"

Porter relented, softened. "They're great people. Proud of Shep. Strong. It was hard, but I think they're in a good place."

"And you?" she said, looking down at her pasta.

Porter thought for a moment. He would have blown off anyone else, but this was Jen.

"I didn't know him well, but I liked him. Solid operator."

"Is that your canned response?"

"Huh?" Porter said, confused.

"That's exactly what you said about the last guy." She waited, unsure whether to speak her mind, but decided to let it fly. "You seem colder about them than you used to."

Porter looked at his hand on the glass. "They come and go faster." He didn't want to talk about it, and only two people in the world could have drawn it out of him. One was a one-legged pararescue jumper out west, the other was Jen.

"It's been a mess lately, getting better now, but…I'm getting pretty sour about it." He decided to risk saying out loud the thought he'd only heard in his head so far.

"I keep thinking maybe it's time to hang it up. Every mission is like, okay, maybe this is a good one to go out on."

"You're up soon," she said, referring to his obligation. It was circled on her calendar, and she knew he would probably blow right past it.

"Yeah," he said. Another long, awkward silence, and Porter decided to put that thought into its box. "Deal with that then, I guess."

Jen put her fork down. She wasn't hungry anymore.

Porter saw her dejection. "Would you like to come by tomorrow?"

"No." She avoided his eyes, knowing she should say more but couldn't. She knew he could use a friend to see him off, and she felt selfish for denying him the support. He had always stood by her and she wanted to repay the favor, but couldn't bring herself to go back into that world. They both knew it, and Porter wasn't angry, but he was sad.

"It's alright," he said, looking at her as she stared at her plate. "Jen?" He reached across the table as he said her name, and for the first time in years he touched the back of her hand. It made her look up.

"Really, it's alright."

She smiled and looked away. "Thank you." She pushed the half-empty plate away and took a sip of her drink, looked around the restaurant, saw families laughing, people at the bar watching sports. The war wasn't on most people's minds anymore. She'd lost the most important person in her life because of Afghanistan, and was terrified she might lose one of the only ones she had left. Unless she already had.

"What's going on over there?" she finally asked.

"Lots of scumbags to kill. Same old."

"You never used to be so calloused," she said in a quiet voice.

Porter didn't answer, nor did he get offended. The hardening helped him do the job, for as long as it was his to do.

Jen looked into Porter's eyes. "He wouldn't have liked it."

Porter met her gaze. "He would have grown calloused, too."

———

"Time of death," the doctor looked at the clock on the wall, "20:47."

After a brief pause, the ER doctor left the trauma room and the nurses commenced clean-up operations, filling special garbage bags with blood-soaked blankets and a variety of medical packaging. Jen gathered the supplies — rubber tubes, clamps, various pieces of plastic — put them together on a tray, and left to dispose of them.

Jen paused before dropping them in the receptacle. Only moments earlier, all of these finely crafted instruments, perfectly designed to save lives, were sitting in sterile packages, ready to go at a moment's notice. How quickly they were now discarded in a heap, those that fulfilled their mission indistinguishable from those that had not.

She looked at her watch and realized Porter's plane back to Iraq was most likely already in the air. She hurried with her business, washed up, then pulled out her phone.

She saw a text message: IM OFF. THANKS FOR DINNER. TAKE CARE

Jen sat on a bench and re-read the message, feeling the lack of punctuation in his last sentence.

He's gone. Maybe for good.

She wondered what she should have said, what she should have done, but not for long. She stood, put the phone back in her pocket, and decided to put Porter in a box of her own. She walked back to the nurse's station, slowly growing calloused, too.

8

Counselors

COB Foxtrot
Kirkuk Province, Iraq

Craig turned the corner and saw Ginger from a distance, arguing with…him. That lieutenant. Craig averted his eyes and shook his head, annoyed.

Come on, Ginger.

He turned to go back to the barracks and almost ran straight into Tim Miller, who was standing behind him.

"Excuse me," Craig said, shifting to the side to walk past.

"If you don't talk to her about this, I will," Tim said, still watching Ginger. Craig looked back and saw her walking away, body language betraying her wrath. It was a look he knew well.

"I have talked to her," Craig said.

Tim turned to face the younger pilot. "And?"

"You know her. She laughed it off, told me not to worry about grownup stuff."

Tim frowned, knowing that was probably exactly what she'd said.

"It's not just about her, Craig."

"I know." He leaned against a pallet and crossed his arms, stole a look to verify they were alone. "I told her she was risking a court martial, that we didn't need all the drama. That it's a distraction to mission focus and all that. On top of the fact that he's a total…" Craig held his tongue, refrained from using the perfect word.

Tim smirked, wondered if he was about to hear Craig swear, and decided he'd rather not hear it. "Yeah."

"Maybe *you* should talk to her," Craig looked away, getting angry again.

"Does Eddie know?" Tim asked.

"Probably. Eddie knows everything, but he wouldn't go there with her. Not unless the guy messed with her, then Eddie would be the one getting a court martial."

"Yeah," Tim agreed. He wondered if he should deal with the guy, instead. *No, you'd just end up breaking his face. Talk to her. She's your responsibility.*

But first he had to get things sorted in his own mind. And for that he needed some advice of his own, and it wouldn't come from human wisdom. *Wait, pray on it. There's something else you can do, too.* He turned to walk back to the barracks.

"So, what are you going to do?" Craig asked after him.

"Call my wife."

———

She was furious. She needed to go for a run, or to the shooting range, but instead Ginger walked down the aisle at the base's PX. She had to know. She paced the aisles and picked up a few toiletries, a couple of food items, then quickly grabbed a test off the shelf as she walked by and made a bee line to the open register.

The young lady manning the checkout scanned Ginger's items and, to her relief, seemed to intentionally avoid looking at her as she put everything in a bag. Ginger didn't speak as she paid. She hurried back to her squadron headquarters, past the common area, and straight to her room.

———

Tim turned off the Skype connection. He was calm again; he had his wife's encouragement and a plan. He thought of his daughters, two of whom were grown women about Ginger's age, both single. He wondered if anyone was looking out for them, and whether they were making similar choices, influenced by their lack of a father figure since he was constantly absent.

Are they making good decisions? Do they have someone willing to call them out if they make bad ones?

Tim hoped they did. So he decided to lay it out for Ginger, and he prayed she'd listen.

———

"Yes sir, I understand," Major Atwood said into the phone while looking at Robinson from behind his desk. "I'll forward you my recommendation today," he said, and hung up.

"Fort Campbell?" Robinson asked.

"Yes."

"Let me guess, Cooper?"

"Actually, I was planning on forwarding Miller's dossier."

"Please." Captain Mitch Robinson said with a mixture of disgust and humor.

"You don't think he's superior." It was more of a challenge than a question.

"Of course he is, but A, he doesn't want it, and B, he's probably going to retire anytime now. And C, he'd probably tell you to go to Hell…and then retire anyway."

Atwood didn't smile. If he ever smiled, it was merely a mask, usually in the presence of his superiors, and never behind closed doors.

Robinson wasn't scared of him, or impressed, or surprised. "And, D," he added, "Miller himself would tell you the obvious choice is Ginger."

Atwood shuffled the papers on his pristine desk, then picked up an expensive gold pen and started writing. "Cooper doesn't have the temperament for Special Ops. They want our best. Professionals, not showboats in dance shoes."

Robinson ignored the insults. "And E, she's been putting in for it for months." He paused. He was toeing the edge of insubordination — his normal tendency when defending his aviators, usually against Atwood or others like him.

He knew it was complete BS; Atwood wanted Ginger right where she was. Pegasus had a reputation for excellence that Atwood had nothing to do with, a perfect operational record and the best unit cohesion either commander had ever experienced, largely due to Robinson's leadership, and Ginger and Tim's flying — things Atwood understood well, and intended to keep in place as long as they served him.

But Robinson knew Atwood better than most people. He was also was a master of managing two things that always seemed at odds: the military bureaucracy, and taking care of his aviators. He waited as the gears in Atwood's mind churned. The major seemed to ignore the last statement.

No matter.

He knew he'd already made a strong enough case, and calculated that Atwood would recommended Ginger, that he would play the role of mentor sending off his star pupil to do him proud, a reflection on his leadership that the commanders at Fort Campbell would remember down the road. Robinson knew Atwood was simply pondering how to make it look as if it were his own decision.

Robinson had to wait it out. He hadn't been dismissed.

"What is the time table on One Three?" Atwood asked.

"Working on it, but it'll be grounded for at least a week, if not a month," Robinson said. "They were pretty adamant about the assist on that one," he added, referring to the testimony Donovan gave during the after-action review, in front of the entire squadron.

Atwood said nothing.

Robinson almost smiled, figured he'd take another shot at the Major…just because. "Cooper saved their lives for sure."

Atwood had had enough. "Thank you. That will be all, Captain," he said, never taking his eyes off the page, or his pen off the paper, though he gripped it tight.

Bingo.

Robinson stood, saluted, and escaped.

—

Tim Miller's heart raced. He raised his hand and knocked on Ginger's door. There was no answer. He waited and wondered if Ginger had left but he was pretty sure she would be in. He knew his pilots' schedules, routines, habits, everything.

He was about to knock again when he heard a faint voice. "Come in."

Tim opened the plywood door and saw Ginger sitting on her bunk, her back to the door, hands gripping the frame of the uncomfortable cot.

"Hey girl, got a minute?" he said, as light-hearted as he could.

She didn't respond.

He walked in, propped open the door with a bag, and moved around her bunk to face her. Her complexion was white. Her eyes had a look he'd never seen in Ginger: fear.

"What's wrong?" he asked, fighting fear himself.

Ginger pulled what looked like a flat plastic thermometer from the cargo pocket of her leg. She handed it to Tim. He looked at it for a second, remembering all the times he and his wife had sat in the same position, but with very different emotions.

Tim Miller sat on the bunk next to Ginger, placed it back in her pocket, and put his arm around her.

She tilted her head toward his chest, fighting tears.

Eventually she managed to speak, but barely more than a whisper. "Don't tell Craig."

Tim closed his eyes, thinking for the right response. "He's not the one you need to tell," he said finally.

"I know."

———

"Hellfire away," Craig said as he pulled the trigger. He watched the missile destroy the vehicle and several insurgents around it. He engaged the remaining stragglers with two bursts of the chain gun. When the dust cleared, there were no targets left.

"Looks like we're done here," Craig said.

"Copy that," Ginger agreed. She radioed the ground troops to tell them they were leaving.

Ginger spoke no unnecessary words on the return. She was rarely quiet, especially on missions, and Craig wondered what Tim had said to her.

Maybe she's pissed at me? Or Tim?

An hour later they walked back to the hangar, still in their flight gear.

"Nice job," Craig said, trying again.

She didn't respond.

He stopped. "Ginger."

She turned. "What?" she said, annoyed.

"Are you mad at me?"

"Why would I be mad at you?"

"You seem pissed off. I mean, you're often pissed off, but usually in a nice way."

The jab gave her the first smile she'd cracked in three days. "Craiger, you're fine. It's me. Sorry."

Tim was waiting for them at the lockers, and Craig saw him mouth something to Ginger. She nodded and finished putting her gear in her locker as Tim went down the hall.

"You good?" Craig asked her.

She turned to him and gave a weak smile that was betrayed by her cracking voice. "It's nothing," she said, and walked away.

Craig watched her leave, knowing that whatever it was, it was very much not nothing.

Ginger walked into the briefing room and saw Robinson, alone, typing on a laptop.

"Got a minute, sir?" she asked.

Her commander looked up, surprised to see Ginger an hour early for the debrief.

"Of course," he said getting up to meet her. "What's on your mind?"

Ginger paused, unsure how to begin even though she'd rehearsed the words for days. She stood with her back straight, chin up, hands behind her back — the normal posture of a warrant officer asking for an audience of her captain — all of it, Robinson noted, completely unnatural for Ginger.

"Sir, I need to make you aware that I've violated my orders."

Captain Robinson stood straighter. "How?"

"Fraternization, sir."

Robinson's eyes softened. He waited for her to continue at her own pace.

"I'm…I'm pregnant sir."

For a fraction of a second Robinson was angry, then relieved, although he didn't show it. He'd feared she may have committed a war crime, one her gun camera footage would soon reveal. This was simpler, but then reality set in and he realized what this would mean for his squadron.

And yet, Robinson saw the pain on Ginger's face and was moved.

He turned away from her and stared at the unit's flag hanging from the ceiling. He began formulating a plan of action, and walked to Ginger, standing in front of her.

"At ease," he said softly.

She unclasped her hands and rubbed the sweat from them.

"Sit down, Cooper," he put a hand on her shoulder. "Ginger."

Ginger sat, looking at the floor.

"Well," Robinson forced a weak smile. "Congratulations."

Ginger rolled her eyes, not sure how to accept the words.

"How do you know?" he asked. "Have you been to the medics?"

"No," she said. "Just a test."

"Tests can be wrong," he said more as a question.

"Yes," she consented, but knew it wasn't.

Robinson thought about his squadron, the ramifications for everyone involved, the reasons behind the rules.

"Who knows?"

Ginger didn't look at him, wondered if she should lie, realized it wouldn't matter eventually.

"Just…Miller." She saw a look of horror in Robinson's expression. "It's not him. He's just…the only one I'd trust. And you, sir."

Robinson considered asking who it was, but realized he didn't want to know.

"Ginger, stay here for a minute."

"Yes, sir," she said, standing up.

Robinson walked out of the briefing room intending to find his senior aviator. But as soon as he walked out the door, Miller was waiting, standing by himself at the end of the corridor, trying to look casual.

They locked eyes. The captain nodded toward the briefing room.

Ginger stiffened when they both filed in, worried about dragging Tim into the mess she'd created.

"Guys," Robinson said, "this is all off the record. We don't have anything official on paper, right?" He looked at Ginger.

"But let's assume you're right. Okay, that presents some challenges for you, and us obviously. We're going to have to deal with them. But here's the thing, Ginger — for now, unless we have an official diagnosis, we need to focus on the mission."

Ginger and Tim shared a look of uncertainty.

"But," Robinson continued, "there's no getting around this, so don't even try, Miller — we need to go to Atwood and let him make the call."

Ginger sank, and Tim exploded.

"Atwood! Are you out of your mind, Mitch." It wasn't a question. "Really?"

Robinson fired a look at him that he normally reserved for the enemy. He motioned calmly to Ginger and mouthed silently to Tim, *Shut up.*

Tim paced the room to settle down, and after a moment he tried again.

"Look, Mitch. I understand the chain of command. But you know as well as I do that Atwood doesn't care about anybody but himself. Not you, not me. Certainly not Cooper."

"Yeah, exactly," Robinson said.

Tim folded his arms and stared at his commander.

"Trust me, guys," Robinson said. "He's gonna be pissed, but he's not going to make a case out of it. I can't promise you much, but I will promise you that."

"So he'll…what?" Tim said. "Give her a medical discharge, send her on a flight home, and say 'Have a nice life?' Wash his hands? That might serve him, but it doesn't do much for her."

"We're kinda limited in our options on this one. We're in a war zone. He could have her arrested."

"For doing something that happens every day all over this Army, war zone or not, and you know it!"

Ginger stood. "Miller, I appreciate your passion, but I don't need you to defend me." She turned to Robinson.

"Sir, I'm ready to tell Atwood, and reap whatever consequences he deems proper. I'm not asking for any favors. I'm just informing you as my duty, sir."

Tim threw his hands up and turned away.

Robinson took a step toward her. "Cooper, look. The United States Army has spent hundreds of thousands of dollars training you to do a job that few people will ever be able to do. I'm not going to just throw all that away. We need you. This country needs you, and there are some very important people in charge who get that."

"There are just as many who don't, Mitch," Tim said. "Don't make promises you can't keep. We've both seen this stuff go the other way."

Robinson let the truth hang in the air as they each considered the next move.

"Ginger, I want you to hear me. The ball is in your court. I'll make sure of that. This may seem like the end of something you love, but don't go down that road just yet. This war isn't ending anytime soon. You're one of the best pilots I've ever seen. Better than me, better than Tim, even. We're going to need pilots with your skill for decades to come, in all sorts of roles from Apaches on down. You can still be part of that if you want."

Ginger shook her head. "How?"

"It's going to have to be delayed for a while, a year, maybe more, who knows. I've got a few ideas. But what happens after the baby is born, you decide. Not me, or Atwood, or the Army. You. Hooah?"

Ginger nodded. "Hooah, sir. I'm not gonna suck up to him or anyone else for leniency."

"I would never ask you to. But let me work some things out first, then we'll go to him together. I just need you to trust me. Okay?"

Ginger nodded again. "Thank you, sir."

"Cooper, we're a family. We take care of each other, up there and down here. I'll be in touch, and guys," he paused, "tell nobody. Don't go to the medics, or the guy, whoever he is, or Craig…anybody. Alright?"

She and Tim nodded, and walked out together. As they left, Tim turned to look at Robinson and shook his head.

Robinson hoped he could manage Atwood as well as he thought he could. But he had to admit, Tim might be right.

9

Command Decisions

Porter walked off the C-17 and went straight for chow. He would only be in Baghdad for as long as it took to wrangle a helicopter ride back to Al Asad, and the base complex in Baghdad was a resort in comparison. The remnants of Saddam Hussein's palaces served as a backdrop for the American command structure, with all kinds of amenities, including a variety of restaurants.

On recommendation from senior officers, Porter settled in for a five-star steak and eggs at one of the swankiest war zone facilities he'd ever seen. He sat alone, oblivious to everything around him, while he drained two cups of coffee and savored his steak.

Porter had his back turned to the Navy steward when he heard a couple of familiar voices boom out behind him, punctuated by profanity and directed at the steward.

Porter turned to see six operators in full gear — dirty, smelly, and impatiently hungry — arguing with the young steward who nervously scanned the dining area as the operators got louder. He recognized Jenkins as he walked in.

"Who, this guy!?" he said, pointing to the steward.

The Delta operators parted to make way for Jenkins, who got in the steward's face. "Walk your scrawny little legs back into the linen closet, change your steam-pressed underwear, and go file a report to your CO! If you ever deny one of my guys food again, I'll drive you twenty miles outside the wire and leave you there!"

A trickle of sweat was evident on the steward's forehead. He opened his mouth to speak but Jenkins cut him off.

"Did I say you could speak!?"

The terrified steward saluted and held it.

"Move!" Jenkins bellowed.

The steward rushed into the back room.

Jenkins grabbed a plate and made for the servers, his grinning team followed, and the rest of the diners went back to their meals.

At the omelet bar, a civilian server placed a biscuit on Jenkins' plate and ladled a modest portion of gravy.

"Son, I've been eating corn nuts for a week," Jenkins said. The server added a second biscuit and a large pile of gravy. Jenkins didn't move. The server added four slices of bacon.

"There ya go, laddie," Jenkins said, and left to join his men, and noticed Porter. Eric saw him too, and they joined him while the rest of their team took another table.

Porter rose and shook their hands. "Where you guys been?"

"I can't even remember," Jenkins said, sitting down. "You've been livin' pretty, I see." He motioned to Porter's civilian attire.

"Just got back from stateside. Took Shep's body back to his family."

Jenkins and Eric absorbed the news in stunned silence.

"How?" Eric asked quietly.

"First night. Took a round in the back."

"Man. I'm sorry," Jenkins said.

They ate for a few minutes. Finally Porter asked, "Been out this whole time?"

"Since it started," Eric said. "Babysat a highway the first night. Then they sent us out to chase down Muhammad Al Whoever up there in the Breadbasket."

"Get him?" Porter asked.

"What was left of him," Jenkins said, taking another bite off his plate.

Eric nodded and shook his head. "Somebody must've got nervous about losing him and fired a flechette rocket at his SUV. It was a mess. Pieces up in the trees."

"Speaking of trees, you need to tell your guys about this one." Jenkins pointed his fork at Eric, then to Porter.

"Right," Eric continued. "That region's an insurgent paradise. Dense palm groves and ditches. Perfect for hiding and they had traps everywhere. Those infantry vehicles kept getting bogged down and shot up so we helped them clear the place house to house, field by field. So, get this — now the hajjis are rigging up IED's *in the tops of the palm trees* and waiting for us to pass under them before detonating. Killed a whole squad in one shot."

"Creative little creepers," Porter said.

"Right."

"Where to next?" Porter asked.

"Lookin' like Mosul, from what I hear," Jenkins said. "Us anyway. You?"

"Wherever they tell me."

"Heard that," they agreed.

Porter knew it was a matter of keeping the pressure on. He'd seen the war ebb and flow, from a swift rout of Saddam Hussein's army, to the occupation that followed, then the deterioration characterized by a clever insurgency of brutal foreign jihadists. It was clear to the troops that the only way to beat them was to kill them, and the insurgents would never stop. Porter hoped American leaders would keep their foot on the gas, or the jihadists would soon infest the same places all over again like cockroaches.

Jenkins' Delta operators and Porter's SEALs were the American military's spear tip, targeting the enemy leadership and causing confusion, while their brothers in the Army and Marines provided the muscle needed to sweep up the mess. Both the special operators and conventional forces were finally playing to each other's strengths: quick precision strikes on the one hand, the ability to overwhelm and control territory on the other. One group was an arrow; the other, a bulldozer.

Porter checked his watch, then stood. "Well ladies, gotta go check up on Denny." He reached across the table and shook their hands. "See you in sandbox."

He paused at the other table, slapped a couple of the guys on the back, and helped himself to a slice of bacon from one of their plates as he left.

———

Al Asad Air Base

Porter entered the SEAL section of the base and noticed several of his men seemed haggard. Some noticed him, but most kept to themselves. Porter went to his room and dumped his gear on the floor next to his bed, changed into shorts and a workout shirt, put on his Oakley sunglasses, and pulled his ball cap tight onto his head. He needed a run.

Outside, he spotted Denny running around the fence line. Porter caught up and tapped him on the shoulder, keeping pace.

"Welcome back, boss," Denny said, without breaking stride.

"How they doing?"

No chit chat, no banter. Porter wanted an unfiltered, no BS report and only Denny could give it.

"Pissed," Denny said simply.

"Shep?"

"The whole thing." Denny downshifted into a walk. "What the hell did they send us out to that plant for if they didn't give a damn enough to occupy it? Typical BS, but this time it cost us Shep. Getting a little tired of wasting good men on stuff they don't even care about. That's what I hear 'em saying, anyway."

"All of them?"

"Pretty much."

"You?"

Denny stopped and put his hands on his hips, thinking.

"Yeah, I guess. What about you?"

Porter looked around at the dozen or so planes and vehicles actively working around the base.

"Got a job to do. It doesn't get any easier whining about it."

"Come on, they know all that. Nobody's sore at the work. Bring it on. They just don't want to be wasted on meaningless 'maybe-something-might-be-there' missions."

"Me either. Keep them busy," Porter said.

"No problem there," Denny said.

COB Foxtrot
Kirkuk Province, Iraq

Atwood processed Robinson's proposal.

Robinson could see the wheels turning in his boss's head, and though he was confident Atwood would see reason, he decided to play one final card.

"But mind you, the politics on this could get real ugly. We don't need publicity."

Atwood tapped his expensive pen on the desk as he looked out the window toward the flight line.

He's a calculator, not a leader. Break it down for him again.

"The first thing Fort Campbell is going to do when she gets there is give her a physical," Robinson said, holding up his thumb. "Since she'll be on U.S. soil, that puts the issue entirely out of our hands." *Your hands.*

He put up his index finger. "She gets her Night Stalker tryout like she's been wanting, so we get to be the good guy." *Meaning, you.*

He held out the middle finger, wishing he could extend it by itself. "If they want her bad enough, they've got the connections to work out an arrangement to wait nine months, and if they reject her outright on those grounds, we get her back and can do likewise."

"And," he held out the fourth digit, "it protects the squadron's reputation." *Your reputation.*

"She put herself in this situation," Atwood said.

"So did the guy, but he gets to skate, no repercussions on that end. That's a BS double standard and we all know it. She's not calling him out."

"Assuming she even knows who it is."

Robinson wanted to put his fist through his commander's face but kept his cool. "She's accepting responsibility, came to me, followed the chain of command, willing to subject herself to a medical discharge, or even a court martial if they really want to go there."

"Campbell's just gonna think we're pawning our problem off on them."

"Not after they see her fly."

There was a long silence. Atwood considered the nature of the current war, the unprecedented media access, the sexual politics…the conventional politics.

"Fine, go fetch her. I'm done with this," Atwood said. *Checkmate.*

———

Ten minutes later, Robinson and Ginger walked into Atwood's office and closed the door. Ginger stood at attention.

"Have a seat," he ordered them, but remained standing himself.

Ginger was strangely relieved. After several conversations with Tim over the past few days, she was ready to let the chips fall where they may. She had almost no fear, and even a hint of hope for the future.

"Sir, I—"

Atwood cut her off. "Cooper. I understand from Captain Robinson you've been feeling a little sick lately." His tone was harsh and it immediately put her on guard. "If you're too sick to perform your duties, see the medics. Otherwise it's none of our concern."

Robinson lowered his eyebrows, and a tinge of nausea started in him as well. *Where is he going with this?*

"Sir," Ginger tried to interject, but Atwood held up a hand.

"That's not why I called you in, Cooper. I've got good news," he smiled, picked up a piece of paper, and handed it to her.

"You've got orders to report to Fort Campbell for evaluation with the 160th Special Operations Aviation Regiment."

Ginger was stunned. She'd been asking for this assignment for over two years. As much as she loved flying the Apache with Craig, she wanted to operate at the absolute top of the pyramid, and the SOAR Night Stalkers were the best in the world. She'd dreamed of flying a Little Bird while watching *Magnum P.I.* with her dad. Now, the little girl who'd constructed plastic models of *Blue Thunder* while other girls played with Cabbage Patch dolls was about to get her chance with the most exclusive helicopter squadron on earth.

Ginger looked at Robinson.

"They want our best candidate. That's you," Robinson said. "You've earned it."

Atwood continued. "This squadron has been operating nonstop for months on end. I don't want you to lose your edge. So I've decided to work in a rotation for some R&R beginning with yours and Donovan's crews.

You'll head home, or wherever you'd like, and then report to Fort Campbell after you had some time to get yourself back in shape for their evaluations."

Atwood smiled and both Ginger and Robinson felt a chill in the air at the way he'd phrased that last part.

"Cooper," he said in the smooth manner of a sweaty salesman, "I'm not going to lie. The 160th is not an assignment I'd hand to anyone. You'll be representing our squadron as well as your own character."

He paused and stared at her. "I have the utmost confidence you always weigh your…" he paused, "choices carefully, and so far you've always exercised the right choice, for the benefit of your country as well as your own future, not to mention the people counting on you – the troops on the ground, and the men flying with you."

Atwood was no longer smiling.

Robinson was ready to explode. This is not what they'd discussed at all. A wave of sickness washed over him that morphed into anger and disbelief of what Atwood was suggesting, or rather, pressuring. He didn't know if he should speak up now, or speak to Ginger alone later.

"You'll leave in two days," Atwood said. "So feel free to make arrangements or appointments stateside so you'll be fully ready for the evaluation. Of course, they'll start with a physical, so rest up well prior to that and get your body back in shape. Believe me, you don't want anything to be a distraction. You'll only ever get one chance with the 160th. They'll fail you for the slightest infraction, and they've got a list of applications a mile long, so do whatever it takes to make sure you're ready." He paused and looked her straight in the eye. "Mentally *and* physically."

Atwood could tell Robinson was about to speak and cut him off. "Dismissed," he said, and sat at his desk, picked up his pen and started writing.

Ginger stood. Her eyes burned with hatred as she saluted the commander who now ignored her, who'd just washed his hands of her. She turned on her heel in crisp

Army fashion and stormed out. Robinson hurried after her, not bothering to salute and not caring if Atwood even noticed.

"Cooper," he said from behind, but she didn't stop. He got close enough to grab her elbow. "Ginger."

She turned and threw off his hand, walking away from him.

"That's not at all what we discussed. Don't listen to him, you don't…"

Ginger turned back, "I don't *what?* Is he wrong!?"

"Yes. He is."

Ginger shook her head, held out her hand to stop him from following her, and slowly walked away.

Robinson watched until she turned the corner. He looked at the ceiling, then walked away in the opposite direction.

—

Tim Miller hit the connect button on the Skype home screen. His wife's choppy image appeared.

"Hey, there's the guy," Renee Miller said, smiling.

"Hey babe," Tim said in a voice his wife instantly knew meant trouble. Her first thought was that someone had died.

"What?" she said quietly.

"Crew issues. Lots of FUBAR."

His wife knew they were about to play a game of tell but don't tell. She knew every member of the Pegasus squadron, all of their wives, and most of their girlfriends and family members.

"Someone close to you?"

"Good kid, getting bad advice. Really, really bad advice."

She knew there were only a few members of Pegasus whom Tim referred to as *good kid.* She also knew only one of them would cause her husband the kind of fatherly angst he reserved for his daughters.

"She alright?" Renee guessed.

"No," he said, then mouthed a few key words that made his wife sink in her chair.

"Oh, Ginger," she said, and put her hand over her mouth.

———

Ginger gripped the phone and forced herself to push the last number. She waited while it rang four times before a voice finally answered.

"Marcus."

"Hey dad," she said, trying to keep her voice from cracking.

"Heeey Gingersnap," Marcus Cooper said with a wide smile. "Keeping those boys in line over there?"

· She bit her lip and closed her eyes. "Of course." She paused and her dad waited. He always let others set the pace of a conversation.

"I've got an assignment stateside for a few weeks, maybe more."

Marcus knew there was really only one assignment that would pull Ginger away from the battlefields of Iraq. "Somewhere in Kentucky, maybe?"

"Maybe," she said.

"About time," he said, laughing. "I can probably head that way to see you if you'd like. When are you shipping over there?"

"No need, Dad. I'm coming home first."

10

Family

Kansas City International Airport

A few dozen people strained to see the faces of arriving passengers who made their way out of the busy terminal. Standing in front of them all was Cecilia Allen, who fought past the throngs, determined to spot her oldest son first.

From a distance, Craig saw his mom and held out his arms, then did a pirouette as the curious soldiers walking with him backed away. He was still a hundred feet away from the security checkpoint, and paused, holding up a finger as if to say *hold on a minute,* and made like he was going to stop off at the airport bar he was walking past.

Cecilia put her hands on her hips, stomped her foot and pointed to the ground in front of her. Craig smiled, picked up his pace, and was tackled by his family as soon as he passed the checkpoint.

"I'll box your ears, boy," his mom said and hugged him for twenty seconds before letting her husband have a turn. Peter hugged his son for a long time, long enough for other passengers to notice the muscular men who didn't try to hide their tears.

"Welcome home," his brother Casey said, taking his bag.

"It's alright, I got it," Craig said, trying to take it back.

"No, no, I got this. Go get him," he said, as their sister handed Craig his six-month-old niece.

"Wow, you really made one of these?" Craig beamed, admiring and cradling the newest member of the Allen family.

"I helped, bro." His brother-in-law hugged him from the side.

"Dude, TMI," Craig said, handing the baby back to his sister.

Craig took turns giving hugs and eventually the Allen family made their way to the parking garage.

"We get him for the ride home, right?" Casey asked his parents.

"Yes." Cecilia turned to Craig. "Do you mind if Casey drives you home? Your dad and I have a meeting this afternoon we can't get out of. See you at the house for dinner?"

"Sure, I guess. I don't know if I trust this kid to drive, though," Craig said, and smacked his little brother's chest harder that he meant to.

"I'd trust him to fly that helicopter of yours," Peter Allen said. "By the way, why didn't you bring our girl home with you this time?"

"She went to visit her dad in Cali," Craig said.

"Well, tell her to come see us too. She can bring him."

"I'll let her know."

Craig watched the industrial areas give way to the green of grass and trees as they moved farther from the airport and closer to home. He thought about Ginger and wondered if he should call her dad's house to check in, but worried about pestering her. He wanted to talk to her, but she'd made it clear she wanted to be left alone, by everybody. Robinson and Tim were keeping something from him. He'd already guessed what it was, though neither would confirm it.

Maybe Tim was wrong. Maybe it's just a rumor, or a misunderstanding.

Craig let himself believe that, but an inner voice kept bringing her to the forefront of his mind and he couldn't shake it. *She's hurting.*

Casey interrupted his thoughts. "So, what do you want to do first?" he asked, both hands on the wheel.

"Eat," Craig said. "In fact, you guys hungry? I'll buy. Let's get some chow."

There was a chorus of approval from the back seat of the minivan.

"I still can't get over seeing you drive. Do you get much practice?"

"Are you kidding?" Casey asked. "The same day I got my license, Mom and Dad were all, 'Casey, can you drive Jane to youth group? Can you stop by Hy-Vee and get some eggs?' I almost wish I hadn't bothered."

"Zero sympathy from me. Why do you think I joined up?" They both laughed.

"It's a bummer there isn't a home game while you're here," Casey said after a few minutes.

"It's alright. I haven't been keeping up anyway. I see highlights once in a while but usually we're just too busy."

"Probably for the best. They stink this year," Casey said.

Birdie spoke from the backseat. "I told some people you'd be home for a couple weeks. Some of us were going to go see a movie tomorrow night if you want to come."

"Oh, yeah? Maybe."

"Emily is going," she added, and Casey grinned.

Craig hadn't thought about his sister's friend Emily in over two years, but he'd thought a lot about her in the past. He looked at his brother who was playing it cool. Craig turned to face his sister.

"What movie?"

—

Palm Desert, California

Ginger was up much earlier than the sun, or her dad, or his girlfriend. She stumbled out of the spare bedroom in a completely unfamiliar house. But as she walked to the kitchen she saw her history on every wall, pictures of her and her dad, childhood drawings, and just about every gift she'd ever given him from the time she was four until last year.

You'll never be able to do all that he's done. You can't be a mother.

Her head hung low as she entered the kitchen and she shook the thoughts away. *Coffee. Coffee will help.*

She rummaged the cabinets for coffee, then paused and realized she didn't want it. She didn't even particularly like it, but drinking coffee with a bunch of aviators was her daily routine. But she was nauseous and suddenly realized it was the last thing in the world she wanted. She found a bag of pretzels instead.

She sat at the kitchen table but almost immediately got back on her feet, antsy with anxiety. She turned around the room admiring the messy simplicity of her dad's kitchen. The man could have afforded a private chef and a million-dollar home, but he kept a box of Frosted Flakes on the counter and put all of his money into the garage. Marcus never went on vacations except for a road trip to see Ginger wherever she happened to be stationed. But her deployments were longer than ever these days, and she hadn't seen him in ages.

And now I need to leave him again.

She looked out the kitchen window; the sky was mostly dark. Her internal clock was still on Iraq time and she wondered how long her dad slept these days, then realized his girlfriend might wake up before he did. Ginger had met her for the first time the night before, and she seemed nice but was obviously nervous about meeting Marcus's only daughter, and clearly wanted to make a good impression. Ginger didn't want to get roped into an awkward one-on-one with a stranger, not today. She quickly took a last handful of pretzels and put the bag away, then tiptoed back to her room to retrieve her sneakers.

A tinge of blue was now on the horizon and she remembered seeing a strip mall and a gas station nearby the night before. She couldn't remember how close they were, but didn't care. She wanted to run, maybe even straight out into the desert and just keep going.

Maybe even die there.

The thought startled her.

Where did that come from?

Ginger rubbed her eyes as she walked out the door. The cold desert air was familiar but the shivers were not. She rubbed her bare hands together to warm them, wishing for her flight gloves, then instinctively put one hand on her belly but just as quickly removed it and shivered again.

Run. Run away.

And she ran.

———

"What are you gonna do in L.A.?" Marcus asked after breakfast.

"See a girlfriend. I know, I just got in, but this is literally the only day that works for her," Ginger lied. "I hope you don't mind." She avoided eye contact. She never lied to her dad. Even when the mall security called to tell him she'd skipped school, she didn't lie about it.

Ginger chanced a look and knew he was thinking. When he thought long enough he always figured stuff out, be it mechanical or emotional. She didn't want him filling in his own blanks.

"You don't know her," she said, wondering if she should add another lie, but figured it would be safer to stick with vagaries. "I can get a rental car. I'll be back tonight, then I'll be here with you the whole time, if that's alright." She looked at Marcus's girlfriend, and couldn't remember her name.

Marcus merely shrugged his shoulders and drank his orange juice.

His girlfriend smiled. "Of course. In fact, I was going to head to Bakersfield for a few days anyway. I'm sure you guys would like some time alone," she said.

Ginger was relieved. "Oh. No, I'd like to get to know you better, too." She had no problem lying to strangers. Marcus looked at the table, trying not to grin.

"It's alright. I'm visiting my sister." The woman smiled.

"You don't need to waste money on a rental car. Take your pick," Marcus said, nodding toward the garage.

Ginger thought about all of the cars and motorcycles in her dad's shop. Every ounce of her wanted to choose the '68 Camaro, but the last thing she wanted to do was draw attention, not where she was going.

"I'll just take the truck, if that's alright."

"Sure," he said, quietly processing the data.

"Thanks." She stirred her soggy cereal, then added, almost in a whisper, "It shouldn't take long."

Ginger was resigned to tell him — but after, when it would be too late for him to talk her out of it.

—

Riverside, California

Ginger parked the truck and scanned out her windows. The parking lot was beautiful, well-manicured by the best gardeners money could buy. She saw the bright blue logo on the business sign directly in front of her, mocking her.

Drive away, now.

Ginger gripped the steering wheel, put her hand to the keys dangling from the ignition.

Don't turn it off. Leave now. Go back. Tell him.

She put her head on the steering wheel, heard Tim's voice, his gentle assurances about her strength, his admiration of her, his pleading with her to see it through, to expect good things. She heard Robinson telling her she's part of a family. How he and his wife would be alongside her every step, for the rest of her life, even going so far as to offer to adopt, a last minute appeal before she stepped on the plane.

Ginger had Mitch's wife's number in her phone. Renee Miller's, too.

Call Cecilia.

Ginger flipped open her phone but heard another voice, an accusing voice:

You're just like her.

Ginger looked up, imagined the mother she never knew. Her mother, who left her and Marcus for the drugs she loved more.

That's what you'll be, a worthless mother who loves everything else more. Only for you, it's helicopters. She'll hate you the way you hated her.

Ginger trembled as she looked at the phone in her hands.

Don't call her. She'll talk you out of it. Atwood is right. This isn't about you, it's about your country, your squadron, the men on the ground getting shot at right now. You should be in the air, keeping men alive, but instead you were selfish, sacrificed their well-being for a momentary pleasure. First you violated your orders, broke the law, now you're thinking of wasting all of the training the nation has invested in you. How dare you. Go, get this done and get back to work. You'll never be able to live with yourself if you let all of them down.

But that was what Tim said, Ginger remembered.

"You'll never be able to live with yourself," he'd told her.

But he meant the opposite of this. They need you. Craig needs you to look after him.

Ginger remembered all of the missions, all of the teasing and heroics. She remembered Craig strapped to the weapons pod, all of the stress, and gore, and times they'd been shot at. He needed her. They needed her. Ginger closed the phone, put her hand back on the key, and turned off the engine.

——

Kansas City, Missouri

Craig and his parents sat in silence. Nobody felt like talking. They'd spent the last several hours enjoying all of the noise and camaraderie of the family dinner, desserts, games, hugs goodbye, and plans for the next few days, until Cecilia and Peter finally got their oldest son to themselves with coffee, and all of the littles in bed.

They spoke about the present and the future, for them and their country. They listened as their son brought up the war and his role in it, unwilling to broach the subject themselves but glad he was willing to open up. They mainly listened, knowing better than to offer advice on something they knew nothing about, until they got to Ginger.

Craig laid out what he knew, which wasn't much. But Cecilia knew, and she also knew what her son needed to do about it.

"When was the last time you spoke to her?" Cecilia asked.

"In Atlanta, when we went our separate ways. I told her I'd call in a day or so."

"What did she say?" his dad asked.

Craig smiled. "She patted me on the shoulder and told me to go home and eat some cookies." He held up a cookie. "She knows us pretty well, I guess."

Peter Allen crossed his arms and sat back in his chair thinking. "Will she talk to her dad, you think?"

"I don't know, maybe."

"Does she ever talk about her mom? How she died?" Cecilia said.

"In a way," Craig said. "I asked her about it once. She told me that, 'the b— ,'" he caught himself. He didn't want to repeat Ginger's colorful language to his mother. "She said that the, um, woman could burn in hell, for all she cared. And she never answered her phone so I was gonna try calling her dad's place tonight. I don't know what to say, though."

"Don't worry about it. Just speak and the right words will come out." Cecilia put her hand to his chin and made him look her in the eyes. "You are strong, smart, and filled with love, and I have no doubt you will say what she needs to hear."

Cecilia looked at her husband as she spoke to her son. "Let her know her family is here for her, always. No matter what. Will you tell her that for us?"

"Yes ma'am."

———

Marcus sat by corner window, one eye on the driveway, the other not watching the hundredth screening of a normally favorite movie. He'd been worried since late afternoon, after hearing her voice on the phone saying she might end up staying the night.

She's a grown woman, a soldier, a combat veteran. Maybe she wants to cut loose a little with her friends?

But her voice betrayed her characteristic confidence. Something was wrong with his little girl. Marcus went to the fridge for a second bottle of beer.

I shouldn't worry about her anymore, right?

His daughter lived a lifestyle in which the most dangerous men on earth routinely tried to kill her. She was trained to deal with them, surely she could handle herself in a bar, or wherever she was. Even before joining the Army, she could always take care of herself. All of the years around roughnecks, watching her dad and his buddies racing anything on wheels while witnessing way more than a young girl should, had conditioned her to expect anything. It was Marcus's greatest regret. Eventually he couldn't let it go on, and when her mother spiraled downward, Marcus had made an ultimatum: Get clean, or get out. Ginger's mother chose the latter, and all he could do was move forward and try and set his little girl up for a better life.

He was aided considerably by the fact that she was smart, smarter than all of the celebrity kids in the private high school he moved her to, smarter than the brainy ones with Latin phrases next to their names in the graduation pamphlet, the "Magna-Get-A-Life types," as Ginger called them. She skipped school at every opportunity, aced every test, and generally spun the heads of countless administrators and teachers, all of whom knew her innate ability to find unorthodox solutions to problems was surpassed only by her disdain for all things academic, whether she mastered them or not.

The connections Marcus made restoring classic cars and motorcycles for influential people in L.A. opened all kinds of doors, doors Ginger cared nothing about because she'd only ever wanted one thing: to be a combat pilot.

Marcus smiled. *But she made it.* He took a sip of his beer. Somehow, despite the drug-saturated violence of her early years and all of the worthless guys she'd wasted time on at beach bonfires as a young woman, Marcus's little girl was finally where she wanted to be. Now she was a little less than two weeks away from a chance to join the most elite helicopter squadron in the world.

Is she scared? Is the pressure taking its toll? But Ginger was never scared, maybe to a fault. *Is it war, or regret?*

Marcus figured he'd just have to wait and ask, and in the meantime, watch the driveway.

He was both relieved and terrified when the phone rang.

"This is Marcus."

"Hello, Mr. Cooper, this is Craig Allen. How are you this evening, sir?"

Marcus waited for the name to register. *Oh yeah, her partner.*

"I'm good, Craig. I'm guessing you're looking for Ginger?"

"Yes sir, is she available?"

"No, she's not here right now. Want me to give her a message?"

"No, that's alright. I just wanted to…" Craig wasn't sure what he intended, other than to make sure she was alright.

Marcus sensed the hesitation, and wondered what their relationship was.

"I just wanted to encourage her, sir." It was the truth. "You must be pretty proud of her. She's going to do great at Fort Campbell."

"Oh, yeah. She usually does."

Marcus and Craig had only met once, at Ginger's first deployment ceremony. Neither of them really wanted to talk to each other, not because they wouldn't get along, but because they were both more concerned about Ginger.

"Okay, well, I'll try her again tomorrow, perhaps. Thank you Mr. Cooper. Goodnight, sir."

"Goodnight, Craig."

Marcus looked out the window. He looked at the clock on the wall, 11:45pm.

Go to bed. She's a big girl. Surely she won't be drinking and driving, she's never been much of a drinker.

He started for his bedroom but stopped, remembered Ginger had once teased Craig for being from the Bible Belt.

Kansas? He tried to remember. Marcus did quick calculation, realized Craig had just called her at almost two in the morning, his time. *He's worried.* He went back to the window.

———

For a moment Ginger couldn't remember where she was, wondered if she was dreaming. She sat up in the bed and immediately buckled over with cramps. She lifted her head from the pillow and looked at the hotel night stand, saw the bottle of medications and yellow and pink discharge papers.

Ginger forced herself up, quickly reached for the nightstand, and downed three pills, remembering everything.

The past twenty hours came into focus; she recalled the hurried discharge from the clinic with minimal instructions and zero sympathy. Driving, finding it impossible to concentrate on the highway. Taking the first off-ramp, pulling in to the first motel she could find. Dialing the numbers to call her dad. But she couldn't remember what she'd said.

At least the clinic had given her pain pills, not included in the quoted price, of course. She'd taken the prescribed dose, then another dose in a desperate attempt to sleep, she didn't care for how long.

But now she was up. She was alive. It was all over.

He's probably worrying. You need to call him, make up a story.

Ginger fumbled for the phone.

"Marcus," he said.

"Hey, Dad. Sorry I never called you last night." Ginger was careful not to lie. "I figured I'd better not try to drive home, so I hung out here."

"Okay. You alright?"

Ginger could hear her dad's disapproval, but couldn't tell if he believed her. She was stuck. For the second time in her adult life she lied to her father.

"Yeah."

"When are you coming back?"

"Today."

"Okay. Take your time. I'll be in the garage. I love you."

Ginger gritted her teeth to keep from wailing. She managed to get out a composed response.

"I love you too, Dad. Sorry," and hung up, feeling sicker than she'd ever felt in her entire life, and cried longer than she knew was possible.

After the waves of pain settled she took slow steps to the bathroom, flicked on the light, and turned on the water. She splashed several handfuls of water on her face before looking in the mirror. An accusing voice gripped her, filled her with condemnation and shame as it mocked her.

You're worse than her. She never killed anyone.

Ginger couldn't look at herself. She turned on the shower, threw herself into the bathtub, and curled into a ball, desperate for the water to wash her nightmare away.

—

Marcus was in the garage when Ginger got home.

"Hey," she said.

He looked up, saw she was still wearing sunglasses, and went back to the gearbox.

"Hey."

She wasn't sure what to say. They'd played out this scene before, and she knew he wouldn't ask her where she'd been or what she'd done. He never did. But sooner or later, she knew he would expect her to tell him what she'd learned from it.

"Are you alright?" he said, this time standing to face her, and lifting her sunglasses.

Ginger summoned the strength that made her one of the strongest aviators in the United States Army. "Actually, pretty tired. And a little sick." She gave a small smirk.

Marcus recognized his daughter again. "Yeah, that happens."

"I think I'll go lie down," she said. She felt like she'd been hit by a truck.

"Alright, I'll check on you a little later."

"Thanks."

Ginger went to the spare bedroom, slept for most of the day, watched part of an old movie with her dad, skipped dinner for another long shower, and slept until the following morning. Sleep was her only craving, the only relief from the accusations and the pain.

———

On day three, Marcus noted Ginger up at a reasonable hour, and dressed in more than sweats and a t-shirt.

"Sorry, you missed breakfast," he said.

"It's alright, I'll probably go get something. I kinda want to get outside and get some fresh air."

"You feeling better?"

Ginger didn't know how to answer. Physically she was feeling pretty good again. "Yeah, I think so. What do you have going today?"

"Work. I'm gonna have to head over to Redlands to pick up some parts. You can come, but it might be pretty boring. Only take a few hours though."

"Actually, I was thinking I might take one of the bikes for a ride. If that's alright."

Marcus grinned. She must be feeling better. "Sure, still got your old Ducati."

"How about the Busa?"

Marcus crossed his arms and stared at her. "Uh huh," he said, picking his teeth with his tongue. The Suzuki Hayabusa was the fastest bike in the garage even before

Marcus had customized it. "She's pretty touchy. Think you can handle her?"

Ginger's deadpan expression matched the insult in her voice.

"Dad. I fly Apaches."

"Yeah, I guess I forgot that. Sure, go ahead." He stood, grabbed his keys, and kissed her forehead. "I'll be back for lunch. Get a warm up, and maybe we can take a ride together this evening?"

"Sure, Dad." *Maybe a ride will help. Something has to help.*

———

Ginger threw her soda cup into a dumpster in her dad's shop. The clean air filled her lungs on the jog down the road; the greasy fast food was a welcome relief and the calories almost made her feel human again.

She admired the vehicles, some in various states of repair, others in showroom condition ready to sell to ritzy buyers who undoubtedly had no clue how to drive them, all with the keys in the ignitions.

Ginger had never been in this shop before — Marcus had high-tailed it out of L.A. and relocated his business in the desert the same month Ginger left for basic training — but everything was laid out in the familiar way, including the location of her old helmet on a shelf right next to his, and her old racing jackets and gloves hanging underneath.

She walked toward the Hayabusa but paused as she passed the gun safe, eying the numerical keypad.

I'll bet it's the same, too.

She entered the numbers of her birthday and the lock opened. Inside were a few shotguns, a classic Winchester 1892 carbine, several handguns, and a few boxes of ammo. Marcus didn't hunt. The guns were for fun, and for protection on long rides in the middle of nowhere that often ended with him and Ginger sleeping under the stars.

Never ride unarmed. Marcus had taught her that lesson as a teenager, and she retrieved a Glock 9mm still in its holster, removed it and checked to make sure the magazine was full.

You'd only need one, you know.

Ginger stopped. Where had that thought come from? She closed her eyes and slammed the magazine back into the gun, attached the holster to her belt, and went to the Suzuki. She pushed the garage door button as she rolled it out of the shop, and the automatic door closed behind her.

She fired it up, felt the power of the machine; it was a familiar sensation she needed. She was desperate to be back in a cockpit but this would have to do for now.

Focus. You'll be in with the Night Stalkers next week. Get your head right.

She took it slow through the city streets, getting a feel for the bike. In a matter of minutes she pulled onto Interstate 10 and gradually accelerated past the sparse late morning traffic of the desert highway. She went around a car that was doing 85 in the fast lane. As soon as she was clear, she gunned it.

The motorcycle responded by lurching forward, and Ginger was back in her cockpit. She pushed it to 100 mph, then 120, then 130 with no intention of slowing down. The desert flew by just as it did from her Apache window, merely background for the mission at hand. She didn't know how far she'd go; at this speed she'd be in Arizona in no time.

Unless I get pulled over by a cop. But no, a cop wouldn't be able to keep pace with me. Not out here.

Ginger knew this stretch of desert, had ridden it with her dad many times. She knew the curves of the road, the rocks, the hills, all of them old friends she was glad to see, friends who knew her before —

Before you were a murderer.

The voice, again.

Make it stop. Faster. Drive faster.

She passed more cars, no longer slowing as she flew past them at 150 mph like they were standing still. She didn't care about cops, didn't care about startling the other drivers. She had only one goal: drowning out the accusing voice.

Murderer.

The voice kept repeating the word, much louder than the music playing through the earbuds under her helmet. It was relentless.

How many people have you killed? Just little black and white blips on the monitor to you. Careless, heartless…selfish. Why do you get to live?

Ginger saw another familiar landscape, the interchange ahead. She slowed just enough to make sure it was clear, took the off ramp, and turned to her left to cross over the interstate onto Cottonwood Springs Road.

That's good. Now you'll be alone.

Ginger went through the gears till she was back up to 120. Another voice tried to tell her to slow down. The two-lane road cut through the desert and she could easily hit a rock, or a roadrunner, or a person. The gradual curves alone could sent her flying off the road, or into a head-on collision with any of the small cars or large trucks. The voice encouraged her.

Death would be instantaneous, an accident. They wouldn't know you did it on purpose.

She went faster.

Do it. Just a jerk of the handlebars. They'd want you to if they knew what you did.

Ginger saw a car. She gripped the handlebars, and drove past it.

Gonna tell Craig? the voice asked.

She tried to argue with it.

Craig would understand. He'd be sad, disappointed, but he'd understand. He's always forgiving. Tim too, and Mitch, and Cecilia.

The voice persisted.

Maybe before, but not now. Now they'll know who you truly are. Now they'll shake their heads and hate you for what you've done. Even your dad will wonder, "How could she?"

Ginger let up. The bike slowed.

No, she countered, *Dad doesn't dwell on the past. He'll want me to move forward, to take responsibility.*

Exactly, it laughed.

Ginger reached back, felt the Glock on her hip.

All around her were desert shrubs and Joshua trees as far as the eye could see. She was alone, as alone as she'd ever been. She wanted to break something, to shoot something, to scream, anything to make the voice stop.

Ginger pulled the bike off the road, creating a cloud of rocks and dust as she stopped, put the stand down, and jumped off. She strode into the brush, kicking small bushes; took off her helmet and threw it into the desert, then pulled her earphones out so hard she broke the cord before throwing them to the ground.

Ginger looked into the crisp blue sky overhead, closed her eyes, and screamed. It shook the air and strained her vocal cords, one long powerful blast until her breath was spent.

And still the unimpressed voice spoke. *It only takes one.*

Tears now. She cried, turning around, desperate to see someone, anyone, but she was alone. She reached back and pulled the Glock out of its holster, felt the weight of the loaded gun, and let her arm fall to her side as she paced and cried out loud.

"God, help me." She'd never said those words before. And the voice laughed at her.

God, help you? Murderer. Stop playing around. Stop being a coward.

She kicked at a Joshua tree like she was kicking in a door, over and over with the flat of her boot. She turned and waved the gun, crying.

Craig, Tim…I'm so sorry…God, help me.

Ginger pressed her finger gently against the trigger. She stared at the tree in front of her, her heart racing, her chest pounding, another scream beginning to crest like a wave about to break. She started to scream as she lifted the gun.

Don't worry. Just one shot and all of the pain will be gone. It's okay. You can do it.

She stared at the tree, breathing heavy and sweating as she brought up the gun.

God, help me.

Suddenly the tree changed shape. Ginger blinked at the hallucination, and in it saw the image of Atwood superimposed in front of the tree. Before she could even register what she'd seen, the image changed to a blue logo, the one she'd stared at while sitting outside the clinic, then changed again into an insurgent with an AK pointed at her.

Her instinct and training took over, her muscle memory pointed the gun at the familiar threat and Ginger loosed a scream louder than the first as the pulled the trigger, then pulled it again and again. Brass flew from the gun onto the sandy rocks under her feet, fifteen times until the slide pulled back, the bullets nearly cutting the Joshua tree in half until the last cartridge was ejected.

Genevieve Cooper fell to the ground, dropped her dad's gun, and curled up, crying as the heat of the sand and the sun above her combined to envelop her, but still she shivered.

11

Forward

Al Asad Air Base, Iraq

Porter caught sight of Ozzy from a distance, working out on a pull-up bar. The muscular Iraqi performed a slow set of five, dropped into a dead hang, then did five more.

Porter looked at Denny. "What's up with Ozzy?"

"I don't know. Kinda keeping to himself lately."

A flag waved in Porter's brain.

"You concerned?" Porter asked, still watching him.

"With Ozzy? No. He's solid."

"Solid?" Porter was skeptical.

"Yeah. Hundred percent." Denny shook his head. "It's something else." He shrugged his shoulders and walked away.

Porter watched him for another minute, still busting out sets of five, and decided to approach him.

"You going for a record?" Porter asked.

Ozzy stopped with his head over the bar, slowly let himself to the ground, and released. He wiped his hands together, stood up straight, and turned to Porter. "What is the record?"

"Couple thousand, I think."

"No, sir. Not that many."

Porter considered their last mission. "How you doing, Ozzy?"

Ozzy thought about the question. He understood Americans well enough to know it was often asked rhetorically, but he also knew Porter didn't ask rhetorical questions.

"Honestly, Porter, sir…pretty distracted. I'm concerned for my family."

Porter was interested where this would go. "Where do they live?"

"Tal Afar. In the north."

"They still there?"

"I believe so. I spoke with my wife about a month ago and she was…scared."

"I would be, too. It's pretty violent up there right now, isn't it? Can't you move them somewhere else?" he asked, remembering all of the fighting he'd done there a year earlier. Ozzy had been a major part of it too, with a different platoon. His performance then was the reason he was with Porter now.

"It's my family's homeland. If you don't mind my asking, sir, where are you from?"

Porter had no interest in telling an Iraqi where he or his family lived, so he kept it vague. "New England."

"I'm not familiar with New England. Has your family been settled there long?" Ozzy asked.

"Generations."

"So, if someone came to New England and started setting off car bombs, and kidnapping and killing the people you love, would you pack them up and move?"

Porter smiled and nodded. "No, you're right."

Ozzy tried to think of how he could explain his life to this American.

"My country has been at war…all of my life. First my father fought the Iranians, then," he paused, "the Americans…the first time." He hoped Porter understood the history, how so many Iraqis had gleefully surrendered to the Americans during Desert Storm, happy to be out from the conscription of Saddam Hussein's personal army, run by thugs and sadistic gangsters.

"When the Americans left, we had some freedom. As long as Saddam had his palaces, he didn't care much about us. We were not free, but things were simpler, as long as you kept quiet and stayed out of his way. My mother, she…was not quiet. She raised us to not be quiet." Ozzy looked away, trailing off in thought.

Porter waited, remembering the things he'd seen while hunting the ousted dictator across his former country. He recalled the prisons dedicated to torture, the mass graves, the unthinkable brutality Saddam's regime brought upon the Iraqi citizens who challenged his authority in any manner. Porter wondered if he had seen Ozzy's mother, or what was left of her, in any of those awful places.

"When your country came back, my father was waving your flag. My brothers and I, we all signed up as police. We wanted to be a part of what you were trying to do here. And have revenge, I guess." Ozzy sat down on a bench. "Porter sir, they're all dead now. I try hard to not hate them."

Porter knew he was referring to the insurgents. No sooner had the Americans established a foothold and a strategy to hand Iraq over to its own people, than the jihadists came from Iran, Syria, Saudi Arabia, highly trained experts from Chechnya and Europe, like scavengers to a warm carcass. Fanatics young and old, all drawn to Iraq, the new ground zero in the fight they salivated for.

"They're savages, Ozzy. It's okay to hate them." Ozzy looked at him, and he saw disagreement in his eyes and felt immature for saying it. Porter believed it was true, but something in him — perhaps from old conversations with Jen or Aiden — knew the thought was wrong somehow. He took a seat next to him.

"Is your family Shiite?" Porter knew the ongoing civil war was mostly being conducted on tribal and religious grounds.

Ozzy let out a laugh. Porter really didn't know him very well at all. "No. No, we are not."

Porter felt out of his element. He understood history as far as necessary to do the job. He understood religion in the abstract, gleaned from the people around him, people he cared about, loved even, but it had no practical place in his life. He decided he had no business speaking to Ozzy about the things he was ignorant of. But he knew how to lead men in combat, and he wanted Ozzy to know how he felt.

"Ozzy, I'm gonna level with you. I can't say what the guys in the big tent plan to do about this mess they've started. Maybe we kill them all and drive them out. I hope we do, 'cause I'd rather kill 'em here than in my hometown like you say. I'm sorry it has to be here, but sometimes you're the bug and sometimes you're the windshield."

Ozzy smiled, nodded. Porter continued. "Maybe my country decides it's not worth it and bails. All I know is that for now we've got a chance to kick 'em in the teeth and take back your neighborhoods, and we're gonna round up the rats for as long as we're here."

"Thank you, sir. It is my prayer that your leaders feel the same way."

Porter knew some did, but many others didn't, and all he could do was the job in front of him.

"Come on, let's go pop off a few rounds," Porter said, getting up.

"Yes. Let's."

Palm Desert, California

Marcus refilled his mug. Ginger watched him open a top cupboard, pull out a dark bottle, and add a small splash to his coffee. He paused, then added another two-second pour. Then he offered the bottle to Ginger.

"No thanks," she said, with the smallest hint of a smile.

He sat down across from her and took a long sip before asking his first question. "And what about the guy?"

Ginger scoffed. "He flat out denied it."

Marcus raised his eyebrow. "Denied it was his?"

"No. Denied it even happened."

Marcus fumed inwardly as she continued.

"Uniform Code of Military Justice. He went into full CYA mode."

"What would have happened?"

"He's a superior officer, and as such could get court-martialed, or stripped a rank for fraternization. For him it was a simple decision, ditch the crazy girl and deny everything."

"Well, there was proof…" He saw her look down, and wished he hadn't said it. "Sorry. What did you do when he said that?"

Ginger took a sip of her own coffee. "Nothing. He wasn't worth it. I went to my commander and admitted my lapse. Figured I'd just take whatever punishment they dished out."

Marcus took a long drink from his mug, thinking before speaking this time.

"So, this decision. Was the guy a part of it?"

"No. He washed his hands of me, so I washed my hands of him."

Marcus was visibly disappointed. "I see," he said quietly.

Ginger was confused, then defensive. "You think I should have told him?"

"What's done is done, but, yeah, you should have told him."

"Why? He made his choice weeks ago."

Marcus answered with a sincere, gentle tone she knew well. "He may be a grade-A scumbag right now, maybe forever, but even so, someday he's going to feel exactly what you've been feeling. He's going to wonder about it, and it may very well haunt him." Marcus looked away. "It affects everyone, Ginger. It just does."

She saw he was on the edge of weeping, and the shame flooded back. She knew she would see the man again at some point. Part of her wanted him to be haunted, but another part of her, the part that woke up almost nightly from nightmares, didn't wish that torment on anybody. He was right. Everyone was affected, Craig, Tim, her dad. She had another revelation.

This was Marcus's first grandchild. Maybe his only grandchild.

"I'm so sorry." A tear rolled down her cheek. Marcus saw it and knew it would speed the healing, but he also saw her dejection.

"I understand why you didn't tell me."

"It was fear," she said with a little strength in her voice again. "I was afraid you'd talk me out of it. I wish I would have told you." They both knew she was right. There was a long pause, the grief heavy in the silence.

"Ginger." He looked in her eyes. "I'm not proud of what you did, or how you got there. You know that. But I am still proud of you. I'm proud of you right now, this minute. You're facing it, speaking about it, and you're going to move forward. You're not going to let shame or past mistakes control your future. I won't stand by and watch that. You're going to go to Kentucky, get back in that cockpit, and show them who you are."

Tears flowed openly, but she pursed her lips and held her head high.

"I don't deserve it, Dad. Not now. I don't deserve any of it. I violated my oath, twice now, and I…"

"No, you don't deserve a reward for this. And maybe they'll disqualify you on those grounds, but you do deserve the chance to stand in front of them. That, you do deserve." He scooted his chair right up next to her, and put his arm around her.

"You will either learn from this, or be destroyed by it."

They hugged tight for a long time before he stood, and then leaned over to kiss her forehead before going back for another cup of coffee.

"Dad?"

He turned.

"Maybe I will take a splash."

Marcus reached over and took her mug.

—

Kansas City, Missouri

Craig took inventory to not miss anyone; practically every family member across two states had come to the barbecue that would send him off, back to work. One of the last hugs was reserved for Emily, who had received an inordinate amount of his time these ten days, something Cecilia encouraged amid his siblings' objections.

Cecilia Allen watched their goodbye, and noticed that it didn't include a kiss. *Not this time, at least.*

Craig walked over and hugged his mom for a long time. She whispered in his ear. "I love you."

"I love you, too."

"Stay sharp. And give 'em hell for your mama, okay?"

"I will."

Cecilia let go and handed him a bag full of cookies. "These are for everybody. Tell Eddie to share." Then she handed him a small envelope. "This is for Ginger. She's family, she always will be. Make sure she knows that."

"I will. I promise."

—

Fort Campbell, Kentucky-Tennessee border

The clock was ticking, the pressure mounting, and Ginger was in heaven.

She zipped past the third waypoint and made a dramatic cut to the left. Her right eye darted from the compass to the map, and back again as she flew the Little Bird almost exclusively with her left eye and paid no attention to the clock. She knew by her evaluator's silent responses that she was flying faster than he was used to. She also noticed he tried not to smile.

Ginger wanted to sing, but also didn't want to appear too cocky. So she hummed instead as she hit the next waypoint and changed direction again. She was completely comfortable, and even though it was hard, it was crazy fun. This was only the second time she'd flow an AH-6; the first was when she was still learning the basics of combat aircraft. That day she'd taken it easy, wondering what the little egg-shaped machine was capable of. But now as a combat veteran, she drove it the way a race car driver would take a test drive, fully aware that the men watching her wanted to be impressed, to see something that would separate her from the rest of the pack.

The past week had been a whirlwind of activity — physical tests, oral examinations, written examinations, a psychiatric evaluation. She even had to take a swim test. She prepared and delivered a mission briefing for an entire room of instructors who said absolutely nothing to her; not even a hint of interest, good or bad.

The instructors threw the book at her and the other seven candidates. There were grueling flight tests in Blackhawks, Chinooks, and Little Birds. She was surprised how much she enjoyed flying the large Chinook, even when they surprised her by turning off her automated flight control system, forcing her to use muscles she didn't know she had just to keep it airborne.

All of it was exciting, but the whole time she was itching to be in the Little Bird. None of the machines were as challenging to fly as the Apache, to her anyway. Walking the flight line of the Night Stalker arsenal, she was like a kid let loose in a toy store.

They put her in situations she'd never experienced, simulated emergencies to see how she'd handle stress, and didn't let up on the pressure the entire week. For her current test they'd blacked out all of the Little Bird's instruments, leaving her with only the map and compass to plot and navigate her course within a tight window.

Ginger passed the final checkpoint twenty seconds ahead of time. She took her right eye off the map and looked at the instructor. He merely took notes and said nothing.

It was time to land. She decided to see if she could illicit a response.

She saw several concrete Jersey barriers near the landing pad, and flew straight to the one nearest her landing zone, lined up the helicopter's skids so they were exactly centered over the eight-inch wide concrete barrier, and landed on top of it with her rotors still spinning.

"Is here alright?" she asked with a hint of snark.

The instructor turned and gave her a look she couldn't discern.

"Oh, am I faced the wrong direction?" She immediately lifted the skids a fraction of an inch off the concrete, rotated the helicopter 180 degrees and set it back down so softly the instructor didn't realize they were balancing on the narrow ledge.

He shook his head, pointed to the landing pad and went back to taking notes.

She saw several of the ground crew pointing at her, and she knew she'd either cemented her acceptance or her rejection by the world's best helicopter squadron.

She landed, and as she powered down she started singing, wishing Craig was there.

———

Two days later, Ginger stood in front of a horseshoe-shaped table full of men with dour expressions. They let her wait for several minutes, standing at attention as they reviewed a pile of papers. She was ready for anything, and knew what would probably be first.

The unit psychologist led off. "Cooper, are you pregnant?"

"No, sir."

"Your urinalyses says otherwise."

The psychologist knew she wasn't — a sonogram immediately administered after the physical had confirmed the positive test result was due to hormones from a recent, but not current, pregnancy. Ginger had told the doctor everything at the time. She knew the regiment psychologist was trying to rattle her, knew all of the questions were intended to rattle her, piss her off, get her to cry, become defensive — anything that would disqualify her from performing at the level they required of her.

"I had an abortion thirteen days ago, sir." She could have left it at that, but she knew this line of questioning wasn't about her body; it was about her mental state, her character as an officer, her ability to learn and adapt to new challenges. She knew she had to be fully honest, to open the box and let them in if she had any chance of being invited into their fraternity.

"It was the worst decision I've ever made in my life. If I could go back and change it I would, but I can't. I have to live with it now. And I'm ready to move forward, sir." Ginger held her emotions in check, wondering if this direct and honest response would illicit follow-ups.

It did. The regiment knew she could fly; they needed to know if they could trust her — about everything, scars and all.

"Do you lack self-control, Cooper?" a different officer asked.

"Are you a home wrecker?" asked another one from across the room.

A torrent ensued as the instructors questioned her willingness to follow orders, to accept responsibility. They asked personal questions that mocked her, the kind that in any other business setting would have dragged everyone through a human resources nightmare.

"You're not married, not attached to anyone, no friends, no social media involvement. Cooper, why shouldn't I consider you a loser?"

Ginger knew the special operations units had to know she was able to keep mission focus. It was terrible, morally reprehensible, but she knew the rest of the male pilots were also being prodded for their own unique weaknesses. Finally they turned to flying, and the questions got even more brutal.

"You fly the Chinook like it's an ice cream truck. Do you think we're going to let you carry men to their death?"

Ginger was quick to retort. "Sir, I respectfully ask you to refrain from disparaging ice cream. As for forty-sevens, sir, I rather like the big uglies. And I can fly that big girl through the front door of Grand Central Station and back out the rear without scratching the paint, sir!"

They questioned her service record, her combat experience and decisions, critiqued her mistakes in battle, quizzed her on mechanics, questioned her physical prowess. They mocked her technique, called her reckless, told her people were lucky to be alive in spite of her failures. With each question, she became more and more confident.

For two hours it continued, and she watched men who were hell-bent on making her cry at the outset soften and become fully professional, and then casual. She could see them exchanging looks with one another, trying hard to give her nothing to go on.

But she knew. Her honesty and confidence were winning them over, to say nothing of her flying, which she knew was exceptional.

A long pause ensued, and she wondered if it was all over.

"Cooper," the president of the evaluation board said finally. "I'm going to be honest with you. We are not going to make a decision today."

She was disappointed but not surprised, and kept it in. "Yes, sir."

"You will return to your squadron this evening. If we choose to invite you to join the regiment, we will contact you." He stood, and the rest of the board followed suit, ending the session as abruptly as it started.

Ginger saluted and walked out of the room.

—

"See what I mean?" one of the instructors said when the door closed behind her.

There was a general murmur of approval. Some of them sat back down, others stretched, all recharging for the next applicant. When they were seated again, the board president looked down the line of his officers.

"Any objections?"

All of them shook their heads. He looked at the psychologist.

"Doc?"

"Not from what I've seen. I think she's ready to move forward."

Several of the men grunted agreement.

The president wrote *Genevieve Cooper* on the number two spot on an unofficial list he was compiling on a scratch pad. He had another week of evaluations with another class of candidates to fill five spots. He still had a number of men to evaluate, and their individual aptitude would determine which pilots were placed in which air platform. It was clear that Cooper was a natural fit for the AH-6, but she could fly anything, and he might need her elsewhere.

Also, he'd just gotten a strongly worded email from his own commander, a ball rolled downhill from a four-star general in Iraq who wanted his pilot back. Until he got it all sorted, the war needed Warrant Officer Cooper back in her Apache.

—

Contingency Operating Base: Foxtrot
Kirkuk Province, Iraq

Ginger walked into the squadron headquarters and was immediately confronted by Eddie, whose frame blocked two thirds of the hallway in front of her. He crossed his arms and scowled.

"I heard a rumor 'bout you."

Ginger paused, tilted her head. "Oh yeah?"

"Yeah, some people sayin' our little sister gonna up an' leave us. You fixin' to be a Night Stalker. Well?"

She smiled. "Yeah well, I guess we'll see."

Eddie wrapped his left arm around her and ushered her toward the common area. He leaned in and whispered into her left ear, "Take me with you."

———

Ginger stood near the flight line sipping coffee from a paper cup. The smell of jet fuel, cheap coffee, and garbage was strangely comforting. She heard someone come up behind her.

"Welcome back."

Tim Miller stood next to her but she didn't turn to face him. She had rehearsed this moment, had dreaded it.

"I did it," she said.

Tim let the statement hang in the air for several seconds. "How did it go with the Night Stalkers?"

"They said they'd let me know." She took another sip of coffee. "I should have listened to you...and Mitch. I guess I blew everything."

He moved closer and stood with his arms folded, leaning over to her. "Want a lollipop?"

Ginger scoffed but smiled. She turned and looked up at him. "Yeah. I think maybe I do."

They watched another Apache lift off.

"Let's get back to work…I'm glad you're here, kiddo."

"Yeah, me too."

———

Ginger made her way to her sleeping quarters. She sat on the bunk in her flight suit, grateful the war would be calling any minute; she wanted to fly.

The squadron was in constant demand and the air crews were cycling through shifts at maximum allowable air time. There were rules about how many hours a pilot could fly versus when they were forced to sleep, and the rules were being stretched almost to the breaking point. Ordinary pilots would spend anywhere from twenty to forty-five hours per month in the air. Most of the Pegasus pilots were well past eighty.

"Sorry, you missed the cookies."

She turned to see Craig in her doorway eating a sandwich. With his mouth full he added, "They were good, too."

She stood, walked over to him, and noticed he was holding a small box.

"This is from Dad."

She took the box, an inflatable kids-style floor seat with an image of Mulan. "For his warrior princess, he said."

She laughed. "It's perfect."

Craig pulled an envelope from his chest pocket. "And this is from Mom," he said, handing it to her.

Ginger took the letter, her eagerness to open it stifled by the desire to read it alone.

"Thank you."

Craig put his hand on her shoulder and got serious. "Are you good?"

"Yeah. Yeah, I'm good…but Craig," she leaned closer, drawing him in. "Take a breath mint, will ya," and she slapped his belly.

"Jealous," he said, taking another bite of his sandwich.

The PA system came alive. "Portia, Hamlet, Stage, Curtain." This week's Shakespeare-themed coded message translated to: Cooper, Allen, Flight Line, Immediately.

"I guess I'll read it later," she said, tossing the box onto her bed and tucking the letter into her pocket before sprinting toward the flight line. Craig crammed the rest of his sandwich in his mouth and did the same.

12

Rover

Tal Afar, Iraq
One Month Later

"Sheep manure or dead camel?" the Marine asked.

"Sheep manure *and* dead camel, and a probably a few buckets of human waste thrown in," another squad member predicted as they approached a dilapidated shanty in a row full of dilapidated shanties, every one of which they had to visit.

A toddler peeked at them from behind a broken wall, watching them with vacant eyes. He was barefoot and wore a shirt several sizes too big for him.

"Hey buddy," one of the Marines smiled.

Sergeant Taylor began his sixth "knock and talk" of the afternoon, fully expecting this one to be the same as all the others — useless.

A man in a white robe and cap answered, cigarette in hand. A familiar exchange ensued as the Marines passed a series of questions through their interpreter, all of which were answered with an immediate "no" and emphatic head shaking, but zero eye contact.

Taylor knew it was pointless. He had no confidence in what the locals said, only what they did. And hiding terrorists is what they did; most of them, anyway.

There were some good elements in the larger cities where the awakening was taking place, where Iraqi Army platoons were getting trained and supported by the Americans, which sometimes flushed out the hardcore insurgents who fled to concealed areas where they regrouped, plotted, and came up with new ways to kill, like the new chlorine IED that took out two Marines a week earlier right down the road.

But Americans were not the only ones getting killed.

Tal Afar was a hotbed of sectarian violence with suicide bombers detonating themselves almost every day. Insurgents attacked the civilian population, the Iraqi police, and other local authorities. Anyone who had the audacity to collaborate with the Americans was a target. Kidnappings became frequent, as did mass executions, and IED attacks of increasing destructiveness and ghastly creativity terrified average citizens into silence.

The Army controlled two thirds of the city and the Marines were responsible for the rest, and they both knew this was a city of experimentation. Tal Afar was a perfect hub, situated by a major highway into Syria to the northwest and Iran to the east, and within reach of friendly remote villages and other major population centers like Mosul. It was a prime location for terrorist research and development.

The Marines were confident everyone in the neighborhood had information about the bomb makers they sought. They had names and faces of the suspects but it hardly mattered anymore; everyone was an enemy, because everyone in the neighborhood lied and claimed they didn't know anything.

Sometimes Sergeant Taylor could see the conflicting spirit in their eyes as they lied. He hated them for being afraid, even though he himself was always afraid of this city, and he wondered if he would lie too, in a similar situation. Would he do whatever it took to stay off their radar and protect his family?

He tried to shrug it off. Sympathizing with them only made the mission harder, and yet his job was to win their trust, make friends, and earn the intel via relationship with people he hated. It was the last thing in the world he wanted to do.

The Marines would patrol, and talk, and patrol and talk some more. They had become cops, and it galled them. They wanted to just kick in the door and search the place, but to do that they needed actionable intelligence — essentially probable cause, as a cop might say. But they were not cops, they were United States Marines, and they prayed their leaders hadn't forgotten that.

From behind Sergeant Taylor, Lance Corporal Jackson listened to the typical exchange while scanning the faces of several men watching from across the street. They seemed passive but Jackson knew most of them probably wanted all of the Marines in his squad dead. It was maddening. The Marines spent money in their shops, gave toys to their kids, gave food and clothing to people who received it with grateful smiles; and still the Americans got no cooperation. Worse than that, they were hated.

What is that smell?

Taylor broke off the conversation.

"What's in that shed?" he asked his men.

Three Marines pulled off, and when they opened the door to the shed the stench was almost overpowering. A cascade of flies was thick in the darkened room and they turned on their flashlights, pointing their weapons into the shed. Faces stared back, blank hollow faces, like creatures from a low budget horror movie. Flies and fleas crawled over them. At first the Marines thought they were bodies, but they knew the scent of death and this was different.

One of the undead creatures blinked, and another stirred.

"Sarge! You've gotta see this."

The sergeant walked to the opened door and saw six bodies, four of which were completely naked, two wore filthy rags. Taylor wasn't sure what to do. He had no intention of going into the swarm of flies, but this wasn't natural. Red flags began waving in his head. He decided to call his superior officer on the radio.

"Rover Five, this is Rover Zero Niner. I need you to see this."

"See what, Zero Niner?" Staff Sergeant Reid answered, annoyed.

"Rover Five, I've got a shed full of dying people, sir. Not sure what to make of it."

The other squad was patrolling the street parallel to theirs, and one of the Humvees would have to break contact to make its way over.

"Copy."

A minute later they saw Reid's Humvee turn the corner and head toward them. When he got out he immediately noticed the smell, stronger than ever now that the shed was open.

"In the name of..." he said, followed by a slew of expletives. After a cursory look in the shed he barked at the Marine interpreter. "Standifer, get him over here!" he said pointing to the man in the doorway.

The interpreter spoke to the homeowner, who waved his hands and shook his head.

Reid had spent most of the last three days listening to guys like this one telling him no. He unholstered his pistol and stormed toward the Iraqi with the gun in his hand and got in the man's face.

"Now!"

The man lowered his head, still waving his hands in protest, and made his way to the shed.

"Ask him what these people are doing in here." Reid ordered his interpreter.

Standifer and the man had a fast conversation that grew more animated as each spoke.

"He says this is where they keep people who don't think right."

"What?" Reid asked.

There was more conversation. Standifer seemed to understand, and got angry. "Nut jobs, sir. They put the mental cases in here. Pretty much just leave them there till they die."

Reid got an inch from the man's face. "Get in there and pull those people out. Now!"

The man fell to his knees and waved his hands.

"Tell him to go in there or I'm gonna arrest him and everyone in this house," Reid said, and pointed to the truck the Marines had brought with them for that very purpose.

A crowd of onlookers was growing on both sides of the street. Reid pointed to two military-aged men leaning on a wall in front of the house next door. "Tell those two to help him."

The Marines barked orders and eventually coaxed the young men at rifle point to join the homeowner in carrying the unfortunate people into the open. Reid turned his attention to Taylor and his dismounted squad. "Search every house on this block."

"On it, sir," Taylor said, as Reid got back into his Humvee to rejoin the other squad.

The Marines entered the house and rounded up the residents for questioning. Taylor surveyed the block and saw angry faces everywhere he looked. Robed women walked toward their destinations faster than normal. The streets had teemed with people when they arrived, now it was as if the population had drained after a tornado warning, creating an ominous stillness. Taylor knew what was about to happen. Dozens of firefights over several years in this trash-covered hell taught the Marines how to predict how this day would end.

Taylor was already surveying the terrain for his next move.

Here comes the suck.

—

"No weapons here, no," the professional-looking Iraqi said in flawless English. Two Marines pushed past him and saw a row of 20mm shells on a kitchen table.

"What do you use these for, then?" one of them asked. They flex-cuffed all three people in the apartment and continued searching, and added five rifles to the cache.

Other Marines found similar ordinance along the block and before long Taylor's squad had nine men in custody, flex-cuffed and waiting in the back of a seven-ton armored truck.

Jackson walked through a house and found a double metal door toward the back of the building with a large lock on it. "Bolt cutters!" he called. One of the Marines moved up and cut off the lock, then backed away while another opened the door.

"Get Taylor," Jackson said. "Go, grab him now."

A runner took off and Jackson crept toward a long metal table in the center of the room. He eyed the body laying on it, wearing an American uniform.

———

Dwura stood at the store counter and sensed the commotion on the street behind her. She hurried to pay and grabbed her daughter's hand, rushed to the exit, and noticed her son staring out the shop's front window.

"Goriel," she snapped in Arabic. "Stop staring. We need to go home, quickly."

Her fifteen-year-old felt the buzz on the other side of the glass generated by people hurrying, some toward, others away from…something. He wondered if his father was near. He knew there were Americans down the street, and his father was always with the Americans, but neither Goriel nor his mother ever knew what he did with them, or where.

Dwura ushered her children out of the small grocery store, her son's arms filled with fruit, milk, and a small bottle of overpriced vitamins. As they stepped across the road, they saw the American vehicles in the distance. Dwura paused, putting a hand on her belly, and wondered if Zayno was with them.

The last time her husband was home, he mentioned fighting in Ramadi and training outside Anbar Province. But he also spent time in Baghdad, or near it. She had no idea where he was, and it was odd but the fact that she hadn't heard news of him lately must mean he was still alive. His last visit was brief, but it brought joy back to a home that lived in fear whenever he was absent.

He spent those few days with his son in sober conversation. Dwura had listened from the other room as her husband went over practical ways to stay out of trouble, like never, ever, picking up a weapon on the street. He told him to pay attention to all the neighborhood talk, to avoid certain areas and people. He passed on to him lessons the SEALs were teaching him about self-defense and situational awareness. But mainly, he charged his son to protect his mother and sister, to the death if necessary. It shocked her, but she knew he never overacted, and the day he left she began making her own preparations, just in case.

"Home, children. We need to get home right away."

She tugged Hazail along and other mothers did likewise. But there was another urgency on display, one that resembled wild animals converging on prey; the faint sound of Arabic battle cries carried across the landscape like a wolf pack's howls, down alleyways and across rooftops, drawing them out of their dens.

A pair of insurgent trucks flew past the store, and she wondered if she could warn the Americans, or if she should. Goriel stared at the vehicles as they turned the corner.

He's thinking the same thing.

"Let's go, son," she said.

He turned to face her, and Dwura saw a mixture of fear and hate in his eyes, the same look she'd seen in the eyes of so many of her friends, and even some of her family members as they turned into…them.

Love, son. That is why your father fights them. He doesn't hate them. He loves us. She wanted to say the words out loud but there was no time. *Later. First get them home, to rest, to eat, to pray. God, protect him. Protect the men with him.*

"Remember what your father told you," she told the boy who was already taller than she was.

A subtle change showed in Goriel's eyes and he immediately scanned the road from right to left, then the rooftops. He nodded to her, took a step in front of his mother and little sister, and led them home.

———

Taylor entered the room, but as he got closer he saw the body was actually an Iraqi, similar in appearance to the destitute souls in the shed. Flies buzzed, and lice crawled over the newly dead body.

"And we've got these." One of the Marines pointed to several opened boxes in the corner, revealing US military uniforms, either stolen, purchased illegally, or given to the insurgents by sympathetic — or coerced — members of the Iraqi Army.

"Bait," Taylor said.

"Exactly," Jackson agreed.

It was an old tactic; the room had all the markings of a kind of laboratory for IED research and development. The poor souls in the shed were simply living bomb casings, supplied to the terrorists by a culture possessing little value for the mentally disabled.

"Gonna need to comb this place. Get the butter bar on the line —" An explosion nearby cut Taylor off. "Move out!"

Outside, the Humvee pounded its .50 cal into a truck across the street while rifle fire rained down from a half-dozen shooters. Across the four-block stretch of the two parallel roads the Marines had been canvassing, the firefight raged in all directions. The Marines, scattered along the roads in groups of twos and fours, returned fire and took any cover available.

Taylor heard an explosion a block away. The cab of the 7-ton was in flames, detainees scrambling for their lives out of the back, some burning, others scarred but alive — all were now his responsibility. The same men would have been shooting at him right now if he hadn't arrested them, but now he was responsible for keeping them safe until they could be removed from the battlefield.

I wish I could just shoot them and be done with it.

"Pile them in the Hummer," Taylor ordered. The Marines grabbed the cuffed men by the arms and threw them into the back of the nearest Humvee.

We need to move, get out of here now. Mobility saves lives. Keep moving.

Through the smoke he saw the setting sun behind a building. They would soon be fighting in the dark.

Taylor fired his weapon and through his scope saw a flaming object roll down the street. *A burning tire.* Then he saw other tires rolling in from multiple directions, and the stench of the smoke joined the eerie fog of battle as pitched battles continued all around them.

"All loaded, Sarge," a Marine said, referring to the detainees.

The Marines pulled the body of the 7-ton driver free and moved him to the side of the road. A corpsman pulled out a body bag and loaded it into a second Humvee, amid the frantic cries of the detainees.

Taylor got on his radio. "This is Rover Zero Niner, we've got one KIA and nine detainees, moving out."

"Negative," Reid responded. "QRF in route. I'll move to you to link squads and move together."

"Copy that, Rover Five." *But we need to move.*

The first Humvee started driving slowly and the second followed as most of the Marines jogged behind them, pissed off beyond the boiling point at the loss of their driver and itchy for revenge.

"Move to that intersection and set up a fire position to wait for Reid's squad," Taylor said on the radio.

"Copy that, Sarge. Let's go. Stop before the intersection," Jackson said to the lead Hummer's driver.

In their wake, the Marines detonated an explosion, making the 7-ton just another piece of flaming garbage on the dank street.

———

A block away, Reid's Humvees fought their way down the street to attempt connecting with Taylor's squad. Massive rounds impacted one of the Humvees, tearing through the armor and shattering the glass. The Marine on the .50 swung around to meet whatever was shooting at them. The barrage of large rounds from the Soviet DShK immobilized the Hummer's engine and flew through the flesh of several Marines.

Reid scrambled out and returned fire with his men.

"Rover Zero Niner, we're disabled. What is your location? We've got wounded men and a busted Hummer."

"Copy that, Five. We're on the corner to the East of you. We'll come to you."

———

Taylor got out of his Hummer, ran out and pounded on the hood of Jackson's vehicle.

"Need to link up with Reid. Turn down there," he said, pointing to the cross street that connected the two roads the squads had patrolled.

The driver took a hard right-hand turn and immediately saw Reid's squad down the street engaging the enemy. Taylor held the corner, ensuring that his men were all accounted for as they made the turn and joined the others, some of whom were tending to the wounded in the chaos of flames, muzzle flashes, and smoke.

"I'm all turned around," Taylor said, trying to regain his bearings. "Which way is out?"

"That street's blocked." Reid pointed in the direction he'd just left. "What's that one look like?"

"Same. Maybe we can barrel through, though." Taylor saw a pile of burning debris at the end of the road. "QRF?"

Reid shrugged. Both men knew what the other was thinking.

We need to move.

"Sir." Reid's radio operator handed him the receiver.

Jason Carpenter increased the throttle and the city came into view in his heads up display. The highway and surrounding desert were dark, but the city was illuminated with several bright spotlights that played havoc with his infrared.

"Rover Five, this is Falcon Two Seven, I am an F-16. Can I have the ten-digit grid of your locations?"

He knew there was little he could do to help the Marines surrounded by buildings filled with civilians. He had plenty of bombs and missiles, and 500 rounds in his cannon, but the reality was he couldn't shoot without causing mass casualties. What he could do, however, was watch enemy movements, and direct others, and warn the men on the ground.

"Copy, Falcon Two Seven," Reid said, and let his radio operator give their location.

"Rover Five, I see you. Be advised you've got multiple vehicles converging on your position from all four directions. They appear hostile."

———

Taylor and Reid shared a look. "Copy that, Falcon." *What the hell am I gonna do with an F-16 here? Where's the Cobra?*

They were being boxed in, their reinforcements were boxed out, no doubt engaged as well. Reid had detainees, his own casualties banged up and bleeding, and only two options. Either he continued moving against enemy positions that were growing stronger by the minute, and hope he could keep the remaining Hummer from getting taken out, or he could get his men into a strong defensive position and give the enemy hell from there.

Reid scanned the buildings and saw a two-story across the street that would probably give the best fields of fire he could hope for.

"Strong point that building. Let's move," he said, then turned to his radio operator. "Call it in."

The sergeants and several other Marines ran to the building, fired at the courtyard gate, and kicked it in the rest of the way. At the main door they paused to throw two flashbangs into the opening and waited for the percussion to abate as the three intact Humvees set up near the courtyard entrance. A Marine set a demolition charge on the courtyard wall, blowing a hole large enough for the Hummer with the detainees to drive through.

Reid's men entered the home, cleared the first floor, and moved upstairs where they found four civilians.

"Tell them to get out," Reid ordered Standifer. The interpreter spoke quickly, and the man grabbed his smallest child and ran down the stairs with the rest of his family. Taylor followed to ensure they left the building, and returned to his men on the ground floor.

"Get the detainees into that bedroom," Taylor ordered two of his men. "Haskins, Thrombull, babysit 'em. Jackson, Smith, Esposito, come with me." Taylor led the three

Marines around the eerily quiet courtyard; the only sound was of their heavy breathing.

"Set up here," he said to the young man carrying the SAW machine gun. "You and Esposito own this corner. Keep the fire hot, call if you get low on ammo." He turned to Jackson. "Let's go."

Taylor and Jackson had just turned to assess the other corner when they heard Smith open up with the SAW.

The house was now a fort, and they intended to keep it that way.

———

The detainees huddled together in the corner of the ground floor bedroom. Standifer instructed them to stay put to avoid getting shot.

Reid entered. "They injured?"

"Some more than others. Looks worse than I think it is," Standifer said.

Reid looked over the detainees, some of whom had burn marks on their clothing, others had blood from various wounds, but none seemed too serious.

"I'll have a corpsman check 'em out when he gets a chance."

Reid walked to another room where their corpsmen were patching up the wounded Marines, most of whom were antsy to get back into the fight as soon as they were no longer bleeding out. The only critically wounded man had blood-soaked bandages on his left forearm below the elbow. Reid looked at him.

"Langford, did I say you get to die today?"

"No sir, Sarge," Langford said with weak confidence.

"Let him patch you up. You've still got one good arm and we may need it later. Oorah?"

"Kill, sir," Langford said.

Reid rubbed Langford's sweaty head and went back upstairs.

"Rover Five, I'll be your relay for now," Reid heard the pilot say to his radioman.

He was relieved to have eyes overhead, some air that wasn't entirely useless, but the radio network was going to cause a major delay. Reid and Taylor had two long range radios between their squads that could communicate with their lieutenant on the outskirts of the city, but the open radio channel was alive with activity as the QRF was fighting its way in against heavy opposition.

"Rover Five, you've got two Apaches approaching from the west. Let me know how they can assist you and I'll relay it to them for as long as I can."

"That's more like it," Reid said.

———

Carpenter circled the Marine position and saw steady shooting, but it was hard to tell exactly which building was theirs. Additional units were moving toward them from Qaryat al Ashiq, and by morning the entire neighborhood would be owned by the Army and Marines, he hoped. But until then, anything could happen.

"Falcon Two Seven, this is Pegasus Eight," he heard on the radio.

"Copy, Pegasus," he said as the Apaches came into view. "I see you. I've got plenty of fuel to keep eyes on Rover. Multiple targets converging on their position. They're all yours."

"Copy that," Ginger said. "We've got forty minutes on station. There's a ton of smoke down there and I can't see their strobe. Can you get Rover to sparkle their building for me?"

"Copy that, Pegasus. Stand by."

"I'm pretty sure it's that one," Craig said as he watched one building shooting in all four directions.

Ginger watched the chaos below. People and vehicles were moving everywhere; the fight had been raging for over an hour and all of the civilians would have holed up long ago, so everyone on the street was probably a target. But that fact was only somewhat useful. Since her return to Iraq a month ago she and Craig had been in non-stop action, and it all looked the same.

They were high enough to see another battle underway on the outskirts of the city, several miles away to the east, where a Marine Cobra helicopter was circling.

"What's going on over there?" she asked Donovan.

"Probably Rover's QRF. Gonna take them a while. Army'll probably get there first," Donovan said.

"I'll take that bet," Craig said.

"Me too," Rico chimed in.

"How we doing, Falcon?" Ginger asked. "Oh wait, I see it." The infrared laser beam on her screen was fixed at a 45-degree angle into the sky. "Falcon, have them snake it."

"Copy that, Pegasus. Standby."

The beam began to oscillate like a searchlight on the roof of the Marine's building, and Craig locked it into his computer while Rico did the same. Now they had a good half-hour with which to rattle the cages of the city and convince the local population to back off.

"Falcon, I've got 'em." Then she said to Craig, "Let's dance."

"I've got at least twenty military-aged men on foot and four vehicles converging on Rover from every direction."

"Copy that, Pegasus," Falcon said. "Was that an RPG?"

Rico saw it fly from the balcony of a nearby mosque into the Humvee outside the building. The explosion destroyed the vehicle, and the Apaches watched, helpless, as injured Marines fell out and retreated toward the building.

Donovan took a chance on his radio. "This is Pegasus One Three, I've got Marines taking rockets from the mosque. Request permission to fire." He knew what the answer would be.

"Pegasus One Three. Negative, do what you can within the rules of engagement."

Donovan swore, but only Rico heard him.

———

Several miles to the west, six additional Rover Humvees and two Bradley fighting vehicles slugged it out block by block, until one of the Hummers ran over a package in the center of the road, igniting an explosion that halted the already tender advance. Marines poured out of the Bradley behind it to collect the men from the disabled vehicle.

"Get 'em in there fast," a Marine shouted to the corpsman.

Three Marines lifted the wounded into a good Humvee as the others returned fire within the shadows. Above them they could see occasional bursts from the Cobra's guns and the impact its projectiles made into the ground around them.

"Let's roll. Eyes sharp," the lieutenant said, getting back into the Hummer and wondering how many more IEDs had been tossed into the road since sundown.

A truck rolled into view and shot its recoilless rifle at the Hummers, catching the back of the trail vehicle, disabling its forward movement as the Hummer limped and lost speed, gears grinding underneath it.

"Transfer any wounded to one of the Bradleys," the lieutenant said. "We need to keep moving."

The other vehicles continued as the Marines again moved weapons and ammunition from the damaged vehicle into a Bradley.

"Blow 'em," the lieutenant said. A hummer fired its grenade launcher at each of the disabled vehicles and they were on the move again, losing two vehicles in five minutes.

"Rover Five, this is Rover Two Two, taking heavy fire but moving."

He listened to static.

"Rover Five, do you read me?"

"Copy…taking accurate rocket fire," Reid answered. They heard explosions in the background.

———

Another blast hit the ground floor, shaking the building. Taylor saw his men shooting at the street, heard an almost constant drum of machine gun fire below him.

"Sateurn, go below and see if Jackson and Cordero need more ammo."

The corporal disappeared down the stairs.

Taylor climbed the staircase to the roof and found Reid kneeling next to the radio operator and scanning with his NVG's. He crouched next to them.

"Where's the RPG?" Taylor asked.

"There. Balcony of that mosque," Reid said, pointing.

A crowd of armed military-aged men ran down the street but disappeared in a cloud of dust as the unmistakable sound of a 30mm gun fire passed above them. An inky black hulk passed overhead, followed by its engine noise.

"'Bout time they shot at something," Reid said.

"Sir, Falcon says they can't fire at the mosque per the rules of engagement."

"He's right there," Reid said pointing. "If I had an M40, I could take him out myself."

"It'd be a hell of a shot," Taylor said.

"Where's the armor?" Reid asked the radio operator.

"Army says acknowledged. That's it."

"I only need one tank. One." A bulldozer, or even a big truck could break through the roadblocks and allow them exit.

"Find a truck in the neighborhood, maybe?" Taylor asked.

"Tried. I don't see anything nearby."

Reid and Taylor watched another Apache rocket shoot toward the street.

———

Ginger and Donovan took turns circling the city, taking pot shots at targets in the open. Trucks were moving around the main intersection toward the mosque on the corner.

"Military aged men, all armed," Craig said. "Hellfire away." He fired at the first truck. The explosion lifted it airborne and also took out the two behind it.

"Three for one," Ginger said.

She hovered at 3000 feet, watching rockets continue to fly toward Rover's position from one of the mosques down the street.

"Pegasus One Three, we've got a surge of people on foot heading toward Rover."

"Copy that, I see 'em."

"Falcon, let Rover know they've got shooters heading from the east," Donovan said.

"I can't get a clean shot, Eight. They're using the building for concealment."

"Same here, One Three," Ginger said frustrated.

"Draw 'em out into the open somehow?" Craig asked.

"How exactly do you propose that?"

The road was deserted but for the broken Humvees and the fires blocking traffic. Crowds of fighters were streaming toward Rover's position through alleys, darting across the roads and back to the shadows, running from one building to another.

Craig loosed a hellfire, timing the impact of the rocket to perfectly intersect a truck speeding around the corner toward the Marines.

"Nice shot, Craiger."

"Yeah, I played a little quarterback in high school. I threw a sexy deep ball."

"Craig," Ginger said in a tone intended to get him to focus.

"Here's another one," Craig said, firing into a courtyard of shooters trying to scale a wall.

"Don't get cocky," she said.

"Look who's talking."

Ginger felt pinging on the bottom of the aircraft. "Taking fire," she said, pulling hard to the right.

"Copy, same here, Eight," Donovan said.

Ginger leveled out and turned back to re-center Rover's position. There was so little they could legally shoot at, and they were running out of time.

"One Three, we're out of fuel in five."

"Copy Eight, better give them the bad news," he said.

"Falcon, this is Pegasus Eight. We're at five minutes remaining on station."

"Copy, Pegasus, I'll pass it along," Jason answered.

Ginger looked at the buildings around Rover. People were all over the place, hiding in the shadows, running through yards and on the rooftops. She magnified into one of the rooftops, trying to figure out what she was seeing.

"Craig, do you see that?"

"Yeah, not sure…"

"That's not a weapon? Is it?"

"I don't see any," he said confused.

"One Three, you see this on the rooftops?"

"Copy that, Eight."

Ginger looked harder. Suddenly the image registered in her mind. She realized what it was at the exact same time Craig spoke.

"Searchlights."

13

In The Light Of Night

It was as if someone flipped a light switch. Searchlights on several rooftops clicked on and poured their high luminosity beams at the Marines. Others shone down at the street and still more aimed skyward, toward the helicopters. Taylor and Reid pulled up their NVG's, rendered useless in the bright lights, rubbed their eyes to shake out the disorientation. From multiple angles the Marine sergeants saw tracer rounds heading skyward, followed by the unmistakable sound of their source.

"Dushkas," Taylor said.

———

The spotlight caught the glass Ginger was looking through and she swore, wincing at the bright burst in the night vision. The alarms sounded, followed by large impacts as rounds hit her aircraft from two sources she couldn't see. Instinctively she pulled the stick to the right and began evasive maneuvers.

———

As soon as the insurgent operator saw the Apache he unloaded, screaming a war cry. Pegasus Eight was peppered by several 12.7mm rounds from a Soviet DShK that had been waiting, concealed, opening up with everything it had into the sky at the lights' signal. The Dushka could deliver a lethal blow to a helicopter up to 4000 feet away, and the

Apache was well below that. But worse than that, a twin-barreled 14.5mm ZPU mounted on a large pickup pulled out of a garage five seconds before the sky lit up.

The guns walked their rounds via tracer into the helicopter, hitting its engines and tail from two directions, effectively killing it in midair. All that was left was for it to crash.

———

Taylor watched in horror as the Apache flamed and tipped on its side in the direction of the mosque. The Marines fended off what was clearly a coordinated attack, just when he'd felt like they were gaining control of their real estate.

"Sir, we've got some reinforcements," the radio operator called out. "QRF almost here. Having a hard time finding us."

"We're the one in center of the lights," he roared.

Reid's first instinct was to organize a squad to move on the crash site, but he had no such luxury. He had injured men, prisoners to secure, and an attack of his own to deal with. *Maybe when the QRF gets here, if it ever gets here,* he thought.

The realities of war came slamming home. He couldn't help them even if they survived the crash, which was doubtful. Maybe the Army could get there. He knew this would get their alarms blazing and all sorts of things were going to happen much faster than they had earlier. *Get your men out alive.* As much as they hated it, Taylor and Reid knew that the second the dust cleared on the crash site, the savages would swarm it, and there was nothing they could do about it.

———

"I'm hit. Mayday. Mayday. Mayday," Ginger said, and swore again.

She worked her controls and tried everything she could think of in the span of seven seconds that somehow felt like an eternity. Everything was in slow motion and nothing worked. For years, this machine had been an extension of her body, she could make it do anything she wanted. But now it was dead. She'd trained for this, she knew all the lessons about surviving a crash, but all of the protocols assumed some measure of control. She had none.

The Apache was simply falling sideways, hurtling. The rotors continued to spin as it decreased altitude, and she and Craig could only hold on.

"Craig." She saw her canopy fill with the sight of concrete structures in dark green night vision. "Craiger, hold on."

But Craig said nothing, and Pegasus Eight's voice was replaced by static across the radio net of northern Iraq.

———

The F-16 saw the helicopter tip over and fall toward the city. It caught the edge of a one-story structure and tore a portion of the roof off as it fell between it and the next building. Through the dust cloud, Carpenter saw pieces of the main rotor chew the ground and spin the aircraft in a violent thirty degrees, causing its tail to break off completely into yet another house, which collapsed onto the skids and buried much of the helicopter from view.

"Pegasus Eight, do you read me?"

He keyed the emergency open channel that would let everyone know. "This is Falcon Two Seven, I've got a helo down. Pegasus Eight is crashed. Repeat, Pegasus Eight is down."

He watched as the dust settled, hoping to hear something or see any kind of movement.

"This is Falcon Two Seven, I've got multiple individuals running toward the crash site."

"Acknowledged, Falcon Two Seven. Pegasus Eight down," a sober voice replied. There was silence, then, "Any sign of survivors?"

Jason Carpenter gave the hard response. "Negative," then he added, "except for civilians. They're about to swarm it."

Donovan didn't see the crash; he was making his own evasive maneuvers. He heard Ginger's mayday as he was repositioning, and by the time he could react she was already on the ground.

"Pegasus Eight, do you read me?…Pegasus Eight, do you read me?"

Static was the only response.

"This is Pegasus One Three, I have visual on the crash site. No movement," Donovan said.

"See anything?" he asked Rico.

Rico ignored him, concentrating on every little speck of white on his screen. There was so much debris, so much smoke, and so many individuals in the surrounding buildings, some of whom were laying down, probably injured or killed, and Rico couldn't tell who was who.

"Beacon?" Donovan said.

Rico zoomed out from the crash site to take in a larger picture and his heartbeat quickened. "Donny, contact!"

Donovan saw it too. Ginger's helicopter was crashed on a block between two mosques that were a little more than a block away on either side. On the other sides of the crash were two major roads that bisected the city, essentially boxing the helicopter in, and the locals knew they had a prize delivered straight to their doorstep.

An additional roadblock went up on the street to the south of the crash, and figures poured out of both mosques.

Trucks and vehicles came from other directions contributing to the roadblocks.

"Take those out!" Donovan said. "We've got to keep a lane open to them."

Rico fired and a truck exploded, which only contributed to blocking the intersection. Rico fired his cannon and cut down advancing fighters but there were too many to target so he ran strafes into the road, then Rico noticed something even worse.

"Donny, fuel."

Donovan looked at his status; they'd just passed their maximum time over target and had to break off. What remained in the tank was only enough to get them to the next refueling point. He didn't know what to do.

"Rico, they're gonna kill them."

"I know, Donny…let's land."

Donovan blinked at the response. He was an officer, and his duty was to break contact, refuel as soon as possible, and get back here to search for what might remain. But these were his friends. Rico's option — ignore protocol, risk court-martial and their own lives, maybe stay till their fuel tank was dry, protect Ginger and Craig as best they could, then land nearby and pray they could protect their own Apache from another swarm of bad guys till the Army could save them — no, it wasn't an option after all. It was a fantasy, the likelihood of either of them surviving the crash was remote.

"Screw it," Rico finally said. "Let's land. Or just let me out. I'll get to them myself and you take her back."

Donny wanted to do the same thing himself but knew it would never happen.

"Donny, I'm serious. Please," Rico said, his voice cracking.

Donovan made the only call he could make, and ended the conversation. "Negative." He was sick to his stomach. "Falcon Two Seven, Pegasus One Three, breaking off to refuel. Do what you can."

"Copy that, Pegasus."

Rico wanted to say something as they pulled away but the words wouldn't come out. They flew in silence until a text message came in on the display.

ON OUR WAY. HOW BAD? -TM

Donovan read the message from Tim Miller and his eyes watered as he typed a response:

BAD. OVERRUN. FIND THEM FOR US.

He waited impatiently for a response from Tim.

I WILL.

14

Pegasus Eight

Ginger heard faint yelling, like in a dream. She tried to open her eyes and her right eye throbbed with muscle spasms. She reached for her head but pain seared through her right arm. Her head hung to the side and her helmet was cracked. She pulled it off with her left arm and the jagged, broken monocle fell apart from her blood-caked eye. Everything was dark.

As her other eye adjusted, she tried to comprehend where she was. She realized she was partially upside down, and the blood rush was making her head throb. The latch of her seatbelt harness would not open, and she felt for her Asek Egress knife. She grit her teeth from the pain as she slid the hook-shaped razor blade around the straps and pulled with what little leverage she could muster. As it sliced the harness, her body contorted to the new tension points.

She started to panic, cut another strap in haste, then a third, desperate to get free of the inverted trap as her head swelled and the pain intensified. She began to see stars as she cut the last strap and her weight succumbed to gravity. Like water, her body slithered in the direction of least resistance, through the broken glass and twisted metal of the partially-sheared canopy, cutting the length of one side of her body until she came to a sickening thump on dark concrete.

She lay shuddering in bristling pain from head to toe. Several things were broken. After the initial wave rushed over her, she managed to take a deep breath, followed by violent coughing and another wave of pain. She tried to lift herself up, managed to get to a half-sitting position but shock made her queasy and again she saw stars as she fell onto her back.

She was still in darkness but could feel the clouds of dust she was breathing in as her eye continued to adjust.

I'm alive. I think. Yes, I must be alive because there's pain. I crashed.

Ginger remembered the flashlight in one of the front pockets of her survival jacket. She opened the pocket, twisted the head of the flashlight and shone the beam around. Directly above her she saw Craig.

Craig!

She couldn't believe she'd forgotten about him. She excoriated herself for being consumed with her own survival and the anger gave her strength. She tried to call his name, but the lack of air in her lungs rendered it little more than a whisper.

Is he alive? Is he breathing?

She rolled over, adrenaline fueling her determination to aid him. She pulled herself to a knee and put all of her strength into her left leg, managing to get close enough to shine the light at his helmet.

"Craig, can you hear me?"

He didn't respond.

I have to cut him loose. Should I? Will I injure him more? Should I leave him until help arrives? No, he's upside down. The bad guys will be here any minute.

She reached into her jacket and unholstered her pistol with her left hand.

Good luck shooting straight with your left. Ginger, you moron.

She swore, realizing she still hadn't done the first and most important act. She fell into a sitting position, set down the gun, and reached deep into her front left pocket. She pulled out the ground-to-air radio and activated the beacon. It immediately fixed her position on the Army's GPS, letting them know she was alive, and allowed her to securely communicate in burst transmissions to anyone listening.

"Pegasus Eight," she whispered, coughing.

A voice in the other end of the radio blared out so loudly it rang in her ears and filled the darkness around her.

"Pegasus Eight, we copy, over."

She tried to reply but her throat swelled. She clicked the transmit button but let go without saying anything and tried to catch her breath.

Get it together. You need to get him free. They're coming. They're going to be here any minute. You need to get away from the aircraft.

She looked again at Craig, then heard voices, many voices, yelling in Arabic.

Run. Run, or crawl away. Get into the shadows. Leave him. Is he even alive?

Ginger looked at the back of Craig's helmet, so familiar for so many years. In a way he was the best friend she'd ever had, a comfort to her, comic relief in a life postulated by focused intensity. She felt Mrs. Allen's letter in her breast pocket.

No. I won't leave him for them to butcher.

Ginger remembered all of the times she had made fun of him. All of the times he made her laugh, even when he was trying to be sincere. She teased him mercilessly, like an older sister should, or so she thought. Ginger thought about Cecilia Allen, the closest thing she'd ever had to a mother.

They won't touch him.

Ginger remembered laying in the desert, feeling like a murderer as shame and regret had washed away all sense of purpose and identity. What was she? What did she have left to give to the people she cared about?

Those Marines are probably getting overrun too, or maybe they're on their way here now. It's my fault. I've failed them all. But Craig might still be alive, or at least, if he's dead, I can still protect his body, give his family something to bury. They won't get him. I'll die first, but they will, too.

Genevieve Cooper picked up the gun and stood, screaming from the sudden pain. She put weight on her right leg, realized it was broken. The pain was more formidable than any she'd ever encountered but she didn't fall; she dropped the gun on instinct and grabbed a piece of the canopy to steady herself, propping herself against what was left of the airframe. The flashlight lay in the dust and its illumination allowed her to catch sight of the Apache's submachine gun hanging in the cockpit by a harness. She tried to reach for it, but her dominant arm was broken. She shifted to lean against her right shoulder and used the other hand to try and release the harness latch but had no grip. She lost her balance and fell again.

Get up. Man up. Do it. Now!

She heard voices, clear voices nearby.

There's no time left. The pistol.

She searched the ground for her pistol but couldn't feel it in the dark.

The knife.

Ginger pulled the knife from its sheath, and as the first voice came within striking distance she spun around on her knees, wielding wide, sweeping slashes at the air. A cornered animal will fight with a vehemence unparalleled in other arenas of nature, and so it was with the last desperate strikes of Marcus Cooper's daughter. She spun, and struck, and screamed in a manner worthy of any soldier current or past but for five rotations only, and with little effect on the hordes of predators who swarmed her. Her wounds were too great, and she fell as her vision blurred again as the sounds of angry voices approached in the dark.

15

High Resolution

Contingency Operating Base: Foxtrot

Mitch Robinson paced behind the radio operators who could only direct traffic and listen in. He heard Tim Miller communicating with three of his other pilots, leading the flight of four Apaches, his trademark coldness filling the airwaves. But Mitch knew Tim well enough to listen past the professionalism and he could feel the seething in Tim's voice, short and in no mood to answer questions.

The radios were alive with other transmissions from the ground and the air. Mitch monitored them all — the F-16 as it gave monotone play-by-play, watching throngs of locals swarm the crash site; the Army commanders whose tanks pulled top speed as they crashed over concrete barriers and through the multiple fires that barricaded the crash site; all of them agitated with a sense of universal helplessness.

By the time Mitch's four Apaches were over the site, he could do little more than hope Tim and the others could identify Cooper's and Allen's bodies from the air. Maybe they could direct the Army units on the ground to them. Ginger's radio had been silent for ten minutes, the beacon still at the crash site. It became clear to almost everyone, from the general in command of Northern Iraq on down to Mitch Robinson, that this had transitioned from a mission of rescue to one of recovery.

Tal Afar, Iraq

Tim Miller was completely focused on the crash site. The DShK was dead, so was the ZPU and all of the other trucks that the Apaches discovered around Pegasus Eight's carcass. Tim and his wingman circled the neighborhood at 4000 feet, first taking out the spotlights the Marine snipers couldn't get at, then the trucks, and then anything else that moved out in the open.

The enemy had partially retreated. They had their prize and were smart enough to know when to fight and when to disappear. For ten long minutes before the Apaches arrived the crash site was overrun with bodies. The enemy quickly secured a perimeter around it, but just as soon as it was erected an onslaught of Army units eliminated the uncoordinated resistance and hastened to establish dominance as soldiers geared up to go house to house in search of the aircrew. But they still hadn't reached the crash site.

Miller hovered and watched, his front seater targeted the mosque's upper deck with his finger on the trigger, the chain gun selected. The helo was out of small arms range; both he and the jihadists knew it. Miller and his gunner were unified in their willingness to fire at the mosque if necessary, almost savored the notoriety that might come from an international incident given the circumstance, and could care less about a potential court-martial that might follow. The Rules of Engagement meant nothing to them at this point, ROE's that were responsible for hundreds of American deaths or worse, including whatever was currently happening to the bodies of Ginger and Craig, be they alive or dead. Miller was more than ready to tell everyone what he thought about it, prison or no prison.

Miller searched with the TADS and hovered it over every figure he could see. Iraqi men stood next to the Apache, others searched Ginger's cockpit or rifled through the various compartments in the rear of the aircraft. Tim saw a few dead bodies as well in the surrounding rubble and people hovering around them. Tim flicked a switch with his thumb and activated the Field of View option, magnifying the images by a factor of five but he still couldn't tell from this range.

"What do you think?" Miller asked his front seater.

"Not enough detail."

"Taking us to 1500, be ready."

"Go ahead," he said.

Miller dropped elevation to within RPG range, allowing the image of the bodies to fill two-thirds of his screen. He examined every detail: their clothing, their hair, what the people around them were doing with the bodies. He flicked on the FLIR to check for heat sources. Three bodies on the ground were cold and lifeless. It was morbidly comforting.

It's not her, not him. None of them are. Where did they take you?

"Alright, that's it," Miller said and elevated to 4000 ft again. He contacted the Army unit that approached less than a block away. "This is Pegasus Six, they're not there. No sign of Pegasus Eight's crew. Request you search the surrounding structures in force."

"Copy, Pegasus Six," was the only response.

Tim knew most of those people on his screen knew something, may have contributed to whatever fate his friends were suffering. They were scavengers picking at the carcass of the Apache; the true predators were savoring their feast, somewhere. Now, Tim prayed the boots on the ground could locate what he and all of his worthless technology could not. He wondered if they might unleash some revenge of their own, if they could find them.

Do the job.

Tim and his gunner searched the surrounding buildings with the TADS, zooming in on anything that resembled a body or a weapon. Soon the only elements of war he saw were two tanks and four Bradleys coming across the main intersection and spreading out along parallel roads. He got on the intra-squadron frequency to speak to the other Apaches.

"If they're still on the site, our boys will find 'em. But if they're being moved, this is our only chance to head 'em off. We stay till the last drop is in the tank. Hooah?"

"Hooah," they agreed.

By the time the Army reached the crash site, all of the civilians had retreated and tried to disappear. Tim Miller knew the guys on the ground would be thorough in the extreme, tearing apart the neighborhood house by house. That was their job, and for the first time in his life since climbing into a cockpit, Tim Miller wished he could be on the ground kicking in doors with them.

Taylor pounded the side of the replacement 7-ton and the truck pulled away, followed by an escort of two Humvees. He was finally free of the detainees, and for a moment he thought he might get a chance to stop and collect his men. He took a drink of water from his bottle and then let several ounces shower his face. The sun was barely up but already the heat was a nuisance.

An Army tank turned the corner, and soldiers following it on foot ran into the first building as it stopped. He saw Reid speak with the lieutenant, then break off and walk in his direction.

"Army's got this block, he says. They want us to fall back and set up a perimeter two clicks to the east. Semper Gumby," he scoffed.

Taylor surveyed the destruction the two squads had created over the last several hours, knowing soon he'd be right back here or somewhere just like it, doing the same thing. He'd be back at it, knocking on doors, hoping to get some assistance from people who, for the most part, resented him. Some might have been willing to sit down and talk yesterday, before he'd destroyed their neighborhood. The fact that the insurgents had initiated the carnage wouldn't matter.

Taylor shook his head. "Wilco."

He climbed back into the passenger seat of a Humvee, blinking the dirt out of his eyes, ready to start another hot day on zero sleep in a desert town that reeked of garbage and dead bodies, a smell that somehow didn't squelch his appetite because it was simply a part of the landscape. It would stay with him for a week even after he got home, whenever that would be. There was no escaping the smell or the heat, or, at least for the next several hours, the hunger.

He remembered a bag of Skittles in his pocket. He poured a few into his dirt-smeared hand and gobbled them up, then put his head back and emptied the rest of the contents into his mouth. Proper chow would have to wait.

16

The Hole

The White House, Washington D.C.
00:23:00

The president stared at the secretary of defense as he finished the emergency briefing, and didn't hesitate with the first question.

"Media know?"

"They know there was a helo crash, but not exactly where or what kind," CIA Director Green answered.

"Family?" the president asked.

"Too soon," the chief of staff said. "We've got nothing to offer them other than that the helicopter crashed. No bodies have been recovered. We haven't contacted them yet."

The president looked at him without speaking.

"Both pilots have living parents, but are unmarried, no kids. We —"

"Tell them." The president cut him off. "Tonight. Immediately." He looked away. "Give them a chance to start praying we find 'em, alive." *Or at least in one piece.*

Several sober faces looked at the president and nodded.

"Tell 'em we're doing everything in our power to find their loved ones and bring them home." He locked eyes with Green. "Right?" The decades-old political allies shared a look that communicated their mutual disdain for sugar coating anything.

"Mr. President, yes sir. We are."

The president shifted his gaze to General Shields, the new head of Joint Special Operations Command. "It's been how many hours?"

"Ten, Mr. President."

The president thought for a moment. "No bodies," he said. "They've moved them somewhere, got something planned for them." He took a deep breath and addressed Green and Shields. "It's your rodeo now. Find 'em."

"We will, Mr. President," Shields said with confidence. Green only nodded.

———

Contingency Operating Base Foxtrot
Tikrit, Iraq

Tim Miller climbed from the aircraft. As his feet touched the tarmac he stretched his back. None of his arming crew talked to him; none dared. He walked to the hangar and took a warm water bottle out of an opened case, downed it, then went to find a bathroom. Before retiring to his bed for the mandatory rest period, he entered the Tactical Operations Center. He locked eyes with Robinson. They stared at each other for a brief moment; there was nothing to say and so they soon looked away, Robinson back to the monitors and radios, Miller toward the hallway and a shower.

As he was leaving, Eddie caught a glimpse of Tim and ran him down.

"Miller," he said.

Tim paused to face him but didn't speak.

"So?" Eddie asked.

"Nothing," he said shaking his head and looking down.

"Whatcha mean, nothing!?" he said and took a step closer. Tim tried to walk past, but Eddie grabbed his arm and got in front of him. "Dammit, don't tell me 'Nothing.' Not me! What'd they do to them?"

Eddie got in close enough that Tim could smell his breath.

"You need to *tell* me," he seethed. "What did you see?"

The elder veteran of three wars had spent the last several hours bottling his own violence. Tim Miller was a pressure cooker of rage and Eddie had just broken the seal. He shoved Eddie backward and shouted loud enough to turn every head in the TOC.

"I mean, nothing! Nothing! No Allen no Cooper It's like a damn hole just opened and swallowed them up! We looked at everything, looked till our tanks were dry, then went back and looked some more. We watched guys on the ground kick in every door around. Nothing! You follow? Hell, I'd still be looking if I hadn't been ordered to break it off. I don't know where they are! I never saw them, just their broken ass helicopter!"

Eddie put his hands on his hips, fuming.

"See for yourself," Tim continued, motioning to the tarmac. "Go watch the gun camera tape with Atwood if you want. I'm gonna go take a shower and sleep my mandatory minimum so I can get back up there and look some more. Alright with you?"

Eddie looked at the ground, shaking his head, and Tim walked past him to the showers. Eddie stormed over to Robinson in the TOC.

"What they doing about it?" he roared, pointing at the screens.

"Everything they can. Trust me," Mitch said.

"Oh, I'm supposed to trust all that?" Eddie said mocking. "I want to go. Send me and J.T. and Tony and the boys up there to look for 'em," Eddie said, waving his arm in a circle. "Let us rattle a few cages and I'll find out something, I guarantee you!"

"Eddie, believe me, they know what they're doing. You have to trust they're doing their job just like I need you to do yours."

"They *are* my job, Mitch," he said in a voice that filled the room, and his eyes welled with tears as he regained his composure. "Sir."

Robinson went to him, standing with his head high, motionless, tears streaming down his cheeks. Robinson felt every bit of his pain and anguish. Individuals they both loved were missing, maybe dead, and neither had any ability to help them. Robinson meant to speak, but instead he pulled Eddie's hulk forward and let him cry on his shoulder as the rest of the squadron's intelligence officers turned their attention back to their monitors, looking absently at familiar screens, listening in on radio chatter that merely reinforced what Tim had already said. There was simply nothing.

Muhallabiyah, Northern Iraq

The door exploded into the room, taking out the insurgent behind it. In a heartbeat, six figures rushed inside, and in another heartbeat, ten insurgents lay dead. The American special operators moved over the bodies with careful but hasty steps, and spread out to search their segment of the compound. In less than a minute they linked up two additional assault teams that had breached from different entry points, one a British SAS unit.

"Bravo lead clear," the Ranger captain heard in his ear.

"Charlie lead, clear," a British voice said.

"Razor One, Alpha clear," Captain Lanier answered. It was all over.

Lanier looked around the room, lowered his rifle and surveyed piles of IED making materials. Explosives, miscellaneous jugs of liquid, M-16's, rockets, uniforms, mortar tubes and shells, and rows of artillery shells were in abundance. The Ranger couldn't care less; it wasn't what they were looking for.

"Spread out, watch for booby traps," he instructed the eighteen men of the task force.

Across the long compound men got to work, and after several minutes one of them called from an open doorway to his right.

"Captain?"

Lanier walked over and followed his man through a maze of ordinance, equipment, and dead jihadists. On any other day this would have been cause to celebrate. It was the largest cache the task force had ever discovered, but it was a hollow victory.

The captain walked into a room and saw several men under guard wearing orange jump suits, flex-cuffed, and kneeling along the wall. A video camera stood in the center of the room on a tripod, behind it the Ranger saw television equipment and rows of VHS video tapes, as well as a computer and a stool. It was the most basic of makeshift television studios, and Lanier had seen them before.

"Sir," the operator motioned him toward a side room.

The captain entered and saw two operators kneeling next to a Caucasian body. The man was stripped down to his boxers and shirtless.

"Lyons," Lanier snapped.

As Jake Lyons approached, the other operators backed off to give the pararescueman space. The PJ knelt over Craig Allen's lifeless body and felt for a pulse even though he knew the man was long dead. He checked for any sign of life but instead felt the firm, cold flesh left behind by a soul departed.

"How long?" Lanier asked, knowing as well.

"Day or two," Jake said. "He may have even died in the crash," Jake said, examining the numerous indications of trauma along the length of Craig's body.

Captain Lanier pulled out a picture of Craig Allen to compare with the body in front of him. Despite his injuries it was easy enough to positively identify him by physical characteristics, hair, build, and a unique tattoo on his forearm — three interlocked triangles, the Celtic symbol of the Trinity.

"Get him ready to move," Lanier said, and backed out of the side room.

As Jake and a corpsman slid him as gently as possible into a body bag, the Ranger turned his attention to the men in the jump suits. He asked the interpreter, "They saying anything?"

"Yeah, mostly 'Thank you.'"

Lanier knew he'd just saved all of the poor men's lives, a small comfort he wouldn't fully appreciate until years to come. He reached into a zippered pocket in his vest and pulled out a large, black satellite phone. He looked up a number on a laminated card and dialed.

Over his shoulder Jake heard the conversation as he worked to secure the soldier for a dignified return home.

"This is Captain Lanier. I need to speak with General Dawson." A pause. "Sir, positive identification, KIA. Negative, intact. Negative sir, no sign of the other one."

Jake zipped up the bag, unfolded an American flag, and draped it over the litter. He heard the captain conclude the phone call that many people were eagerly waiting for.

"Yes, sir. Out," the captain said and hung up.

"He ready?" Lanier asked Jake.

"Yes, sir."

"Good, get those guys clear and move out. Razor One Eight?" he asked on the radio.

"Copy, Razor One," the attached Air Force Combat Air Controller answered from a different part of the compound.

"Get a fast mover overhead. Get 'em to drop the biggest bomb they've got on this place." He turned to the team around him, laden with trash bags full of the intel, as well as blood samples from the room for DNA testing. "We good?"

"Yes sir."

"Good. Bury this damned place."

Lanier looked around the room and saw a bloodstained table next to him. In disgust and rage he raised his boot against the edge of the table and shoved it across the room, tipping it over with a crash into the lighting equipment.

"Clear out," he said, and walked away.

Kansas City, Missouri

Peter Allen walked into the study and saw his wife sitting in a rocking chair in the dark. He'd seen her there so many times, usually with a baby, and usually like now, in the middle of the night. He pulled up a chair next to her; neither of them could sleep and they'd been in bed for hours, thinking, praying, waiting for good news, resigned to the worst.

He took his wife's hand and she continued to rock. After a few minutes, he asked, "How's your heart?"

Tears started to flow and she looked at him without saying a word, confirming the sinking feeling he'd had from the moment they first got the news of the crash. They knew their son was gone.

He pulled her close, knowing her answer. For a long time they simply wept, until the grief suspended long enough to voice a long-feared conversation. He asked her, "How do you know?"

Cecilia Allen wiped her tears with the last tissue in the box. "Because God's not telling me to pray for him."

Peter nodded. She went on as her voice cracked.

"He's only telling me to pray for Ginger."

———

Palm Desert, California

Marcus Cooper paced the shop in a daze. He looked at his phone. *No, they won't call if she's dead. They'll come in person.* He knew he should be sleeping while he could, knew if the worst were to happen he'd need strength. He sat on the stool and examined his workbench, strewn with several parts in various stages of rebuild. Marcus realized he was in no position to fix anything; he couldn't concentrate.

He walked inside and got a beer from the fridge, paused as he was about to twist the cap and closed his eyes wishing he was in a nightmare. He sat at the table and took a long swig with his eyes closed. Images of Ginger at various ages flashed in his mind. He was desperate to do something to kill the time but was utterly rudderless.

He stood, looked at the pictures of her on the fridge. One was a picture of them camping when she was a little girl, taken by someone Marcus couldn't remember. The other was of her in Iraq, with her arming team — a motley collection of dangerous looking men in camo with weapons that looked larger than Ginger. The men held large machine guns and lounged on the hoods of Humvees, Ginger sat in the center of them, with her arms crossed, wearing aviator style sunglasses, her Apache in the background.

Marcus took another swig, followed by a deep breath. *She's strong. She'll fight. Don't let them break you, Ginger.*

He wanted to fly to Iraq and start turning over tables. He wanted to put his fist through any man who dared lay a hand on his little girl. *You've got some pretty influential clients, Marcus. Maybe call in a few favors?*

He studied the faces of the soldiers, the stern power in their eyes. *No, they'll find you. Don't give up.*

He sat and finished the rest of his beer in one long draught. *Please find her.*

17

Voices

Ginger curled up tighter, desperate to retain some warmth. She instantly regretted it. It hurt to move even a few inches; the pain was complete. From head to toe, inside and out, her body hurt, but she no longer cried, she wasn't hydrated enough to shed a tear. She had some water, just enough to keep her alive, doled out in a putrid, plastic bottle that her captors left with her whenever they concluded their business. The small scraps of stale flatbread they gave her provided little sustenance. Each passing hour drained her energy and she was losing the ability to think. Resistance — which she initially tried — only served to exhaust her resources. It was out of the question now, and she resolved to conserve as much energy as possible, to use whatever they offered to formulate a plan to at least stay alive if escape was impossible.

Her ankle was broken; so was her right arm. Both eyes now functioned, though one was badly cut around the eyelid, and dried blood and swelling obscured the scant amount of light that penetrated beneath the little door. The sliver provided just enough illumination to see she was well caged in a small room with that door as the only exit; her initial probing had produced nothing to use as a weapon and no hope of escape. The room was always dark except for the light that fell in the opened doorway when they were with her, and she'd lost all comprehension of time.

They don't want to look at you, that's why they keep you in the dark. How long have I been here?

The still sticky wounds up and down the right side of her body told her it could only have been a day or two, or else they would have scabbed by now. Yet they grew more painful as time passed, and she realized infection must be setting in. *So maybe it's been several days. Days become weeks. The more weeks that pass, the less likely you are to ever be rescued.*

She deflated.

How long will they keep me here? Do they want me dead? No, they wouldn't feed me if they wanted me dead. Maybe they plan to use me for propaganda, get me on camera hating on America? But first they need to break me. Get me to the point where I'd do anything just to be warm, no longer hungry.

Ginger got angry. For all of her time racing motor-cycles, she was never an athlete. She didn't like sports or running. Her strength had always been her intellect, and Ginger's brain went to work, utilizing every calorie to work the problem. There was always a solution to every problem; her dad had taught her that. *Maybe I can kill the next one, somehow, hurt him at least. Maybe he has a weapon on him.*

She tried to pull herself to a sitting position, feeling along the cold concrete in search of a sharp piece of rubble, or something, anything that she could use. *Maybe the plastic from the water bottle. Maybe I can get enough strength the smash his trachea? Get him to put his hands on his throat and take his gun? An AK has thirty rounds. Surely there aren't thirty of them. I could take them one at a time.*

She could almost hear a voice laughing at her, mocking her. It was a familiar voice, the same one she heard while looking at her reflection in the mirror that day after the clinic, and so many times since.

Fool, it said. *You can't even sit. How could you even think you could take on a full grown man? Give up.*

Her pain overwhelmed her and sent her back to the floor in despair.

The voice continued. *You can't even walk and yet you want to fight this? You deserve this.*

Ginger closed her eyes and would have cried, instead she shivered. *It's right.*

It hammered her. *You've killed hundreds, thousands of men, women and children. You even killed your own child, yet you want to escape? Death is too good for what you've done. This is justice.*

She tried to take a deep breath but the air was foul. She rolled her head to look up but that was an even worse position, and for the first time in her life Genevieve Cooper wished for death. *Is this God? Is this retribution? Was I wrong? Please let me die.*

She had never been to church, had no notion of God and wanted none. All she wanted was to be rid of the pain. Now, in her grief, she wondered if this God whom Cecilia had told her about was indeed real, and this was what He did to those who harmed others.

I'm sorry for what I've done. I'm sorry. I'm ready to die. Take me please.

But she didn't die. She merely lay on the cold floor and heard nothing. She thought about her father. *He'd say, don't give up.* But she'd already done that, in her heart anyway. *How could he ever understand that? Dad never quits.*

She thought about Craig. *Is he here too, somewhere? Still alive. Maybe I can find him, and escape together.* Ginger remembered the stories she had read of POW's in wars past, and how they managed to communicate via Morse code by tapping on walls. *If not Craig, maybe others?*

The voice returned. *You killed him too, you know.*

The pain tore through her and she remembered the words of Cecilia's letter. How could she ever face her? *He's right. I killed him too. God, please let me die. I'm so sorry.*

Her thoughts were silent for a long time and Ginger's heart rate slowed, her breathing became normal, and she felt herself begin to rest. Slowly, as if drifting in from a distant place she began to hear an old but familiar song, one she hadn't heard in years, one she'd listened to on an old tape in her youth. The music was so completely out of place she wondered if she was dead. The voice was not the same as it was on the tape but the words were the same, and sung softly:

Love of my life…

As the song played in her head, Ginger began to tremble but not from pain. The lyrics seemed directed at her but she couldn't imagine anyone would sing them to her. *I deserve this. Nobody can love me. I killed Craig. I killed my baby. I killed so many people. Who can love me?*

In answer, she heard the voice again but this time it wasn't singing.

I still love you.

She let out a deep wail, a cry from a depth never before accessed by her, and she knew who was singing to her though she still couldn't believe it. But she wanted so desperately for it to be true.

I still love you.

She shook and wept in the dark until her own voice was silent again. She'd never been so scared to ask a question in her life — not of her father, not of an instructor. She pulled every last ounce of strength she could muster to ask a silent question to the voice in the dark: *Is this really you?*

Ginger closed her eyes and took a deep breath. Somehow the foul odor was gone, and she let her lungs fill with air that seemed to be from a clear mountaintop. The pain in her body subsided just a little, just enough to lay down without shivering, and for the first time in weeks she was able to sleep, but not before dozing off with a whisper from her cold lips. *Thank you.*

18

Elders

He was an old man, hated and loved. He walked the sidewalk not caring that his teenage grandson beside him was terrified. The boy wasn't a coward or a fool in anyone's eyes, but their actions today would mark them and the boy was nervous. The Sunni leaders might very well murder them on the way back, or tonight in their home along with everyone else in it. Or, if not everyone, maybe just the grandfather. Someone was going to die as a result of this errand.

So be it. The boy will need to take a stand eventually. The old man looked at his grandson. *Do not fear them. Never fear them.* He turned and walked on.

The grandfather didn't fear them. He had taken a stand from the beginning, and would have been killed in violent fashion if he were a younger man and less well respected. Even still he was a threat, and so they merely bombed his store. Failing to stop his obstinacy, they tried a different tact, and took several of his fingers as well as his thumbs.

He responded by smoking cigarettes with his remaining fingers, something their version of Islam forbid. The grandfather mocked them with his four fingers and carried on, opposing them every chance he got. The leaders had written him off as a crazy old man, but this would change that.

His wife knew it, and even as she wrote the note she wondered aloud if this was a step too far. But he stood firm, even in his demand for the boy to accompany him; he needed the boy to deliver the instructions in the best English anyone in the family could manage. The boy's mother, a teacher in Sadr City, was actually the most educated member of the family until a suicide bomber detonated himself just outside her school. The boy witnessed her death, along with most of his peers, and was swiftly sent north to his grandfather.

He's been watching this for four years. He needs to know we can't let them win.

Whether or not the Americans would take them seriously he never doubted. Others had ordered caution but the old man was never cautious and was adamant they act, and act quickly. The Americans could defeat them — would do so, he believed — and this was more than the right thing to do; it was an opportunity.

But first they would need to get the message into the right hands, and nobody knew which of the Americans blanketing the outer rim of the city was the best to contact, or how to approach them without getting killed.

The boy looked much older than his thirteen years. The Americans would see him as a threat. *But perhaps not with an old man by his side.* The real trick was in what to say, and for that the old man prayed for the boy's wisdom, and his courage.

When they left the house, the boy was sweating, and his grandfather half expected him to run away before they even got off the bus. But he managed to endure the ride, and as they took their first steps toward the new American military outpost, he almost dared the young man to desert him.

What the old man couldn't see was the confidence growing in the boy with every step, remembering his mother's death. Finally, after all the years of nightmares and fear, he was grateful to be doing something to strike back.

The grandfather's single aim was for the Americans to root out the insurgents, to clear away this troublesome lot who destroyed his business, maimed his body, and killed those who offended their distorted version of his ancestral religion. They were losing, the old man knew it. He'd watched them scatter over the past year, desperate and forced to the margins, or forced to meld into large populations and hide like cockroaches among them. The old man simply wanted them to leave; the boy wanted them dead.

The grandfather slowed as he approached the massive American vehicles. He studied the faces of the soldiers, most of whom watched the streets from behind dark sunglasses or goggles, and weapons. The old man set his will and boldly headed toward a tank, behind it were two additional vehicles just as menacing. Atop all three, soldiers watched him from behind machine guns, though they weren't pointing their weapons at him, not yet.

Most of the dismounted soldiers surveyed the street, eyes constantly on the move, ready for anything. Two men stood in the center, speaking with a local.

"The man with the long antennae. Do you see him?" the grandfather asked the boy in Farsi.

"Yes."

"He is in charge. You will ask to speak with him."

The boy's heart raced and he answered weakly, "Yes."

The grandfather took several confident steps toward the commanders and quickly drew the eye of all of the soldiers on that side of the street, including the tank's gunner, who was now looking at an old timer and a military-aged young man through the sights of his .50-caliber machine gun.

—

"See pops there?"

"Yeah," the sergeant said, wondering what the old man was up to. He took all of three seconds to size up the duo, neither looked to him like a threat. The old man wore loose-fitting garments that revealed much of his collar and chest, no bulk from concealed weapons or a bomb vest, both hands visible — hands missing fingers, and a lit cigarette between two of the fingers he had left. The boy looked terrified, but not in a getting-ready-to-kill kind of way. That look, the veteran soldiers knew well. This was just a scared kid.

Great, now I have to deal with a crazy old man.

The sergeant kept his index finger extended above the trigger, leveled the rifle and said in a firm, but conversing tone, "Whoa there, sir."

The old man stopped and started speaking in Farsi. The sergeant lowered his rife and tried to gauge what the old man wanted when the boy spoke.

"We speak him," and slowly pointed past him.

"You speak to me, son," the sergeant said not taking his eyes off the boy. "What can I do for you?" *This is new.*

The boy spoke to his grandfather in hushed tones. The old man answered in animated fashion and waved his cigarette around as he spoke. The words were agitated and he pointed several times at the commanders behind the sergeant.

"He say message is for leader. Only leader."

Three soldiers now surrounded the pair, and the sergeant sized them up again.

"Perkins, check them out," he said to the soldier behind them. The soldier performed a pat down, first on the boy whose eyes widened with terror, followed by the grandfather. In a manner of seconds they were cleared.

"Come with me," the sergeant said to the boy.

—

The old man leaned against what was left of a wall and smoked his cigarette, seemingly without a care in the world. *The hard part is over. We're in.*

He saw the sergeant speak with his lieutenant and then point in their direction. He noticed his grandson give a nervous smile to them along with a respectful head nod. *Don't overdo it boy. We still need to walk home, and the soldiers aren't the only ones watching.*

The lieutenant seemed annoyed by the interruption.

"Don't draw attention," he said to his grandson.

"Yes, grandfather."

Several more minutes passed before the lieutenant got around to the pair of civilians. He and his subordinate walked up to the grandfather, the sergeant behind them.

"Good day, Sir. You wanted to speak with us?"

The old man waited for the translation, then said to his grandson, "Give them the note," and dropped his cigarette butt on the ground.

"I have letter," the boy said in English. He slowly reached into his pocket and handed the folded scrap of paper to the commander.

The lieutenant watched the boy's body language and understood he was frightened. The grandfather looked at them, expecting him to read and understand the message.

The lieutenant unfolded the paper and was further annoyed when he saw foreign script.

"What am I supposed to do with this?" he asked the boy, but didn't wait for a response. "Get Bashar over here," he said to his subordinate, who left for a minute and came back with another soldier. The lieutenant handed the note to his interpreter.

The interpreter read one side of the note, then turned it over and examined a hasty drawing on the other side. "Uh," he said, then asked the old man a question.

The man looked the interpreter in the eye and nodded, then added in Farsi, "For now."

———

The drone operator zoomed his camera. The target buildings were located in the center of what from above looked like a series of nested boxes, or like a maze running in a square pattern toward the center. To the north and south of the neighborhood were two major highways, and no fewer than thirty separate buildings between. All he and his team could see was the typical city traffic and routines of normal life in Northern Iraq.

"It's gotta be one of these three," his commander said, comparing the high resolution images on the screen to the photocopy of a hand-drawn map.

"Eyes on. Twenty-four seven, until you hear otherwise. Give us something to go on."

"Yes, sir," the operators replied.

—

Washington D.C.
03:50:00

"And we know nothing about this old man?" the president asked, still rubbing his forehead from the hasty wake up.

"A little. From what we've been able to gather he's been harassed by the insurgents for years so revenge may be a motivation. He's well respected but not politically connected. He just walked up and handed our boys a note. We do know *somebody* is there, somewhere in the vicinity, but nothing concrete to confirm it's her," Green said.

"How? You have a secondary source?"

"Of sorts. Since we pushed Al-Qaeda out of the major population centers, the money flow has dried up considerably. You know that. We're seeing that they don't pay their underlings as well as they did a few months ago. Consequently their low level guys are turning to street crime to line their pockets – robberies, black market sales, etcetera…"

"And kidnappings," the president said.

"Right. And we're fairly convinced the police force in Mosul is fully infiltrated by AQI, which is bad, but it also allows us to get more intel because they're not as disciplined in their communications as the true believers."

"So you've got someone talking about her?" Shields asked.

"Not her specifically. But they're definitely feeling out the market for how much they can get for whoever it is they've got."

"That could be anybody, though, what makes you think it's our girl, or even an American?"

"Because the old man says so. That's not public knowledge, and the timeline goes perfectly with what we suspected. We just didn't think they'd move her this far this fast. Also, the intercepts give a pretty good indication that whoever they've got, they want a lot for. We're talking in the millions. Foreign journalists or tourists aren't worth millions, but American pilots are."

"They're worth even more as the star of a public execution, though," Shields said.

"Which is why we don't have much time," said Green.

The president looked at Shields. "What do you think?"

"Some of them would prefer the propaganda angle. They'd figure something like that could end our public support, which is already shaky. My guess is that the AQI leadership is probably doing a cost analysis as we speak. There are probably two camps. One that wants her dead, the other that wants to cash her in. Whatever they decide, they'll do it soon. We don't have much time."

"How much time?" the president asked.

"A day, maybe two?" Shields said. Green nodded.

The president looked at the black and white image in his hand and made a mental note of the value of the CIA drones; the four million dollar flying cameras were worth every penny. "And this is from?"

"Twenty minutes ago," Green said.

He studied the image, then set it down and took a sip of water. "And that's all you've got."

"We can keep shaking the bushes," the CIA director said. "Or the other option is to go in with a broadsword, close off the area and kick in every door, but if we do that, odds are they might just kill her and fade away."

"With footage delivered to Al Jazeera before our guys even got close," Shields said.

He picked up the image again. He still had the Allen's phone number on a sheet on his desk, and he looked at his watch.

"No. Let's do it fast. But do it right." After several years of war he knew the time difference in every operational theater. It was late morning in Iraq, optimal time for a mission like this was in the middle of the night.

"Can you get a plan worked up in time for the next window?" he asked Shields.

"Yes, sir."

"Let me know when it's ready to go. I trust you with the details, you have my full authority to use whatever resources you deem necessary," the president said.

"Understood, sir," Shields said.

"Have a good flight back to Florida," the president said to Shields.

"Thank you, sir," he said, as he and Green left the small seating area.

The president picked up the phone.

"Good morning Mr. President, what can I get for you?" the White House operator asked.

"Good morning, Sheila. Can you please call up Larry for me?"

"Certainly, Mr. President."

The president hung up and rested in a chair. He took a sip of water and debated whether to order some coffee or try to get another hour or two of sleep. In less than a minute the phone rang.

"Larry?"

"Yes, sir. Good morning. What's up?" his chief of staff asked.

"Clear everything off the calendar today after fourteen hundred hours. Round up the crew and make sure they're here by then."

"Roger that, sir." He knew it meant something major was about to happen. "Want me to quietly book some network air time?"

"Negative. Not this one."

—

Al Asad Air Base, Iraq
09:15:00

Porter and Denny stood in the hangar examining gear when a Jeep came to a stop in front of them. Admiral Buchanan stepped out, and the SEALs saluted and shook his hand.

"Just the men I came to see. Come on, we're making a hop to Mortaritaville," and turned back to the Jeep, whose engine was still humming.

The SEALs shared a perplexed look but followed. "So, what's in Balad?" Porter asked as they climbed in.

"You've got a mission to plan. Your team is being directed now to get their gear ready for transport up north."

"When's the mission?" Porter asked.

"Tonight," the admiral said.

Porter and Denny looked at their watches and realized they had around fifteen hours to plan something, somewhere. The Jeep came to a stop in front of the open staircase of a C-37A, a military version of a Gulfstream private jet, and Buchanan led the officers up the stairs and into it. The door closed and the jet was moving before Porter had even had time to find a seat.

"Don't get too comfy, we've got a lot of intel to go over and not a lot of time to do it. Sorry, no champagne and caviar today."

Porter immediately wondered what would precipitate a SEAL admiral being granted a VIP transport instead of a Blackhawk. "What kind of assets will we have to work with?"

The admiral looked at him. "All of them."

"UBL?" Porter asked.

"Negative, that's still priority number one."

"And this is?" Denny asked.

"According to POTUS, this is number two."

"So who's the bad guy?" Porter asked.

The admiral shook his head as he opened his briefcase, and handed the SEAL officers a stack of satellite images and a dossier. Porter opened the file and saw a picture of Warrant Officer Genevieve Cooper.

———

Joint Base Balad, Iraq
10:10:00

They landed, briskly passing through security checkpoints and guards with an authority even Porter was impressed with. Soon they entered a secure door and were back in a familiar world.

Jenkins rose to meet them. Behind a shabby conference table stood General DeBerg, the most powerful American in Iraq.

"Sir," Porter said.

"Lieutenant Dawkins, Lieutenant Lowery, Admiral, have a seat," said the Commanding General of Multi National Forces Iraq. Porter saw a number of satellite images and recognized the Tigris River.

"Lieutenant, you and Colonel Jenkins will plan a combined assault." He pointed to a building on the image.

"Admiral Buchanan has briefed you on the target and the timeframe. You and Jenkins will work out the details and present the plan to me as soon as it's ready." He stood, and the other men rose with him. "Gentlemen, use whatever you need but this has to be fast and it has to be spot on. That's why I want both of you on it. If you need to move units into place, don't waste time asking for approval, my aide will make the arrangements on my authority. Lieutenant, Delta will catch you up on what you don't already know. Clock is ticking so I won't detain you any longer." With that, General DeBerg left the room.

Porter looked at the images on the table. He picked up the hand drawn map and studied it before looking at Jenkins.

"What do we know about the intel source?" Porter asked.

"Sounds like not much," Denny said.

"He's right. Not much, but it's all we've got."

"Then it's all we need," Porter pulled his hat tight over his head, and pointed to a section of the map. "For starters, I want to take a closer look at this area right here."

19

Wonderland

Joint Base Balad, Iraq
15:00:00

Porter walked through the plywood maze toward the noise of booming voices and teasing laughter in the planning room. He entered and walked past several men in various forms of dress, some in uniform, some in hoodies and flip flops; most had beards. As Porter walked to the front of the room the laughter died down, and those who were sitting sat up straight. A few nodded.

"Skipper," they said, as he passed them.

He looked over the crowd of smelly, dangerous men and settled in at the front. A large projection screen was to his left. In front of him was a relief map on a table with a layout of long streets and several cardboard model buildings. Porter noticed three of the highest-ranking officers in the city slide into the room — General DeBerg among them — and stand along the back wall; they were not smiling.

His gaze fell on Tim Miller, standing in his flight suit next to three other pilots. His arms were folded. Porter made eye contact, gave a respectful nod. Tim just stared.

Porter took in the rest of the crowd, including Jenkins beside him, and began his briefing.

"Alright ladies, shut up and listen up. There's gonna be a lot of people watching this one, so dial in. We're moving on this fast and there are a bunch of moving parts, so speak up if you see something. We're calling this op, Wonderland."

Several of the men took notes as he spoke. Porter continued as an image emerged on the screen.

"Many of you are aware that three days ago an Apache was shot down in Tal Afar, in the north. Chief Warrant Officer Genevieve Cooper, shown here, and her front seater, Warrant Officer Craig Allen, went down in the city. The site was quickly swarmed and by the time the Army got to the wreckage the pilots were MIA."

The rows of special operators leaned forward to pay closer attention, resisting the temptation to look at the four Apache pilots standing along the wall.

"Yesterday Task Force North recovered the body of Allen in a little village south of there. There was no sign of Cooper."

The images changed to a picture of the old man. "This morning, an Iraqi good Samaritan of sorts and his grandson walked up to an Army checkpoint in Mosul and handed them a note that read, quote, 'American woman is here,' unquote, and on the back was a hand drawn map with labeled cross streets."

The projection changed to a split-screen image: the hand-drawn map on one side, a satellite image of the map's reference point on the other. Side by side, the two were quite similar.

"The map refers to this neighborhood in Mosul, as the source confirmed. Additional intelligence sources have concluded with a high probability that this is where Cooper is currently being held." The image changed to a close-up of just the target buildings.

Porter could feel their next question as he watched thirty SEALs and Delta operators study the map. "However, the old man couldn't say for certain which of these three buildings she's in." A collective groan issued from men who had seen this movie before and knew how rarely it turned out well.

"So we're going to take all of them at the same time."

Several heads nodded in approval. Another image went up.

"We're going in with three teams, eleven each, call signs Rabbits one through thirty-three." Another image replaced the map, this one with lines overlaid on the roads. "A C-17 will insert us in six assault vehicles here," he indicated with a laser pointer, "and from there, we separate. Lowery and I will take First and Second Troops in four vehicles to the first checkpoint and prepare to advance on buildings Alpha and Bravo." Porter paused.

"And I'll do the same with Third Troop," Jenkins said. "All three troops will give the checkpoint code word and wait to move onto phase three, where we'll make our way to the target buildings on foot, leaving the vehicles manned to cover our six."

Porter waited for the men to finish taking notes before continuing.

"As soon as we're in position, the Army will move Strykers to block off these four intersections to wrap up anyone trying to flee or reinforce. They will serve as our QRF if things go to hell, and the Apaches —" he looked at the pilots, "— call sign Pegasus, will be in constant contact with each troop to provide any air cover we require."

A list of radio frequencies and call signs went up on the screen, and the various operators, pilots, and Army ground commanders noted the network designations.

Porter waited for the scribbling to subside. "Any questions up to this point?"

The Delta sniper spoke. "Overwatch?"

Porter motioned to the men at the back of the room, and an Army Major answered the question. "As the Rabbits near the target, we'll insert a sniper team via Little Bird to cover the entire courtyard, plus this side of the target buildings."

"And we'll cover everything else," Tim Miller interjected. The comment was out of order, but nobody doubted its truth, and nobody seemed to mind.

Porter continued. "Once the Rabbits are in place, I'll give the order to execute. We breach and start looking for Cooper."

Another image of Ginger went up on the screen. This one was a casual picture of her sitting on an ammo crate in an Army t-shirt, smiling next to Tim Miller who wasn't. The image made Miller shift and he had to bite the inside of his lip to hold his emotions in check. Robinson noted his posture but didn't respond.

"This is Cooper. Pay attention to her facial features and build. Caucasian, 120 lbs, 5' 7", light skin, hair just above the shoulder. She has a unit tattoo on her left calf, looks like this —" two additional images went on the screen, "— and another tattoo, the symbol of the rebel alliance, on her right shoulder blade."

"Damn right," one of the operators muttered, and several guys grunted agreement.

"We may encounter other captives, other women, even. Follow protocol, but keep searching until we positively identify Cooper, at which point we'll use the radio designation ALICE." The word went up on the screen.

"That will be the code word to extract your team. Once you hear that, all three troops move to the street and we take Alice here." He pointed to a square-shaped courtyard one street away from the target buildings. "A SOAR Blackhawk will land and extract her, and only her." More notetaking, and the room was silent again. "Once Alice is safely away, the Rabbits will move out, and the Strykers will move in to exploit any intel, and take over any detainees.

"Gentlemen," Porter spoke directly to the operators. His voice took on a different, almost angry tone, like a father giving life and death instructions to his sons. "We get her on that helo no matter what. However it goes down, Cooper gets on that bird." The implication was not lost on the men; Porter was expecting them to give their own lives to bring Ginger home, even if only her body remained.

The words hung in the air until a soft, Middle Eastern accented voice broke the silence. "We will find her," Ozzy said, looking at Porter. They locked eyes.

"We will find her," Ozzy repeated quietly to himself, looking back at his paper.

———

An hour later everyone packed up their notes and dispersed to filter instructions to their individual subordinates. Porter noticed DeBerg and the other high-ranking officers were gone in a flash. Tim Miller, alone, looked at the relief map on the table, studying the building patterns.

Denny walked up to Porter. "Those additional intelligence sources you mentioned? They never did tell us what they were."

Porter noticed out of the corner of his eye that Miller had heard, and turned and waited for an answer from across the room as he picked up one of the small cardboard buildings.

"Does it matter?" Porter asked, annoyed.

Denny made a face and shrugged his shoulders as if to say, *Maybe, maybe not.*

"If she's there, we bring her home tonight. If she's not," he looked at Tim, "we go after her somewhere else tomorrow."

Tim tossed the piece back onto the table and walked out.

———

Ba'quba District, Iraq
22:00:00

Phil Elliot turned the M118LR rifle round in his fingers, feeling its weight, the perfect symmetry of the brass cylinder. He took care to set the round in the magazine, a process he repeated nineteen more times. He'd had his fair share of jams over the years, and was finally in a position to be extremely choosy over his ammo and his weapon. The 175-grain Sierra Match King bullet was fine with him; the bullet was still supersonic at 1000 yards, more than accurate enough for his standard overwatch missions. Tonight's field of fire would be even less than that.

When he was satisfied with the magazine, he examined the length of his SR-25 sniper rifle, checking for dirt, wear, and occasionally speaking to it out of superstition. Elliot sat the rifle on the table, bipod extended. He finished consolidating the less important gear and ended by fastening his helmet and donning his gloves. He was ready. He picked up his rifle, joined Jeff, the other Army sniper, and they made their way to the tarmac. They listened for the sound of a Little Bird, their ride to a rooftop nest somewhere in Mosul.

Mosul
01:15:00

"One minute to touchdown," the pilot said.

The lights inside the C-17 turned from red to green and the operators moved from their mesh seats along the aircraft's interior and into their vehicles. Porter climbed into the passenger seat of one of the three Special Operations Vehicles, which were essentially modified Land Rovers. Denny and Jenkins took the shotgun seats in the other two SOVs. The rest of the SEAL and Delta operators mounted their designated Lightweight Tactical All Terrain Vehicles. The dune buggy style LTATVs held four men each, and their drivers waited in the line of six vehicles for the slightly larger SOVs to begin.

Porter felt the bump of the C-17's tires touching down as he braced for what was to come. The pilot put the massive aircraft's thrusters in reverse and in less than five seconds they were moving backward. The pilot made a three-point turn on the short, deserted, narrow runway on the northeast outskirts of Mosul. Air Force crew chiefs removed the straps holding the vehicle tires to the transport jet as the final pivot concluded.

Through night vision Porter watched the back ramp of the C-17 open. The second it was down, the aircraft's rear flight engineer gave a thumbs-up to the forward SOV's driver, who started the engine and drove down the ramp. Once clear, it accelerated away from the aircraft, followed by the remaining five vehicles in a tight line. As the last vehicle in the procession fell clear of the ramp, the pilot pulled away, and before the ramp was finished closing the C-17 was airborne and on its way to meet a refueling tanker. Afterward it would circle the empty desert until Operation Wonderland was over and the Rabbits were ready to go home.

The insertion of thirty-three special operators took all of three minutes, and before a curious resident would have had a chance to put on his slippers to inspect the noise, the dark night was silent again.

Washington D.C.
16:20:00 EST

The president, Green, and most of the senior cabinet members sat around the Situation Room table. Radio chatter from a number of locations played out on the speaker phone, and a video feed from a CIA drone was displayed on the wall. An additional phone line was open to General Shields at JSOC headquarters in Florida, should the president choose to speak directly with the man orchestrating the operation. The president sat in silent prayer, watching along with his staff, all of whom knew the best thing they could do was remain quiet.

—

COB Foxtrot, Kirkuk Province
01:25:00

Mitch Robinson and Major Atwood watched a similar feed from the TOC, listening in as their four Apaches approached the buildings.

"Four clicks to target," Tim Miller said.

"Copy that, Six," his wingman answered.

"This is Pegasus Six. Rabbit, we have you at two clicks from target, can you confirm?"

"Copy Pegasus, this is Rabbit One," Porter answered. "ETA five minutes. Any street traffic? Over."

"Negative Rabbit, streets are deserted. Over."

Mitch heard Tim's voice on a different frequency as he made a radio call to another helicopter.

"This is Pegasus Six. Star Three, do you read me?"

"Star Three, I copy, Pegasus."

"Star Three, you are clear for insertion."

"Copy. Star Three inbound," the Little Bird pilot answered.

Mitch leaned back in his chair and put his hands behind his head, took a deep breath, and prayed it would all be over soon.

—

Mosul
01:30:00

The landscape looked different. Porter's driver moved along the rural roads following the GPS, trying to reconcile the land details with the satellite images he'd studied all day. The lead SOV intended to use a rural farm road that didn't seem to exist, so he cut through the brush, trusting in the GPS and the off-road capabilities of the small vehicle. Soon he recognized the physical road markers and breathed easier.

The other vehicles followed his lead. A few minutes later the tires caught the surface of a dirt road and the ride was somewhat smoother. The driver slowed, hoping the locals wouldn't hear or smell the unusual procession moving along their backyards at this time of night. The special operations vehicles, though darkened and as stealthy as could be, were nonetheless distinctly American. Jenkins had wanted to use common civilian trucks to blend in but Porter vetoed it; he wanted as much firepower as possible, and both the SOVs and the LTATVs were stacked with enough firepower to take on anything and get away unscathed.

Consequently, a convoy of six of them at this time of night was a dead giveaway that something was about to go down. Speed was imperative.

Porter studied the map on his computer screen and saw the turn ahead.

"This is Rabbit One, first turn coming up."

"Rabbit One Two, copy," Denny said from the second SOV.

"Rabbit Two Three, copy," said Jenkins.

"Here we go," Porter said to the driver.

The SOV climbed up from the sand onto the hard surface of a paved road and took a casual right hand turn followed by the LTATV driver. They traveled along the curvy road passing a number of dilapidated dwellings, some of them mere lots with only a remnant of a structure remaining, two miles from the target.

Tim Miller saw all of it. The Apaches watched the ground vehicles move as one long snake from the makeshift landing strip, across rough terrain between structures, and finally onto the main road. Tim targeted everything along their path long before they passed it. He saw nothing — no people, no vehicles, only animals asleep in their pens. When they were within a click of the target, he called up the Little Bird pilot.

"Star Three, Rabbits five mikes out."

—

"Copy, Pegasus," the Little Bird pilot said.

Phil Elliot put his right arm on the strap that clipped him onto the helicopter, the only thing standing between him and a thousand-foot fall onto the pavement below. The Little Bird increased speed in a direct line to the rooftop. It was like a terrible and amazing roller coaster ride, and for a brief moment he allowed himself to laugh. He was actually having fun.

The roof was there faster than he anticipated and he felt a heave in his chest as the helicopter came to a sudden stop. The strap tightened against his torso and he realized the helicopter was not going any further.

Phil looked down expecting to see the rooftop, but instead he was hovering above the street. Only the very front of the Little Bird's skids touched the roof, but the aircraft was entirely stable. He and Jeff would have to scoot along to get their feet to the front of the helo in order to get on the roof. They unclipped and moved to the front of the bench, then Phil stepped on the skid, swung himself around, and jumped onto the roof. Jeff did the same. The second they were clear, the Little Bird leapt into the air and was gone.

They immediately realized that garbage and debris had prevented the helicopter from touching down, and the stench almost knocked them over. The snipers moved, crouching, until they got to the eastern edge where they got down and set up their weapons. They surveyed the courtyard and dialed in the distance of the structures adjacent to the target buildings. From his vantage point, Phil would be able to cover every angle of the landing zone.

"Whoever chose this spot knew what they were doing," Jeff said.

"I know, right."

Phil Elliot keyed his mic. "Madman in position. Eyes on target."

———

Jenkins looked at his watch; they were right on schedule. He studied the street layout on the tablet for the hundredth time even though he'd already committed it to memory. He wished they'd had a chance to practice a mock assault on a similar layout. High profile missions like this one could involve days or weeks of planning and practice, but tonight they were going off experience and calculated guesswork.

They were almost there. Jenkins recognized an indentation from an irrigation ditch off to the right and knew, or rather hoped, he would see a mosque on the corner.

There it is. This is the street.

All six vehicles slowed to a crawl as they crossed the four lanes. Porter's SOV made a tight circle and pulled to a stop at an angle with its front end facing northwest. Its gunner stood, activated the minigun, and surveyed his field of fire. The LTATV pulled in behind the SOV facing the opposite direction, toward the target buildings ten houses away. Denny's SOV and its trailing LTATV made the same maneuver, but faced northeast. The four vehicles turned off their engines.

Porter looked down the road at the last pair of vehicles performing the same maneuver. The Delta team would hit their building from a different direction. For decades the Navy SEALs and the Army Delta operators had been rivals, but that was another generation. First in the mountains of Afghanistan, then later in Iraq, Porter and Jenkins always seemed to be on parallel missions; Polaris or Yamaha, Farah or Fallujah, they fought the same war in different places and leaned on each other's experience. Though their areas of expertise varied and their dress uniforms were different colors, they were brothers.

Denny and Porter could see them from a distance, poised and ready. The SEALs heard the radio chime in their ears, "Rabbit Two Three, Looking Glass."

Phase two was complete. All three teams were ready for the next step.

———

"This is Pegasus One Three, Rabbits in position," Donovan said.

He asked Rico, "See any bad guys yet?"

"Negative, place is a ghost town. Hope they got the right grid," Rico said, uncertainty in his voice.

Donovan was thinking the same thing.

———

Jenkins swung himself out of the SOV. He confirmed the vehicles were in the right position and had clear fields of fire, then turned to his team as they crouched behind the vehicles.

"Rabbit Two Three, ready," he said into his mic.

"Copy," Porter replied. "Rabbit One moving."

"Rabbit One Two, moving," he heard Denny say.

Jenkins gave a hand signal to the drivers, one now manning a minigun, the other an M240 belt-fed machine gun. They replied with a thumbs up.

"Let's go," Jenkins said.

———

01:32:00

Porter looked at his watch, almost amazed at the timing. Everyone should be set. "Madman, do you read me?" he whispered.

"Copy, Rabbit. I don't see you yet but I read you. Over," Phil answered.

"Pegasus, do you read. Over," he said softly.

"Copy Rabbit, we've got you. Clear to target," Miller said.

Porter looked at his team, made a chopping hand motion in the direction of the target. Sixteen operators slowly crept down the dark street, leaving six men in the vehicles to cover the intersection behind them.

"All Rabbits, proceed," Porter said.

———

Tim Miller watched the heat signatures of twenty-four men move along the narrow path between the buildings. He wished they could run, get to her faster, but there were plenty of obstacles to negotiate and he knew a single careless step could cause a noise and commotion. *Slow is smooth and smooth is fast.* It was true in old westerns, and still true on modern battlefields. *Do it right, boys.*

For all the firepower at his fingertips, he felt helpless, desperate, but at least he could direct the men who could do something about it.

So he lined up the front door of building Alpha in his sights, and pulled the trigger.

20

Rabbits

"What is that?" the White House Chief of Staff asked, pointing to one of the screens.

"They're sparkling the target," the president said.

There was confusion in the man's face, and Green explained.

"The helicopter is holding an infrared beam at the target. It's a laser sight only visible in that spectrum. It'll confirm for the assault team which door to kick in," he said. "The other team should be coming into frame from the bottom. See, there they are now. Here we go."

It was the last thing spoken in the Situation Room for many minutes to come.

———

01:33:00

Porter took slow, deliberate steps along the street, careful to avoid obstacles. He came up behind what was left of a parked car, briefly glanced inside to verify it was empty, and moved past. Across the narrow street, Denny's team moved with them in a double column formation. When Porter slowed, Denny slowed, and vice versa. All sixteen operators kept their weapons trained on the street across from them, so every angle, window, and door was in someone's sights at all times.

Porter came to an alley and held up his fist at the corner, then stepped one foot to the left. Taggart slid in next to him on the ground with his rifle pointed to the corner, then slowly peered around it, giving anyone who might be there as small a profile as possible.

Through his scope, Taggart could see the alley was empty. He got to a knee and stayed there as the rest of the team moved across the space between the buildings.

Denny's team performed the same maneuver in the opposite direction and soon both columns were on the move again. They were halfway to the target buildings when Porter saw the Apache's bright green beam illuminate in his night vision. He didn't really need the marker — he had the buildings mapped out perfectly — but knowing the Apache was there gave him a sense of relief.

"Pegasus, I see your sparkle," Porter said.

"Rabbit One Two, sparkling Bravo."

"Affirmative, Pegasus. Confirmed," Denny said.

"Roofs are clear all down the street," Miller said.

———

"There they are. Three Bravo," Jeff said when he saw the first operator peer around the corner to check the alleyway, exactly how the SEAL's had done on the other street.

Phil watched through his scope. A Delta operator on the ground was looking down the empty alley as the rest of his team passed by him. Phil counted off eight operators before they disappeared again. He cataloged everything along that alley, knowing that in a few minutes most of both assault teams would probably be running down it toward him and the landing zone he protected, hopefully with ALICE, whoever that was.

"And there they go," Jeff said. "See any movement anywhere?" his spotter asked again.

"No," Phil said, "But that'll change. And Jeff?"

"Yeah?"

"Shut up, will ya."

Just the targets, moron. Let me concentrate.

———

Jenkins saw a different beam from Pegasus Nine illuminating target Charlie. The leader paused for his team to get in close behind him, and then they moved again, crouching under a window as they inched up to the heavy steel door. Jenkins, Jimmy, Lance, and Chad crossed to the other side of the door, Topher took a knee in front of it and removed an explosive charge from his right leg pocket. He pulled back the adhesive cover and stuck it to the door near the handle, then stepped back. The three operators to the left of him put their backs against the wall.

"Rabbit Three One, set," Topher said. "Fire on your command, Rabbit One."

———

"Rabbit One Five, set. Ready for your signal, Rabbit One," Jonathan said from Bravo, a few dozen feet away. He looked across at Porter with the detonator in his hand.

Porter looked at Denny who gave him a thumbs-up, then at Taggart who also held a detonator at Alpha's front door.

"This is Rabbit One, on my count. Ready in three…two…one…execute."

Three simultaneous explosions interrupted the silence followed by the sounds of three flying doors, six panes of shattered glass, and the boots of twenty-four of America's most lethal warriors storming the buildings.

Porter entered his building third in line and went directly to the inner right side of the door, followed by another operator who took up the left. The room was empty and they moved forward to inspect the adjacent rooms. A door opened, and the light inside silhouetted a young girl in the doorway. From behind him, Porter heard Ozzy yell something in Arabic. The girl screamed and moved to the side as the beastly figures rushed into the room, leaving the door open behind them.

Two SEALs aimed into the room in a cross pattern and saw a man standing with crying children all around him. At the sight of the guns, he put up his hands and spoke rapidly over the children's noise.

"Taggart, Ozzy, secure them!" Porter turned and moved on to another room.

She can't be here, not if they are. Damn.

Denny's team entered, fired nine fast shots, and three men fell dead where they slept, with hands not quite on the rifles they'd been reaching for. Denny paused to survey the piles of ordinance as his team continued to clear the first floor. There were piles of ammunition, RPG rockets and launch tubes, and several mortar shells with base plates.

"Move to the upper deck," he told Mario and Jonathan.

They turned up the staircase covering the dead space to the right and took the stairs cautiously. Denny heard the action mechanism of Mario's suppressed rifle — three shots followed by a body rolling down the stairs past him. They stepped over the shooter and his weapon, continuing up the stairs. Denny heard more shots from suppressed rifles as the team finished searching the lower rooms.

"Search this floor, every inch of every room," he ordered.

At the top of the stairs were a number of dead men, and he heard wailing in Arabic. Several SEALs were searching with laser sights while stepping over bodies, some still alive. Denny lifted his NVG's to get a clearer picture.

"Turn on the lights. Check 'em out," he said, then spoke into his radio.

"This is Rabbit One Two, nothing so far."

<hr>

As soon as the door blew, the firefight commenced. Jenkins and Topher dropped two men each as they reeled from the bright light of the flashbang grenades. A spray of bullets rained in from the right, dropping Lance to the ground before the additional operators shot through the thin wall and took out the insurgent they couldn't see. A Delta operator threw another flashbang into the room, then stormed in and shot two additional insurgents. Half the team took to clearing the lower rooms, killing men in every room they encountered. The other half fought their way up to the second floor, doing likewise.

To Jenkins everything was commencing in slow motion, the sixty seconds it took to overrun the stronghold felt like an hour. The rounds diminished, occasional shots rang out that reminded him of a bag of popcorn in the microwave when it's almost done. He reached for a light switch and flipped it on.

"Rabbit Two Three, I need a medic on the lower deck," Jenkins said, walking to Lance and putting a hand on his shoulder.

"I'm good," Lance said.

"You're bleeding pretty bad. Let Eric patch it up." Jenkins keyed his radio. "Rabbit One, Charlie clear. Searching now. How's it look over there?"

"Rabbit One. Nothing yet."

"Rabbit One Two, Bravo clear. Can I get Rabbit Four over here? I've got a couple live ones. Maybe they can tell us something."

———

"Come on, Ozzy," Porter said.

"Keep an eye on them, and finish searching the place," he said to three of his team members. "Everyone else on Bravo."

Porter lead five SEALs out the door. As they moved to the next building, they could sense eyes watching from neighboring windows. Denny met them on the lower level.

"Place is loaded," he said, referring to the cache of weapons, "but no sign yet."

Porter saw their men walking back and forth down the hall.

"Got a couple of insurgents bleeding out and making a racket. Negative Alice, maybe they know something?" Denny said, looking to Ozzy.

Ozzy walked away from them down the hallway.

"Ozzy?" Porter said.

He kept walking as if he hadn't heard, entered a room, and Porter and Denny followed. It looked like an office with two desktop computers, file cabinets, and several heavy bookshelves. Two dead men lay on the floor with papers strewn about. Ozzy stood in the center of the room for several seconds.

"Ozzy, we don't have much time. Those dudes are probably gonna die any second," Denny said.

"She's here," Ozzy said, still looking around.

Denny and Porter looked around the room. The hair on each of their necks stood up and somehow they knew he was right. Porter got a nauseated feeling in his throat. He went to the desk and looked at the papers, seeing nothing out of the ordinary. He went to a double-wide file cabinet and opened a few of the drawers, not sure why. The cabinet was full of maps, and one stood out. It was a square nylon map of western Iraq. He felt the material with his fingertips — waterproof and tear-resistant, the kind of map a pilot might keep in their survival gear, a dual-use map and rain shelter.

He let his arm fall, still gripping it in his fist, and hurried out of the room to look down the hall. The door to the next room was a dozen feet away on the right, and he went to it. He entered and got chills. The room was tiny, little more than a broom closet. He turned around, then rushed back to the room he'd just come from, running his hand along the hallway that separated them. When he got inside Ozzy was still where he'd left him.

Porter did a mental calculation of the square footage.

"This room's not big enough."

Denny looked perplexed. Ozzy turned to face him.

Porter pushed past them toward a pair of heavy oak bookshelves. He wiggled his fingers behind the shelf, looked down and noticed scratch marks on the floor. He dropped the map and thrust his fingers between the bookshelf and the wall and pulled it down with a massive crash, revealing a small door behind it.

Porter pulled out his pistol, activated the attached flash light, and pointed it at the door. Behind him, Ozzy leveled his rifle, ready to fire into the hidden room from the opposite angle. Denny knelt next to the handle, put his hand on the knob and slowly turned, then thrust the door inward and stood back while Porter aimed into the dark. The beam of light caused something to move.

Denny and Ozzy saw it through their rifle scopes, but as they recognized the frail shape of a woman's body they both lowered their rifles, and instinctively looked away.

Porter holstered his pistol. He turned on the light mounted on his helmet. Every masculine instinct told him to avert his eyes but he had to be sure. He looked at the woman's leg as he entered the small room and noticed sickly purple and yellow bruising. As the light shone on her, Porter caught sight of a distinct tattoo, the unit tattoo he had committed to memory ten hours prior.

"Denny, get a blanket," Porter said, taking a knee next to her. "Ma'am, I'm an American. Can you tell me your name, ma'am?"

The woman turned her head and tried to look at him, shielding her eyes from the bright lights. Porter clicked off the light from his helmet.

"Yes," she said, barely in a whisper but clear enough. "Cooper...Gen...Genevieve." There was a pause while she caught her breath. "Warrant...Officer."

Porter shifted his balance to access his radio. "All units, this is Rabbit One. ALICE. I repeat, ALICE."

———

"That's it," the Blackhawk copilot said.

"Copy that Rabbit One, Caterpillar, ETA to landing zone, three minutes," the pilot said, and transitioned to a descent, angling the Blackhawk to allow him to hit the landing zone hot. He saw a perfectly square clearing in the center of three square rows of buildings. He also saw two Apaches below him, circling like sharks.

———

Tim Miller closed his eyes when he heard the code word ALICE, but only for a single second. He went back to studying every shadow on his screen, wanting to shoot anything, everything to make a path for Ginger to escape. He saw lights illuminate in several buildings up and down the street, curious neighbors peeking out their windows, some even stepping outside.

———

Around the landing zone, Phil saw similar movement as the surrounding buildings seemed to come alive. He zeroed in on several faces, looking for any kind of weapon. So far all he saw were confused onlookers, but with each second the locals got more and more confident. He saw the first weapon, briefly, in the hand of a man passing a window facing him, then another. Phil put his crosshairs on the door below the window. He moved his finger to the trigger just as he heard Porter's radio call.

———

Washington D.C.

The brief celebration from the less experienced staff members — exuberant when they heard the code word, the only thing they really understood about the last several minutes — was instantly stifled by the president's silence.

He stared at the screen, his fist under his jaw, and didn't move a muscle, save for his thumb's occasional click of the pen he was slowly crushing in his hand.

One by one, his civilian staff realized what he and Director Green knew. This was far from over.

21

Today and Yesterday

"Chief Cooper, we're going to get you out of here and get you home safe," Porter said slowly. "We're not going to let anyone harm you again." He waited for her to respond but she said nothing. "Are you able to stand?"

Denny tapped him on the shoulder and handed Porter a blanket.

Porter draped it over her and Ginger felt its weight cover her. Instantly she felt a degree of warmth and like a scared child she pulled it with her good arm and clutched it tight. Porter, still on his knees, shuffled back to give her some room as she attempted to sit up. She collapsed and let out a cry.

"No," she gasped. "I think my leg is broken."

"Okay, no problem," Porter said. "Try not to move too much. We're gonna get ya outta here in just a minute, okay?"

"Affirmative," she said, shivering, then added, "Did you kill them all?"

"Affirmative," Porter said, "but there may be more."

Porter turned to Denny. "We ready to move?"

"Affirmative," he answered.

The operators in all three buildings started moving toward the doors at the sound of the code word. Every military-aged man in the other two buildings was dead, and the family in building Alpha was left alone. At the same time, the six men manning the guns on the Rabbit's vehicles dropped behind their wheels, started the engines, and drove to their next checkpoints. Four of the vehicles bounced over the littered, narrow corridor, made their way to the open courtyard, and took positions on each of the four corners. The other two blocked off the street just north and south of building Bravo's front door.

———

01:47:00

"Chief Cooper, I'm gonna have to carry you. I'm sorry if this hurts but we need to get you out right away," Porter said, scooping Ginger into his arms as gently as possible.

A wave of pain and terror immediately washed over her and she let out a cry that burned Porter's ears. He closed his eyes and wished there was room for a litter, but there wasn't, nor was there time to linger. He shifted her, getting his left arm under her shoulders and his right arm under her thighs. Most of her body was tucked under the blanket but her feet hung out, and her left arm clutched Porter's tactical vest with a death grip. Every ounce of strength she had left was routed to that arm, determined to hold on.

He felt it and he tightened his own grip as Denny put a flack jacket over her. He held a helmet as well but Porter shook his head. She was cradling her head against him, so Denny pulled the flack jacket up to cover her head as well.

Porter took slow steps out of the putrid room as he maneuvered with her through the narrow doorway. Denny and Ozzy cleared a path for him, and as they moved toward the entrance they picked up speed. At the front door they paused.

"You've got the comms, Den. I can't reach to transmit," Porter said.

"Right," he said, looking into the dark sky.

"Pegasus, we're ready to move Alice to the landing zone. Watch for friendlies."

"Copy that, Rabbit, we have visual on your designators," the pilot said, referring to the infrared strobe attached to each man's helmet, a visual aid to show the pilots which of the guys on the ground with guns were good and which ones weren't.

Porter looked out from behind a wall of men with suppressed rifles. To the north he saw Taggart and an SOV facing the right, rifles pointed in every direction up and out. To the left he saw Jenkins' back and another SOV doing the same facing south.

He looked at the satellite image in his head and went over the operation as he planned it. The route to the landing zone was down the street, turning right at the alley, and straight on to the grassy clearing where the vehicles should by now be poised on all four corners, and a sniper should be watching from above, with Apaches covering the perimeter.

We get her on that helicopter. No matter what. Nothing touches her.

———

Tim Miller saw three men on the monitor emerge from a building in the alley. Before he could fire his chain gun they were cut down by the minigun on top of the LTATV covering the corner. Miller looked for other targets and saw another door open in the building facing the landing zone. He centered on the first of three men out the door. Again he fingered the trigger but before he fired he saw the third man's chest explode, followed almost immediately by the second.

———

Phil Elliot moved his cross hairs a fraction of an inch to the right and centered on the last man standing. The insurgent had dropped his gun and was on the ground looking at his fallen comrade, who'd just crumpled. Phil waited while the man made a life or death decision. Unarmed and trapped under sniper fire, he could raise his hands in surrender and save his own life. Instead, the insurgent pushed the dead man's weight from his legs and grabbed the AK-47.

The insurgent's fingertips barely touched the gun before Phil's third shot of the night went through him. The sniper didn't see him crumble to the ground, he was already searching for another target.

———

"Movement on the roof," Rico said.

"I see it," Donovan answered.

They watched a man with a rifle peer over the edge into the street where the Rabbits were consolidated. The SEALs fired from the ground and the man fell backward. Rico saw the body roll away and lay still.

"They better get a move on," Donovan said and moved his camera to the door of building Bravo. He saw a shape come out that was distinctly different from the others. He magnified the image and saw an operator carrying a large bundle, then he noticed a pair of feet sticking out from under the blanket.

Tears stung his eyes, his chest pounded, and his breath was lost in his throat. He closed his mouth and took a deep breath through his nostrils, the oxygen bringing the composure he needed. He keyed the unit frequency.

"This is Pegasus One Three. Eyes on Alice."

"Copy that," Tim Miller said. "Focus on finding targets."

———

Jesus, please get her on that helo.

Tim looked at the gauntlet the Rabbits would have to run. It wasn't far, but the Blackhawk wasn't there yet and many eyes were watching. The Apache pilots knew there was little more they could do from the air without risking friendly fire casualties. And Ginger was right in the center of them. It was up to the men on the ground.

———

Porter heard sporadic fire on his right, and the buzz of the minigun to his left. He saw its muzzle flash as he stepped out onto the street, readjusted Ginger's weight, and heard her gasp from pain. She grabbed his vest even tighter.

"Let's move!" he said to Denny and started to run. Four Wonderland operators in front of him and four behind him mirrored his steps.

"Alice on the move. Caterpillar, do you read me?" Denny said.

"This is Caterpillar, copy, inbound," the invisible Blackhawk replied.

The men moved as a single deadly creature along the street. In twenty seconds they were past the LTATV and making the turn down the alleyway.

Porter ran as fast as he could under her weight, three shot bursts rang out to his side, behind him, and in front. His pace was steady, measured, and brisk, determined to run as fast as he could while also cushioning her from jarring. Shock and internal injuries were every bit as lethal as a bullet; it was the reason he chose to carry her instead of subject her to a bumpy ride in an SOV. He sheltered her as he ran and let his own body absorb the stress. All he could see was a wall of bodies in front of him as he pressed on.

Halfway down the alley. Almost there.

———

Phil saw two armed men run across the street parallel to the south alley. They moved with their backs along the wall, gearing up to make a trademark dash; insurgents almost always sent probers to run across a street and spray a magazine of AK rounds at the Americans to see how they would react.

Phil anticipated their path, and as soon as they took their first steps he dropped them.

"One Bravo," his spotter called out.

Phil turned his rifle to the designated sector on the far left, then moved his sight from Alpha, the ground, to Bravo, the roof. Phil saw lights turn on in several houses around the landing zone. He went from window to window assessing threats. Then he saw the circle of operators emerge from the alley and step onto the grass covered clearing. But he neither saw nor heard a helo overhead.

01:51:00

The Blackhawk made for the clearing but something wasn't right. He saw no strobes or movement around the landing zone.

This is the wrong one.

He pulled up to regain his bearings and double check the grid coordinates. He was over the right grid, but had gotten turned around over the terrain. He had expected to come at the landing zone from a southerly heading, but was forced to circle and hold back when the operators on the ground had taken longer than expected.

Now they're waiting on me. Damn.

The Night Stalker pilot made a hard turn and lined up with the landing zone. Now that there were lights on in the windows he saw the problem — there were two city blocks sitting side by side, each block had roughly three hundred houses laid out in a square maze with a grassy box-shaped clearing in the center. The layouts were identical but rotated 180 degrees away from one another, so that coming from either heading the one looked like the other.

The pilot made another violent turn, and the crew held on for a second approach.

—

Porter held Ginger tighter as he followed Denny onto the grass, her head low against his chest.

Denny stopped short when he realized the Blackhawk wasn't there. He swore, looked around the landing zone, and saw the perimeter defended by Rabbit vehicles and dismounted operators.

Porter dropped to the ground and rolled to cover Ginger. Like a three-pole tent he braced himself with his elbow, thigh, and right leg, contorting her into a fetal position and covering her head and chest with his body, his back exposed to the threats around them.

Denny followed his lead and covered Ginger and Porter with his body from a different direction. Ozzy and Taggart were next, and a second later six SEALs had roughly 1700 pounds of muscle and gear, including twelve plates of Kevlar body armor, around the woman they were all ready to die to protect.

None of the SEALs knew how long it would take for the helicopter to arrive, and none would move a muscle until it did so.

—

It looked like a pile of football players trying to recover a fumble, except it didn't move. Phil Elliot only vaguely understood what they were doing. One thing he knew very well was that they were fully exposed; a bad guy could probably kill all of them with one grenade. The sniper and his spotter scanned from window to window, rooftop to rooftop, assessing threats by the second and moving on, then back again.

"Four Alpha," Jeff said.

Phil swung the rifle to the grid just in time to see an operator on the ground drop a shooter in a doorway. He looked at the windows again, saw people looking out and pointing, heard shouting in Arabic.

"Two Bravo," Jeff called out.

They heard the rotor blades from an Apache and heard it fire its chain gun, saw a large portion of one of the rooftops explode in a cloud of dust as the 30mm shells dismantled the cheap concrete structure along with a man and his RPG.

"Uh, never mind. Wow."

Phil dialed in on another window, saw the end of a rifle thrust out. Phil fired a round at the man he couldn't see. There was no way to confirm the kill, but the rifle fell back into the room. A second later it reemerged and Phil dropped whoever held it. Phil focused again the roof of sector One.

Jeff saw something dart behind a dumpster. "Five Alpha," he said.

Phil turned and looked at the spot.

"Behind the dumpster," Jeff said.

Phil watched, could see only the edge of a foot, the rest of the body probably crouching.

"Two or three maybe," Jeff said.

Phil took a deep breath, stroked his trigger and waited for something to show itself.

———

"Caterpillar coming in hot," the pilot said when he saw all the shooting.

He saw the strobes from several helmets in a pile just off-center from the clearing, chem lights all around the landing zone, and vehicles on all four corners.

He angled up as he passed the roof and got into a perfect hover above the grass. He felt pinging from bullets hitting the side of his helicopter. He looked at the nearest roof and briefly saw a man with an RPG pointed directly at his face as he dropped the helo past the roofline and onto the ground.

———

Rico saw the figure drop to his knee and slide the RPG rocket into the launch tube. The Apache front seater had him in his sights when the Blackhawk turned to hover over the clearing, and pulled the trigger as the insurgent leveled the tube to his shoulder. Both man and roof were destroyed.

———

The Blackhawk landed with rotor spinning at full power as the debris from the Apache's shot rained over the men on the ground.

"Touchdown! Get her up," Mario shouted to the pile of bodies next to him.

The men peeled off of Porter one by one. He lifted his head, searching for the helo, and Mario and Ozzy put their hands on his shoulders to help him up as he repositioned his hold on Ginger. The SEALs oriented him in the right direction, keeping their backs exposed and shielding Ginger from the right and left, Denny in front of them.

Porter stumbled to get his legs under him and clutched Ginger as they made their way to the side of the helicopter. Denny stopped and moved aside to cover them with his rifle. Porter was at the open helo door and tried to lift her in to the men inside, but she wouldn't let go. Two pararescuemen reached their arms around her, but Porter felt the tension of Ginger's unrelenting grip on his tactical vest.

Get her on that bird, whatever it takes.

Porter thrust his knee into the door and lunged forward. The PJ's pulled both of them into the Blackhawk as one large mass.

———

"They've got RPG's! Tim, do we fire?" Tim's front seater was frantic.

While the Rabbits engaged small targets elsewhere, Tim had locked onto the dumpster in the shadows. He'd clearly seen three men with rockets dive behind it. His first instinct was to loose a Hellfire and kill them with one shot. But the rescue helo was too close. The explosion would send shrapnel everywhere, probably killing a Rabbit or two, maybe damaging the Blackhawk, or even crashing it.

A hydra rocket would be less powerful, but might do the same kind of damage. The 30mm was the best option but the rounds might ricochet toward Ginger, still well within the kill radius. One round could fly right through several men, and he didn't know what to do. His next instinct was to put his Apache on the ground to shield the Blackhawk; surely he was a juicer target than it was.

"Tim?" his front seater asked.

The three men on the screen ran out from behind the dumpster and fanned out, two on the right holding an AK and an RPG, one on the left with another RPG.

Tim caressed the trigger.

———

Phil saw them split off. He centered on the man to the left and fired, then immediately moved to the right and centered on the second. He fired again and saw the man fall backward as the insurgent next to him sprayed his AK-47. Phil put a round into his chest and watched him fall to the ground. He went back to the first RPG shooter on the left. No movement, kill confirmed. The Blackhawk's engines increased power behind him as it pulled away, the sound diminishing as it disappeared into the night.

He watched the courtyard for another thirty seconds as men on the ground ran to the LTATVs and SOVs. Phil clearly saw two of the Americans were stumbling, no doubt wounded by that last desperate spray.

The operators continued shooting as they remounted their vehicles for withdrawal. Phil heard another helicopter rotor behind him and felt its wind, and looked over his shoulder to see the Little Bird hovering five feet behind him, its skids perched on the edge of the wall.

"Madman need a ride?" the copilot waved.

Phil and his spotter jumped up, grabbed their gear, hopped onto the small helicopter and clipped in. It pulled up hard to the left, and he hugged his gun, trusting the strap to hold him to the Little Bird as he watched the city get smaller and smaller.

———

Tim Miller waited for the Rabbit vehicles to reenter the waiting C-17. As soon as the last one was in, the ramp closed and the large aircraft increased power for a short runway takeoff. It disappeared into the moonless night along with all of the Wonderland operators, save one.

"All Pegasus call signs," Tim heard Mitch Robinson's voice on the Apache's unit frequency. "We got her. Return to base." Robinson said, his voice slightly cracking.

Tim couldn't speak. Instead he texted a reply.
COPY.

———

The feed ended and the screen went to static. There was complete silence in the room as everyone waited for the president to react.

"Shields, are you there?" he said into the conference speaker on the table.

"Yes, Mr. President," Shields answered from Florida.

"Make sure you get on the phone and let Mr. Cooper know we've got her, and we're taking care of her as we speak. Make sure he hears it first from you, okay?"

"Yes, Mr. President. I'll call him right now."

"Thank you," the president said, getting up.

The rest of the room followed suit. The president made for the door and caught a look from Green.

"What?" the president asked his old friend.

"I just figured you'd want to speak with her dad personally," Green said.

"I'll call him later, when we know more. I want to be able to answer some of his questions," he said, putting on his suit coat. "Plus, I've got to get to a…something, tonight."

"Staff dinner for a non-profit, sir," his Chief of Staff said.

"Right," he said. As he passed, he put a hand on Green's shoulder and looked him in the eye. "Let your people know they did good work today. Let them know I said that, please."

"I will, Mr. President," Director Green said. "Zugzwang," he added, as the president was almost out of the room.

The president turned back and smiled, nodded, and left.

"What does that mean?" a staffer asked him.

Green smiled. "It's a long story."

Northern Iraq
01:59:00

The PJ put his hands on Ginger's shoulders and tried to speak over the noise of the aircraft.

"Ma'am, you're safe now. You can let go. Are you injured, Ma'am?"

Porter felt her grip ease slightly. He unclipped his helmet strap, letting it fall away, and pulled back so he could see Cooper's face. He remembered all of the intel he'd absorbed over the last several hours — her service record, physical features, personality type, and her nickname.

"Ginger," he said.

It was the first time she'd heard her name in days, and it jarred her out of the surreal place she'd been floating in. She had clarity, realized she was holding onto a soldier, and loosened her grip enough to look at him. The darkened skin of his painted face made his blue eyes stand out. He was so close she could feel his breath and she let go a little bit, took in the equipment around her, the aircraft's interior, felt the familiar hum of a helicopter's engines and rotor. She released the vest, pulled the blanket close, and started to sit up. Porter put his hand on her back to help her.

Ginger looked at the PJ kneeling next to her. He motioned for her to lie down. "Do you have any injuries ma'am?" he asked. She nodded. "Where are you injured ma'am?" he asked, as his counterpart took her arm to start an IV.

Everywhere.

"I don't know." Ginger let the PJ's do their job. She didn't know how to answer, didn't feel the IV enter her arm, or the blanket being removed and replaced in a manner that kept as much of her body covered as possible. She saw a metallic coated blanket unfurl as someone placed it on her, and caught sight of an American flag fastened to the ceiling of the Blackhawk.

A thousand thoughts bombarded her — Craig, her father, the men she flew with, and *them*, so many of *them*, mauling and beating her, and worse. She closed her eyes to black out the fear. A voice called to her, the same voice that managed to bring her rest in the darkest place on earth.

I still love you, it said.

She opened her eyes and saw the flag. Grief mixed with relief, and she shook and wept, and whether from the massive dose of pain-killing drugs from the IV or from some kind of supernatural mercy, the red, white, and blue flag blurred, the pain subsided, and a dark helicopter full of dangerous men carried her safely away.

———

Porter saw her face disappear under an oxygen mask, her head fall to the side with her eyes closed. He looked at the PJs and knew by their reactions she must be fairly stable.

Good, let her sleep.

He looked out the window of the helicopter and felt a sense of pride. He was a warrior, and as such, success usually meant someone had to die, or at the very least, violence was used to subdue them. He knew his actions over the past eight years in Iraq and Afghanistan had saved lives, but it was still a lonely calling. Most of the time all he really cared about was saving his own men, accomplishing the mission with everyone alive. He'd rescued people before, Americans even, but this was different. Maybe it was because she was a woman. Maybe seeing her so vulnerable, so desperate, had triggered in him an innate sense of protective duty. He really didn't know why this mission felt so different, and he made a mental note to check in with a friend who could probably break it down psychologically. All he knew was that he felt relieved, and good about what he'd done.

He reflected on the fact he'd left his men on the ground. *You didn't really have a choice. Denny and Jenkins will get them home.* He thought about his career, and about Jen waiting patiently for him to decide how long he wanted to continue. *Is she waiting for me? Has she already met someone who can make her forget all of this? Someone who will allow her to move on from Gator? Am I even allowed to love her? Would it dishonor him?*

Porter looked at Ginger again. One of the PJ's saw him and gave a thumbs-up.

We got her. This would be a pretty good mission to go out on. But the war's not over. Would I be quitting on them? Will it ever really be over? Porter turned back to the window and the darkened desert, wondered what would be in store for him when they landed. There would be after action reports, accounting, maybe fits of shaking as the adrenaline wore off, and perhaps he'd learn of casualties. *So much has happened since this morning. Was it really just this morning?*

He looked at his watch: *02:04:00*

No, it was yesterday.

Porter smiled, leaned back and closed his eyes, remembering the SEAL motto. *The only easy day was yesterday.*

22

Arming Teams

Contingency Operating Base: Foxtrot
02:15:00

Neither of the Apaches spoke on the way back, other than necessary communications. Tim and his gunner were silent throughout the landing and rearming procedures. The aircraft required power to rearm and Tim waited impatiently as they taxied and completed the post-mission necessities. His restless fingers picked at his gloves as he waited for them to finish.

Finally they parked and powered down. Tim raised the canopy and climbed out the side. He was down the ladder before his front seater, and rushed past his silent arming team, past dozens of men, all looking at him. He saw Eddie from a distance and tried not to make eye contact but caught it anyway; Eddie gave Tim a respectful nod and walked away, neither man able or interested in speaking.

Tim went straight through the headquarters and into his personal quarters, pulled the door shut behind him. As soon as he heard the click he fell to his knees and wept. The tears flowed, and days of pent up anger, fear, frustration, and worry burst forth like a dam. He stayed on his knees until the shaking passed, and more than once spoke three words, sometimes silently, sometimes out loud:

Thank you, Jesus.

Northern Iraq

"Ugh, you're right. I don't want to see," Ginger said in disgust, and handed the small mirror back to the Army nurse who was taking her blood pressure.

The nurse smiled. "The swelling will go down soon, and the bruising always looks worse than it is. How's the vision in that eye?"

"Cloudy, but better than it was earlier."

"Good," she smiled again. "Just give it some time."

An Army surgeon walked into the room. "There she is," he said, smiling as he put both hands on the side of her bed and leaned toward Ginger.

"I'm Dr. Arbanas. I heard you were coming around. How are you feeling, pain-wise?"

"Pretty good now, I guess," she said, feeling the effects of whatever magical drug the nurse had just administered.
"Do you know where you are?" Arbanas asked.

"Yeah, we went over that," Ginger said trying to sit up and leaning on her bad arm. She fell back in pain that the drugs couldn't mask.

"You've got a lot of injuries we need to deal with, but for now I just want to get you comfortable and rested. Okay?"

"Okay," Ginger said, grateful to simply do nothing. "First we'll deal with the pain, that will be mission A," he said, "then we'll move on to other things like cleaning out those wounds so they don't get infected, fixing that arm, et cetera. It's gonna take a while but we'll get there." He gave her another gentle smile. Scott Arbanas, a longtime ER doctor in the busiest hospital in Boston before getting called up after 9/11, had enough experience to know what she needed most.

Ginger's questions faded in the stupor of the drugs, but one question, the only one she really cared about, fought its way out. "Am I going to fly again?"

Scott smiled. "I don't see why not. I've seen pilots banged up worse who've gotten back in the saddle. But don't worry about that now. First we need to fix you, okay?"

"Okay," she said. It was enough.

"Is there a family member or anyone you'd like to speak with?" he asked, mindful of the delicate balance, the emotional lift against the potential harm of stress.

"Yes, my father, if that's possible."

"Sure. I actually already spoke to him earlier. He knows you're safe," he said, hoping she'd hold off on that conversation for now.

Ginger wondered what all of this meant for her squadron. "My C.O. maybe?"

"Yeah, he's here." Scott motioned for the nurse to show Mitch Robinson in.

Robinson came up to the bed cautiously but with a strong smile. "Hey there, kiddo. Man, it's good to see you again."

Another wave of emotion came as guilt flooded over her.

"I'm sorry…" she sobbed. "Craig? He's gone?"

Arbanas knew her blood pressure was spiking but he let the scene play out; the grief was necessary and therapeutic, in its own way. A tear fell from Robinson's eye as he pulled up the stool next to Ginger. He nodded.

"He's on his way home now."

Ginger closed her eyes and imagined Cecilia, the rest of Craig's family, and their grief at seeing Craig's casket rolled out onto a tarmac. She asked a question she didn't want answered, but she had to know.

"How?"

"In the crash," Robinson said, and left it at that.

She stared at Mitch, spoke with a strained voice. "I tried to cut him loose. I tried to fight them…" and then she cried, and they waited until she was able to wipe her tears while Arbanas motioned for Robinson to wrap it up soon.

"We know, Ginger. It wasn't your fault. It's just war," Robinson said, putting his hand over hers.

She thought about Craig, the Marines on the ground, the men who had come to rescue her. She thought about the men in her unit, Donovan, Tim, and her arming team. "I think I'd like to try and sleep before calling my dad, is that alright?"

Both men nodded, relieved. They made to leave and Dr. Arbanas lowered the lights. But as Robinson was about to walk out, Ginger stopped him.

"Sir?"

"Yeah?"

"Can you send a message for me?"

"Yeah, probably. To whom?"

COB: Foxtrot

Eddie walked into the TOC and an intelligence officer waved him over. The man stood and gave him his seat at the computer terminal. On the screen was an email from Mitch Robinson:

To Eddie from Ginger: "Sorry I broke your bird?"

Eddie leaned back in the chair and wiped his eyes. He took a deep breath and then asked, "Can I send a reply?"

"Sure, go for it," the officer said.

Robinson smiled. He'd show her the reply later, after she'd had a chance to sleep. Eddie's email read:

We've got lots of birds. We've only got one Ginger. Gonna miss you, little sister.

23

The Only Easy Day

Al Asad Airbase, Iraq

Porter pulled off his ball cap, ran his hands over his throbbing head, and rubbed his eyes. He opened a bottle of ibuprofen, chased four of the pills with a Monster energy drink, and pulled the filthy cap tight down again. He finished with the last of the forms, grateful he could now go for a walk and knock out the headache that always seemed to accompany the dreaded desk work. He'd be at this for the rest of the afternoon, but he needed to clear his head.

He entered a hangar where Denny was overseeing the preparation of several pallets for the return home. There was still so much to do with the platoon scheduled to leave for Virginia that none of the elite SEALs had even bothered to call loved ones back home. Mission preparations were set for the next day, likely to be followed with a redeployment. It was a rush order. *Probably back to Afghanistan. Probably in less than a month.* Wherever JSOC wanted them, and whatever it wanted them to train for, one thing was certain: it wasn't going to be in Iraq — for now, anyway.

He finished his drink and followed it with a water bottle on his way to the chow. He noticed a man standing alone on the tarmac with a large rucksack and a rifle. *I almost missed him.*

Porter was so wrapped up in the platoon's orders he'd completely forgotten the Iraqi was leaving. He jogged over and Ozzy smiled, saluted, and extended his hand.

"Sir."

Porter shook it. "Almost missed you. I got bogged down and forgot you were shipping out today."

"You are busy man, sir. There is no offense. Thank you for seeing me."

Porter wished he'd done something for him, wished he had something to give him from the unit. He wanted to let him know he mattered. If they'd had time, the SEALs would have given him some guff, or pranked him; instead he was just leaving with hardly a goodbye. Denny had mentioned it yesterday, but Ozzy got lost in the shuffle.

"What's next for you?" Porter asked.

Ozzy smiled. "Hopefully home for week or two, but I will see. I was given command of a unit of ISOF."

"I know, I put you in for it," Porter said.

The Iraqi Special Operations Forces, the most elite unit of the Iraqi army, was on the verge of deteriorating into the strong arm of the new Iraqi leader. With the wrong motivations and poor leadership it was destined to morph into a death squad, which is why the Americans were still figuring out what to do with it. A SEAL commander had the unenviable task of turning it into something akin to the American JSOC. That commander asked Porter for a list of potential leaders, and Porter knew just the guy.

"Figured there wasn't anyone better to clean up the dirty brigade," Porter said.

Ozzy laughed. "I thank you, sir. I…" Ozzy choked up. "I will always appreciate what you've taught me…Porter, sir."

Porter got in close so they were almost nose to nose. He spoke with authority. "Don't back down an inch. Tolerate nothing. Get them on board or send them packing." Porter put his hands on his hips in the manner of a drill instructor. "Will you ever quit?" he said almost in a shout.

Ozzy stood tall, and answered in a firm voice. "If knocked down, I will get back up, every time. I will draw on every remaining ounce of strength to protect my teammates and to accomplish our mission. I am never out of the fight."

Porter put out his hand. Ozzy took it and they shared a powerful handshake with locked eyes.

"I hope we meet again, brother," Porter said.

"Me too…Skipper."

Ozzy bit his lip as a helicopter landed nearby. He took his gear and climbed in the Blackhawk, and gave a short wave as the helicopter lifted away and disappeared into the brown sky.

Porter put his hands back on his hips, looked at the ground, shook his head. His stomach growled. He turned around and saw the base was busy with activity, the war pausing for nobody, and he moved on.

Oceana Naval Air Station
Virginia Beach, Virginia

Porter clicked the stopwatch. *Over a minute. Too slow.* He walked toward the men reassembling at the front of the structure, a concrete mockup of a Middle Eastern style compound. He saw Mario limp toward him holding one of the ladders.

"Tell me you know how to use a ladder," Porter mocked, pointing to the rungs. "Your feet go on those."

Most of the SEALs laughed even though they were exhausted from running the assault over and over in the stifling Virginia heat. "Run 'em again," Porter said to the SEAL Master Chief who was spearheading the assault team, and his phone rang.

"Porter," he answered. The Master Chief saw a perplexed look on his face.

"Copy that," Porter said, and hung up. "Here," he said, handing the stopwatch to one of the trainers. "Nobody eats till they clear it under a minute. I've got to go to the principal's office for something."

"Whatever, enjoy the air conditioning," the Master Chief said. Porter splashed him with his water bottle.

A few minutes later he walked into the headquarters building and made his way to the Admiral's office.

"You missed 'em, probably at the range," his aide said when Porter walked in.

"Who's 'they?'" Porter asked, annoyed.

"Better hurry," the aide smiled and pointed.

He shook his head and rushed off toward the shooting range. *I don't have time for this crap.* He walked out the doors and around the compound until he found several officers, including Admiral Buchanan, standing around a man wearing a grey polo shirt and jeans, laying on the ground behind a .50 caliber sniper rifle.

Porter waited among the small crowd of SEAL commanders. He saw several civilians he didn't recognize.

"Take a deep breath," he heard Taggart say, "and when you're ready, pull the trigger. It'll give a heck of a kick, sir."

The man fired and two of the civilians jumped from the sound.

"Wow," the shooter said, standing up and leaving the weapon on its bipod. Taggart safed the weapon. "I don't suppose I even came close, did I?" the man asked.

"Negative, Mr. President," Buchanan said, holding the binoculars. "Would you like to take another shot?"

"Oh, no. I'm good. Damn thing would probably knock my shoulder out of socket," he said, laughing.

The President of the United States turned, noticed Porter, and walked toward him. Porter was stunned and unsure how to react. He saluted, wondering if the Commander in Chief would remember they'd met once before.

"Mr. President, sir. It's an honor to have you here."

The president held out his hand and Porter accepted the handshake. "Lieutenant Dawkins, it's good to see you again, son. The honor is mine, I assure you. I hate to take you away from your business. I understand you're training for a mission."

Porter felt like a fool. "No sir. I mean, yes sir, we are, but another officer is taking care of it. How can I be of assistance?"

The president motioned for Buchanan. "General DeBerg has informed me that Operation Wonderland was your baby."

"Sir, there were many people who contributed. I'm just happy we accomplished the mission."

"No doubt," he said. Buchanan pulled out a long box, opened it, and held it for the president.

"I watched it all play out," the president said, removing a medal from the box. He looked at Porter. "I watched every step as you carried Chief Cooper to that helo. Watched you men cover her." He looked around. "I was real proud of you gentleman that day." He made eye contact with Denny, Taggart, and the other SEALs watching, unsure who else was involved.

"Normally we'd do this at the big house, with all sorts of cameras and fancy clothes and all." The president pinned the Navy Cross on Porter's t-shirt. "I'm afraid that's not in the cards at the present," he looked Porter in the eye, "and I wanted to make sure I caught you in person before you went back out." He leaned in to whisper to Porter. "Plus, this gives me an excuse to come over and play with all of your fun toys," he said, and winked.

Porter grinned. "Yes sir, that's fine sir," was all he could say.

He looked him in the eye again, and got serious. "With the deepest gratitude, your nation recognizes your uncommon valor, and your steadfast determination to place the welfare and security of others before your own."

Porter was speechless and tried to think of a proper response, only to settle on, "Thank you, sir."

They turned to face the official photographer, followed by a round of handshakes.

"Now don't worry," the president said so the others could hear, "I'll have you and your parents over for lunch one of these days and we'll get your mom all teary eyed and such. Then maybe we can watch a ballgame with a beer or two."

"They would certainly appreciate that, sir," Porter said.

"One condition," the president said. "I wouldn't wear that Sox hat if I were you," he said. "My wife is a lifelong Yankees fan. She'll kick you out."

Porter couldn't believe he'd just received the second highest award in the Navy while wearing a sweaty t-shirt and a dirty ball cap, but he loved the president for it.

"I'll leave it at home, sir. Rest assured."

"Mr. President," Buchanan said, "I understand you'll be joining us for lunch, but before that I'd be happy to take you on a tour of the facility."

"Sounds great, Admiral," he said, putting a hand on Porter's shoulder. "Lead the way, we'll catch up."

The procession went ahead, except for the two secret service agents who kept their distance.

When everyone was out of earshot, the president asked Porter, "So, let me hear it. No filter, son. How's it going over there?"

Porter wondered what to say, never imagining he'd have this kind of access to the president. He remembered Iraq before the surge, the daily carnage, and the failing morale. He recalled all of the successes they'd managed to achieve, block by block, tribe by tribe, from small villages to large cities all across the nation. And he remembered Ozzy.

"Sir. It's a long way from good. But it's night and day compared to a year ago." The president said nothing. Porter could tell he was waiting for him to continue.

"I know in a few months it won't be up to you, sir," Porter said, referring to the upcoming election, "but if you have any influence over your successor," he stopped and looked at the president, "let whoever wins know, we want to finish the job." The president nodded. Porter thought about Shep and others.

"Let 'em know that good men have died to get us where we are. We can beat them. They need to let us beat them." Porter took a deep breath, hoping he wasn't out of line. "Sir."

"I know you can, Lieutenant Dawkins. Be assured, I will let em know that."

They walked the rest of the way in silence, the president knowing that for all of his suggestions, warnings, and pleas, it simply might not matter.

———

Porter sat in the deck chair on Jen's apartment patio, slowly peeling the label off the beer bottle. *Tell her. Say something. You owe her something.* Jen sat watching the traffic below — families walking by pushing strollers, couples holding hands, enjoying a normal life. There was only one thing left to say that hadn't been said before and they both knew it. But still, he couldn't.

"Well, I guess I'll see you in a few years, then," Jen said with a tone that was intentionally cold.

Porter wanted to get angry but held it in. He knew she was right to be angry, that he should tell her, now, marry her tomorrow even. At the very least he should tell her he loved her. But he couldn't, wouldn't put her heart at risk. He couldn't let her become a widow twice over, he loved her too much for that. And, there was also Gator. Could Porter ever allow himself to love her knowing she was Gator's wife? She probably, hopefully, always would be the wife of the man Porter had loved most.

Jen stood, paced the railing for a moment, and put both hands on the hot metal bar. She watched the setting sun and remembered all the nights she'd looked out on this beach, praying for Porter's safety as she waited for him.

Years of uncertainty and putting her life on hold. How many more years before he was home for good? And even then, would anything ever happen? She wondered if this was the end, if she should let herself move on.

She turned to look at him and saw him hanging his head in defeat. She remembered with ferocious clarity that she'd only ever seen him that way once before, in a hospital room corner chair, holding her husband's trident in his hands as his best friend slipped away. She loved him then, and she loved him even more now.

Jen made another decision.

She walked to him and held out her hand. He looked up at her and took it gently. She raised him to standing and looked into his eyes, then wrapped her arms around him, burying her head into his chest.

Porter held her gently, but Jen held him tight. She heard Gator's voice as she hugged him, remembering what he always used to tell her: *My word is my bond.* She made a declaration of her own, and only death would change it.

"I'll be here. I'm not going anywhere," she said.

24

Rebuilds

Kansas City, Missouri

Ginger stared out the passenger window. From behind the wheel Marcus stole glances at her. He searched for words of encouragement but had nothing to offer.

"You know," he said finally, "you don't *have* to do this."

"Dad, we've been over it."

"I know," he paused, "but maybe it's too soon…for all of you?"

Ginger squirmed in her seat, shifted her belly over, trying to get comfortable in the Camaro's leather seat and wishing they'd driven the motorhome instead. All she wanted to do was lay down; the tendons in her hip and the newly healed bones in her leg and arm all contributed to her discomfort.

But the Camaro was her idea. They'd get there faster, she'd argued, but deep down she thought it might be therapeutic — like their road trips in the old days. By the time they reached a Travelodge in Albuquerque she was ready to call it quits, but didn't want to worry her dad. He already stressed over her myriad injuries, so for his sake she decided to suck it up and keep the pregnancy woes to herself.

She ate another French fry. Fortunately she was always hungry, and it helped. "If I don't do it now, I might never."

Marcus nodded his approval and checked the directions against a piece of paper.

"Ever think of getting a GPS, Dad? You know, technology?"

"Naw, I'm good." He made a few turns through the neighborhood before pulling to a stop in front of a large three-story brick home.

"Yup, this is it," Ginger said.

Marcus put his hand on her shoulder., and she unbuckled, reached over, and gave him a hug, her belly digging into the gear shifter.

"I'm ready." She smiled through gritted teeth.

They walked up the path as dried leaves fluttered past, others crunched under their feet. The scent of fall refreshed her and she gained courage with each step. *Lord, help me.*

Marcus rang the doorbell. Peter Allen opened the oak door with a smile, and behind him Cecilia put a hand to her mouth, pushed past her husband, and hugged Ginger.

"I'm so glad you're here," she said, wiping her eyes.

"You've been on the road for days," Peter said, motioning them inside. "Let's go on in and get comfortable."

Cecilia held Ginger's hand and escorted her to the sitting room in front of a warm fireplace. "Sit here, and if you want to lay down you go right ahead," she said, taking Ginger to a large loveseat.

"Can I get you guys anything to drink?" Peter asked.

"Coffee would be great," Marcus said.

"Absolutely," Peter said ushering a couple of curious Allen children out of the room.

"You'll meet them later," Cecilia said. "They're all anxious to see you, but we don't want to overwhelm you."

Ginger didn't know what to say. The script she'd been working on through five states utterly escaped her.

Cecilia seemed to read her thoughts and let her collect herself.

"Long drive, but I imagine it was beautiful," she said to Marcus.

"Oh yeah, the southwest is amazing," he said, then stopped himself.

"But it goes downhill after that," she smiled and laughed.

"Well…yeah," Marcus said sheepishly.

"I know. Peter and I used to do road trips when we were younger and had less kids. The plains are pretty boring compared with the rest of the country, but it's home," she said. "Craig was amazed the first time he saw real mountains."

Ginger was terrified to broach the subject of Craig, and couldn't hide her discomfort.

Cecilia patted her on the thigh. "But he loved them," Cecilia smiled, "just like he loved flying with you."

Ginger lowered her head, tears streaming down her face. Marcus began to stand but Cecilia held up her hand and shook her head. He reluctantly sat back down.

"Ginger?" she said, taking her hand. Ginger looked at her. "I miss him so much, we all do. But he's gone, and we have to move on. He would want you to move on."

Peter knelt on the other side of Ginger and handed her a tissue. "Craig used to brag on you all the time. He'd tell us about how you'd start singing a show tune while on a mission. How confident you were and how fun. He was always proud of how much joy you spread." He paused. "You can't let them steal that from you."

Ginger cried some more but the pain gave way to something else.

"They're right," Marcus said.

After several seconds Cecilia asked, "Did Craig give you the letter I sent back with him?"

Ginger nodded, and answered softly. "I kept it in the pocket of my flight suit. They…they took it."

Marcus had to look away. Peter pursed his lips.

"Do you remember what I told you?" Cecilia said.

Ginger looked at her with desperation. "By heart, every line."

"It's true, every line," Cecilia said. "We will *always* love you, Ginger. You were family to Craig and you're family to us." Cecilia put a hand on Ginger's belly. "All of you, forever," and she hugged her, and Peter joined them.

Marcus took a deep breath and wiped tears from his own eyes.

Ginger sat within their arms and reflected on all of the years her father had spent raising her alone. She had no memory of the mother who left when she was too young to understand. Now, she had a mother, and an extra father, and for the first time in a long time she felt a measure of hope.

"Thank you," Ginger said finally. "I really miss that little punk," she laughed through tears. "I…everyone who knew him…they were better for it."

Cecilia choked up. "Thank you."

Peter put a hand on his wife's shoulder. "We'd be honored if you'd stay for dinner. We also have a couple of spare bedrooms if you're weary of hotels."

"No, we don't want to impose," Marcus said.

Ginger looked at Cecilia. "That would be nice, actually. The hotel beds have been killing my back."

"Okay with you?" Peter asked Marcus.

Marcus held up his hands in surrender. "She outnumbers me."

"We'll see to it, then," Peter said. "I noticed your '68 when you pulled up. Nice car. I understand you restore vehicles for a living."

"Yeah, I'm always working on something."

"Here," he said, getting up, "I've got something you might be interested in." Peter led Marcus out, winking to Cecilia as they retired to the garage. Cecilia mouthed the words *thank you*, and rubbed Ginger's back, ready to do what she'd always done best — listen.

In the garage, Marcus saw a near-pristine vintage Chevy truck.

"Advance Design, '47," Peter said.

Marcus peered in the windows, admired the curves of its exterior, and walked around it quietly, careful not to touch another man's baby.

"She's almost done. Still having some trouble with the engine, hard to find the old parts. I've had to have some custom made. Not cheap."

"She's beautiful."

Peter looked at him. "Craig and his brother Casey and I used to work on her, till Craig joined up. I kinda feel like she needs to drive again. For him, maybe. Maybe it's silly, but it helps me deal with it."

"After we found out," he paused, "we prayed day and night for Ginger to make it home safe." Peter put his hand on the hood of the truck and patted it. "She'll be back in action soon enough."

Marcus nodded.

"Casey doesn't even want to look at it anymore. It's been hard. But hey, if you'd like to take a look under the hood, I'd be grateful to get some expert advice."

Marcus was relieved to finally be in a familiar place. "Absolutely. Be a shame to see her bottled up in a garage forever. What do you do for a living?" he asked.

"Actually," Peter smiled, "I do counseling."

"Oh good," Marcus laughed, "maybe we could swap some advice."

"Yeah, maybe," Peter said, and put a hand on Marcus's shoulder.

—

As the minutes passed, Ginger let her guard down completely and unloaded everything. She'd been alone or surrounded by men for most of her life, never realizing how much she needed another woman.

For the first time, she opened up and the long process of healing began — not by the magic words of a mom who has all the answers, but by the attentive ear of a woman with no agenda.

———

Kirkuk Province, Iraq

The base commander finished his speech, and one by one the soldiers filed past the stone pillar. It would stay in place for as long as the base remained. Years later, the memorial would be moved to its final destination, in front of a building at a U.S. Army Apache training facility. But for the time being, it would stand in Iraq at the entrance of the recently renamed Contingency Operating Base: Allen.

———

J.T. finished and handed the can of paint back to Tony, who took it and used the fine brush to write his own message on one of the Apache's Hellfire missiles. When he was done he took a step back and examined it with equal measures of reverence and disgust. He handed the can to Eddie.

Eddie looked up at the empty cockpit, remembering all the times he'd seen Ginger up in a cockpit like this one smiling at him, or Craig doing something goofy. He wondered if he'd ever see Ginger up there again.

Then he remembered Craig, and got angry. He gripped the can, spit on the ground, and took a step toward the machine he loved, the finest instrument of war the world had ever seen, and wrote his own inscription on each of the Hellfire missiles.

FOR CRAIG

25

Ends and Beginnings

The young soldier stood on the street corner, his slung rifle pointing toward the ground. He watched the chaos on the street and tried to mask his anger, wondering what his grandfather would have done. The monsters in front of him had literally taken everyone he loved — first his parents, then his grandparents, then his relatives who fled in terror, all killed. He alone chose to stay, the last remnant of the stubborn defiance passed down from his grandfather, who'd given his livelihood, his fingers, and later his life, all because he refused to let them win.

The young soldier wanted to kill them, all of them, but not yet. First he wanted to defeat them, to relegate them to the gallows and see the fear in their eyes when he and the army behind him retook the country he loved. A martyr's death was too good for such scum. He wanted them to feel the defeat he'd felt all these years. He knew the battle would come, maybe soon, but not today.

He could wait.

He glanced at the men beside him and wondered about their loyalty. His army was falling apart, divided by religious and tribal factions, and some of the same men he served with would no doubt join the other side the first chance they got. What would happen when the Americans left for good? Would his country fall apart, subdued or terrorized into capitulation? Were any of his fellow soldiers concerned more with honor than a quick payday? He feared the answer was no.

He watched as their trucks drove past, teeming with rowdy, bloodthirsty savages boldly claiming victory over the invaders and waving a flag. It was not the flag he and his grandfather fought for, but a new, ghastly black one brandished with malice in white handwritten Arabic script and a white circle with three words in the middle. It was the flag of the Islamic State of Iraq and Syria, an organization quickly gaining notoriety in the west by its better known acronym, ISIS.

As one of the trucks passed, the soldier recognized a man in the passenger seat, a new recruit. The man waved at him, then drew his finger across his neck in a slashing motion, and smiled.

—

Baghdad

A small band played while roughly two hundred American troops watched in silence as the American flag slowly descended. When it was down, the honor guard carefully folded it for the return home. There was no fanfare, no grand gestures, and certainly no smiles.

The enthusiastic hope of the Iraqis who, only eight years earlier, celebrated the flag's erection as a symbol of their liberation from the guiles of a dictator, now watched its lowering with ambivalence.

—

Iraq/Kuwait border

What a waste.

Command Sergeant Major Lewis wondered if this was the last time he'd see this country. He stroked his chin and took a drink of water as he watched the caravan of trucks approach the border into Kuwait.

The irony was not lost on him that for all of his loathing of Iraq, he was nonetheless frustrated to be leaving. He thought back to that day four years earlier — "You're going home," they'd told him after his unexpected medevac inside the cockpit of an Apache. It seemed like a thousand years ago.

"Screw that," he'd replied that day, even as his body languished in the ICU. He'd resolved then and there that he would return to the fight, and dedicated the next six months to recovering. He treated physical therapy like an enemy, his singular focus was on returning to his unit, his awards for valor he felt were undeserved.

"Why am I getting an award for doing my job?" he told the commanders who presented them. *And poorly, at that?* He went over his actions as best he could remember, but the battle was fragmented, fuzzy. The most prominent thing he remembered from that day was death and loss. *Deaths that need to matter.* And so he fought his way back into active duty, stayed in this Army, and returned to Iraq.

But Iraq never remained static. And just as the Iraq of 2003 was a lifetime removed from 2008, so too was the Iraq he returned to. Civilian leaders on both sides of the war seemed unwilling to let him and his men win, piling deadly restrictions on them in the form of Rules of Engagement that seemed anything but. They were a joke, the Army confined by them rendered impotent, for all practical purposes. Then, the last straw — their own government refused to defend American troops against Iraqi civilian courts. It was too much, and so the pompous civilian bureaucrats accomplished what the enemy fighters could never do: remove American soldiers from the field of battle.

Many times in the past few months he remembered his father's frustration. His father had watched Saigon and the South Vietnamese soldiers he'd trained get overrun by an inferior enemy, abandoned by a world weary of their plight, and obtuse of the larger implications.

Then, like now, with all the cards stacked in the Americans' favor, the will to win simply evaporated, not in the men who carried the guns but in those behind oak desks, more concerned with carrying the next election.

Are they going to redeploy my men to Afghanistan? Keep us in Kuwait? Send us home? There was still plenty of fight in him, in all of them, and if tomorrow orders came to storm back across the border, he'd relish the opportunity. *We'll beat them here, anywhere, if you let us.*

They had fought the enemy across Iraq for most of his adult life. *Patton was right.* The command sergeant major smiled as he remembered his favorite quote from the legendary general. *The best way to defend is to attack, and the best way to attack is to attack.*

He looked up and caught a glimpse of an F-16 covering his 4000 man caravan, the last troops to leave this country. He looked at the vehicle ahead and reflected on the billions of dollars of military hardware around him. He thought about his men who had never known defeat, and wondered if they would consider this a victory.

<hr>

Fort Bragg, North Carolina

"Allen, he tapped out…let him up…Allen!"

Casey Allen reluctantly released his grip and shoved the gasping soldier away from him. The nearly-unconscious man rolled over, struggling to breathe before finally coughing face down on the mat.

"What the hell was that, Allen?" one of the soldiers said as Casey jumped to his feet.

Casey took a step toward him. "You next?"

"Chill, Davis, your boy's fine," Demarius said.

"Shut up, Smith!" Davis said, getting in Casey's face. "You trying to kill him?"

Casey didn't answer. He looked at Davis with a detached stare that silenced the verbal portion of their exchange.

Demarius saw the familiar look. "Come on now," he said, trying to defuse the ticking time bomb. "Ain't Allen's fault ya boy can't fight. He called him out, right?" He held out his arms, employing the assistance of the crowd. "Right?"

Davis backed off, inwardly relieved. The other soldiers moved out of Casey's way as he stepped off the sparring mat and into the locker room. Demarius followed him. When they were alone, Demarius spoke to his friend.

"That was messed up, bro."

Casey ignored him, retrieving his keys and wallet from the locker.

"What?" Demarius said, angry. "You gonna trip on me now?"

Casey looked at him.

"Don't play me like that. Not me," he said.

Casey looked at him as he put on his uniform jacket, maintaining eye contact while he buttoned the cuffs. Then he smiled and held out his fist. The bump settled the conflict, and they put on their dark green berets last before closing the lockers and walking out. As they exited the base gym they overheard two of the former spectators, speaking about the match.

"Because he made fun of Allen's tat," one of them was saying.

"What is it?" the other asked.

"Some horse with wings, or something."

Casey Allen took a step toward them and Demarius shook his head.

"It's a pegasus." His voice turned heads across the gym. "And it's none of your damn business," he said, walking out.

Whiteman Air Force Base, Missouri
2012

Major General Josiah McCoy walked under the nose of the A-10 Thunderbolt. He ran his hand underneath the cannon, admiring the artwork as he always did before ascending the stairs to his cockpit. He got situated and lowered the canopy. The General Electric TF34 turbofan engines roared to life and the aircraft turned to start its taxi.

Josiah squared up with the runway, throttled the engines as he'd done a thousand times, and lifted off into a clear Sunday morning sky, shortly followed by three additional Hogs.

Once airborne, Josiah adjusted their heading and took the lead in the Fingertip Formation, with two A-10s on his right and one on his left. He watched the green landscape of urban Missouri pass underneath. It was a short flight, and unarmed, yet the weight of it seemed somehow magnified. His military career had been dedicated to using this machine to save lives in support of men and women on the ground.

This was the first time he intended to use it to show off, and there were five spectators in particular he was anxious to do so for.

—

Arrowhead Stadium
Kansas City, Missouri

"Ladies and gentlemen," Cecilia Allen heard over the stadium loudspeaker. "Please stand as we honor America with the singing of our national anthem."

The Allen family stood along with 76,000 others as the song began. For Cecilia, this was always the worst part. All her life the anthem brought tears to her eyes, but for the past four years, the anthem seared her with memories of Craig whenever she heard it, especially here.

Cecilia sang along loudly, and remembered singing it here with her firstborn son when he was a baby in her arms. She remembered singing it another time, reminding preteen Craig to remove his hat, and remembered watching him sing alongside her as a young man in uniform.

Though it tore at her heart she would never let it play without singing along with it. And she sang today, with Peter's arm tight around her, and all but two of the remaining Allen children beside her — Casey in North Carolina, and Birdie on a Navy ship in the Persian Gulf.

—

Stacy McCoy sang with her hand on her heart but turned away from the flag; she was waiting to see something else. Abigail noticed and joined her, squinting to catch the movement on the horizon. They stood, arguably behind the worst seats in the stadium — the highest row near the jumbotron — but the football game was sideshow. The main attraction for the McCoy family was on approach, five clicks to the rear.

Stacy beamed and Abigail tapped the youngest McCoy on the shoulder. "Look," she told the eight-year-old next to her, who also turned. The music and the crowds singing couldn't drown out the older boys' enthusiasm when they caught sight of the flight of Warthogs.

—

The final lines of the anthem rang out and Cecilia raised her left hand while patting her heart with her right. She emptied her lungs for the nation she loved, the men and women dedicated to protecting it, and those who would never return.

A flight of four A-10 Thunderbolts flew in perfect formation over the stadium. As they passed, streams of fireworks filled the sky with booming sounds that jolted her chest — a painful balm that soothed her spirit and allowed her to let go of what might have been, for what remained: the pride of a mother for her fallen hero.

———

Josiah peered out of the canopy in a vain attempt to catch sight of his family in the sea of red. When he was just about to pass out of view of the crowd, he made good on his promise to his little girl.

This is for you, Stacy.

———

Stacy McCoy was all grins. The jets were so low she could almost see her dad in the cockpit. They passed over the stadium and just before disappearing behind the opposite stands she caught sight of the lead aircraft ever so slightly tip his wings.

She beamed, knowing he'd done it just for her. A tear came to her eye as she remembered all of the years he'd been absent for the first twelve years of her life.

No more.

In an hour or two he'd be back, sitting right beside her. The war was over, and her dad was home.

———

Tal Afar, Iraq

"Hazail, come away from the window," Ozzy said to his daughter.

She peeled herself away from the riotous scene below and sat on the sofa, shaking with fear.

"Where would you have us go?" Dwura asked her husband.

"I don't know yet," he said looking outside, "but we can't stay here. You know what they will do…to you, and…" he motioned to Hazail watching them. The girl turned and worry spread over her pale face.

"We should have left months ago," he said under his breath.

"Oh, so it's my fault!" Dwura said. "I'm not afraid of them."

"No," Ozzy said, frustrated. "It's not about fear." His voice was soft and he took his wife's hand to calm the storm behind her eyes. "I wouldn't have you run. And if I were able, I'd stay here and fight every last one of them."

"Well, maybe you should, then." She pulled her hand away and crossed her arms.

From the other window, Goriel turned to face his mother. "No. No, he must go," the young soldier said. "I can stay, but Father needs to return to his command. He's been gone too long already."

His parents looked at him, both fierce and professional in his uniform, expertly clutching his rifle. "Without him many will simply peel away. He's one of few they trust, the only one they will follow. We can't defeat them without him," he said, looking at his mother.

Dwura paced the room. "I know," she said finally, and went to her son. "They need both of you." She put a hand on his cheek and turned back to Ozzy.

"A few of us have been preparing for this. I'll contact them, and we'll go north together," she looked at her daughter, "tonight."

"We can spare a couple of days," Ozzy said. "We'll take you far enough so we know you're safe. Somewhere where I can keep in contact with you."

"Safe?" Dwura said, looking in her husband's eyes. "There is no safe in this world. But the Lord will protect us." She leaned in and kissed him. "And you must go and fight them," she said with her head against his chest, facing Goriel. "Both of you."

Epilogue

Eagle River, Alaska

Ginger stood from her seat, gathered up her belongings, and joined the crowd as it made its way out of the church auditorium. She shared words with acquaintances, smiled at some people she was beginning to recognize, and headed toward the childcare rooms.

She waited in line as parents took turns picking up their four-year-olds. She scanned the room full of toddlers and made eye contact. She smiled. The little girl's face lit up as she dropped the toy and ran to the pony wall separating them.

"Mommy!" she said, clapping her hands.

"Hi, beautiful," she said as she signed the childcare pick up sheet.

"She did awesome, as always," said the helper.

"Thanks. Ready to go, sweetie?" Ginger asked as the little girl made her way out of the gate.

The woman looked at Ginger. "Your last name is Cooper, right?"

"Yes," Ginger said, smiling.

"So, you work with my husband at Wildman Aviation, Dave Wilde."

"Oh, yeah, he's my new boss. I didn't realize," she said laughing.

"Yeah, I didn't make the connection till the other day. He and Rod were talking about this new pilot, Cooper. Normally I tune out the flyboy talk but the way they were going on...you could tell they were impressed." She lightly touched Ginger's arm. "And they never compliment new guys, like, ever. So I asked about this 'Cooper' and it all made sense."

"That's so funny. Yeah, they certainly have pretty high standards. It's been fun though."

"Well, you must be pretty good. He said he's never seen someone so comfortable in bad weather, that you can land darn near anywhere. He mentioned you flew Apaches. Is that right?"

Ginger put on her brave face, wondered if this woman knew her story. The emotions were fresh whenever the topic surfaced but she could speak of them, though she never wanted to.

"That's right," she said and took her daughter's hand to leave.

Her body language closed the inquiry and the woman took the hint. "There's a few of us women going snowmachining next week. You're welcome to join us if you'd like."

Gingers curiosity peaked. "Yeah, that sounds like it might be fun…but I'm not sure I'd be able to manage a babysitter."

"Oh, no, bring her along! My kids will be there. They can ride too, we'll have plenty of gear. Or, if she's not into it, she can stay with my mom at the cabin while we're out."

"Yeah, maybe. Can I get back to you in a few days?"

"Absolutely. Bye, Miss Shiloh," she called, waving at Ginger's daughter.

They walked toward the lobby and looked at all of the faces, some she'd met, most were strangers. She had moved here to escape, to start over where nobody would know or care about her past. She knew Alaska had a lot of veterans and a quality support structure, but mainly it had aircraft — lots of aircraft, and myriad opportunities to fly. Being a single mother was a challenge but she was making it work. She always found a way to make things work.

But she'd been tepid about making friends, especially women. Cecilia kept encouraging her to make connections, to let others in, to let others help carry her burdens.

As she returned to the lobby she made eye contact with a couple of people, then spotted him.

He turned and made eye contact, smiled. Ginger tried to look away casually, hoping he didn't think she was staring. She glanced back and he was still looking at her. He was still smiling and nodded at her, then went back to talking to his friends.

She felt stupid. She'd seen him a few times but they had never spoken. He seemed to notice her every week, and she wondered what he was all about, not sure if she cared.

"Hey Ginger," she heard to her right. She began making small talk with a woman she'd met last week, while Shiloh swung from the end of her arm, hugging her legs. Ginger listened, but her eyes wandered back in his direction. To her horror, she saw him walking toward her.

Her heart rate accelerated but she couldn't understand why. She wasn't afraid of him; she wasn't afraid of anyone.

He stopped a few feet away, waiting for the other woman to leave. When she finally did, Ginger was left alone, and she turned to face him. She looked straight into his eyes.

Many years later, Jen asked, "What was it about him that drew you in? When did you know he was special?"

Ginger pondered that question, recalling their history and all that had transpired since the day they first met in that church lobby.

It wasn't the way he'd always treated her with gentle confidence, and it wasn't how he interacted with Shiloh during that first lunch date, or how he was careful to get permission before giving simple gestures, like asking to hold her hand on date number three.

Nor was it the way he made three separate trips to California in order to get to know her father, something Marcus found a bit old fashioned but was impressed with all the same. Or the way he loved his family, a family that embraced her from the beginning and never even blinked when she told them her history, piece by agonizing piece.

And it wasn't the patience he displayed as they grew closer, how he let others do the counseling so he could focus on just loving her, and in doing so, helped her regain confidence. And it wasn't how he shielded her from the intrusive questions of others, or how he helped her navigate that difficult first face-to-face with Porter again, not as her rescuer, but simply as Aiden's friend.

It wasn't the way he gently held her, and understood the emotions on their wedding night, while she oscillated between crying and apologizing for hours, and talking, and watching the sun rise together. Or how he knew what she needed whenever she'd wake from recurring nightmares. She understood his, too.

There was a moment's pause and Ginger could tell he was lost for words. He looked her in the eye, seemed to regain a quiet confidence, and said, "Good afternoon. I've noticed you a few times and…I would be honored to meet you."

He held out his hand and smiled. "My name is Aiden."

Genevieve Cooper's heartbeat regained its normal rhythm. A wave of comfort washed over her, followed by a degree of excitement, the embarking on a new adventure. For so long, chains had held her back from taking risks, risks she'd always embraced in the past. Now, finally, something in him made her ready to take one again.

She raised her hand and took his, the contact with his skin more than a cold formality, but rather an invitation, and she was both surprised and relieved. She had no desire to let go.

She cocked her head in a playful manner and smiled in to his beautiful eyes. She wanted to sing again, but instead spoke with a warm confidence of her own.

"It's very nice to meet you, Aiden."

It wasn't the way he tried to hold in his tears the first time they overheard Shiloh refer to him as her dad, or watching him gently cradle their first baby together, or their second, or even their fourth.

"Actually," she told her friend that day, laughing, "he was just really hot. He had the cutest little green tattoo."

a preview:
BOOK IV

Aiden unscrewed a water bottle and used its contents to wash the dirt and blood smears from his forearms.

Next to him, Porter removed the magazine from the AK-47 and reloaded another, tossing the empty one into the fully disorganized backpack loaded with medical supplies. He looked at the weapon in his hands and longed for something, anything else *At the very least, something with more than iron sights.* He sighed and slung the weapon, resigned to make do with what they had.

"Come on. I've got an idea," Aiden said, picking up his own AK and walking into the General's field headquarters. Porter followed.

Once inside, they watched Ozzy giving directions in Arabic to a number of subordinates and paying the Americans no mind.

"What are we doing?" Porter asked wondering how long they were going to stand around.

"I'm just pondering the best way to ask him."

"Ask him what?"

"If we can borrow a tank."

Acknowledgements

I'm constantly amazed by how willing people are to help with creating a book. Many of the early readers who volunteered their time were mere acquaintances, friends of a friend; some were complete strangers. I contacted them with a prayerful hope they'd be willing to take a look, and was astounded when so many of them enthusiastically offered their support. Military families care deeply about how they are portrayed (even in fiction). They want the little things to be right, and they aren't shy about saying so.

To the Army veterans, Brendan, Chris, Dan, Dave, and Clifford: Thank you for teaching me the nuance of your craft, for humbly walking me through the technical aspects of various weapons and tactics, and the practical parts of the job that civilians will never understand, like the best way to fast rope from a helicopter. (*"After roping x amount of times and getting tired of hitting the ground, rooftop, or whatever saying "Ouch! Ouch! Hot! Hot!" you kind of learn that if you keep one hand at about navel level, and one at about sternum level, and pull the rope into your plates/kit, you get twice the braking friction at half the burn."*)

I'd love to try it sometime.

To the Hog drivers, Jeff and Mike: Thank you for teaching me new terms, giving me perspective on how war is fought from the air, and for gently correcting the subtle differences that create major errors. Also, thank you for affirming my long-held belief that the A-10 is, in fact, very much a member of the fighter family, regardless of what Navy aviators may say.

To the Marines, Landon and Sam: Thank you for the hook ups, for the stacks of materials you provided, along with how to apply the information in them during my crash courses in urban combat. Thank you especially for the uproarious stories over coffee that can never be retold, as well as your transparency, and your courageous will in reliving events you'd probably rather shelve. I'm honored for the glimpse through the keyhole, and I hope I got it right.

To Joe: Thank you for spreading the word and for the emotional pick me ups, which always seemed to come at just the right time.

To Rachel: Thank you for your painstaking attention to detail, finding typos and the little things the editors (human and machine) miss, and to her husband Juan for letting me borrow her brain for a little while.

To the readers who continue to encourage, purchase, recommend, and share my books: Thank you.

To Rick, DJ, and Cody: Thanks for the messages and the prayers that keep me on track with this and with the other things as well.

To Vincent: Thanks for taking the time to create the artwork that adorns the title pages of my books. And thank you for the originals — my daily reminders of your talent. The price was worth every bean.

To my wife Shannon, who's read every word, wisely deleted several thousand of them, and added another thousand of her own: I'm blessed to be married to a writer who's better than I am. No doubt she even edited this paragraph (she did).

And finally, to the women who've lived through another kind of fire: Thank you for telling your stories. As heartbreaking and gut wrenching as they are, without them the world might never know the truth about abortion and what it does to everyone involved. I hope that in some way this story will adequately reflect the reality you've endured, and serve as a cautionary tale for other women in similar circumstances. But I also hope it will serve as a reminder that the Lord does not define us by our mistakes, but rather by our willingness to accept forgiveness and restoration with Him through Jesus Christ, so that we may walk with our heads held high, leave the past in its place, and take bold steps in the present, facing whatever the new day brings.

About the Author

Vince Guerra is a writer and author. His work can be found weekly at vinceguerra.com, and he is a frequent contributor on Ricochet.com. He lives in Wasilla, Alaska.

Pegasus is the third novel in a four-book series, including *Beyond the Golden Hour* and *The Stars and Their Places*.

Subscribe to receive promotions, weekly writings, news on other books, and updates on part four at vinceguerra.com/allies.

The Modern War Series:

Book One

The Golden Hour: The hour immediately following traumatic injury in which medical treatment to prevent irreversible internal damage and optimize the chance of survival is most effective.

SEAL team Polaris is on a reconnaissance mission high in the Hindu Kush mountains of Afghanistan when they're led into an ambush. The A-10 fighter providing close-air support is shot down and Air Force pararescue jumpers, dispatched to extract the downed pilot, also suffer heavy fire.

As the clock ticks and casualties mount, the PJs join forces with Polaris – facing subzero temperatures, formidable terrain, and entrenched enemies – to rescue the missing pilot and get them all home.

"A richly synoptic peek into a military operation."
- *Kirkus Reviews*

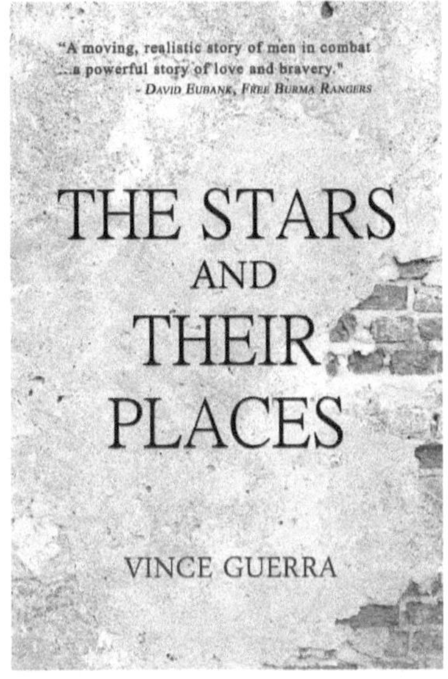

Four years after a heroic rescue mission in Afghanistan, former Pararescueman Aiden McCoy continues to fight for the lives of veterans – this time at home, as they struggle with the physical and psychological effects of war.

Meanwhile in Iraq, Aiden's lifelong friend Jake Lyons impresses everyone with his combat rescue skills. As Jake's reputation grows, so does his exposure to the daily horrors of a chaotic war. Aiden must help his friend confront the challenges of trauma, and get him back in the game.

Spanning two years in locations across the Middle East, American soil, and the shadowlands of intelligence agencies and special operations, *The Stars and Their Places* continues the tale begun in *Beyond the Golden Hour*. It is the second of four novels.

www.ingramcontent.com/pod-product-compliance
Lightning Source LLC
Chambersburg PA
CBHW021105110726
47900CB00007B/2034